The Last Barbarian

by

Mark West

ISBN 978-1-930322-27-1

Cover Design by Sara Dunn
sdunnarts@gmail.com
Instagram: artofsaradunn

MinRef Press

This book is dedicated to
the Barbarians who have made a difference:
N., R., and J.

Book One

The Blood-Jewel of Simathica

Lightning flashed white the yellow hair and fair skin of a young woman. The eyes remained in shadow, black and brooding. The woman, standing in the doorway of a small hut, breathed deep the sweet smell of the first faint glow of morning. A sudden hint of moisture in the air caused the desert heat to become humid.

The dusk rippled with shadows and shadow-like things. Horses and other beasts moved restlessly, uneasily. A storm was coming. It was almost the end of the Long Night. In a week or two, the Long Day would begin, the time of endless sun.

A distant thunder rumble broke the shadowed stillness.

The crudely-built hut lie at the edge of a small desert village, a few palm trees broke up the monotony of sand dunes and rolling hills of barren wheat fields, awaiting cultivation with arrival of the Long Day.

One shadow, fleeting and ethereal, flowed with unseen purpose from tree to bush, corral to adobe wall, moving with an unerring purpose toward the woman outlined in the hut's backlit doorway.

The woman was young, barely past two ten-time celebrations. Her long, golden hair blazed in the lantern light. The hut was made of sun dried concrete bricks, a poor but serviceable combination of sand, small rocks, and clay, with a woven thatched roof that kept off most of the infrequent rain.

The nearby lightning startled her. The loud crack of thunder followed and she stepped away from the door and back into the hut. At the same time, something flung itself into the room. The woman screamed and moved further back as a huge southlands Barbarian flew through the doorway, missed her, and slid under a table on his stomach, scattering chairs.

A soft giggle escaped her lips as she watched the well-muscled man attempt to regain his life's breath. Finally, he rolled over and sat up. He looked about warily, and noticed the woman standing beside the doorway, a long, thin-bladed knife in her right hand.

"Welcome," she said tauntingly, "did you come here to sweep my floor, or to die?"

"Neither, I hope," the Barbarian rumbled, brushing dust from his clothes. He glanced again at the knife. "Do I have to stay here on the floor, or can I get up?"

The woman shrugged. "You seem to have an intimate acquaintance with my chairs; you might as well sit on one."

The Barbarian nodded his thanks, righted a chair, and sat on it. "You scarcely need that blade, wench. I didn't come here to accost you."

The woman stepped closer to the table. "Should I trust your words? You're a man, and by your looks, a Barbarian. You expect me to believe you came here only to inspect my floor? I'm forced to assume you broke into my home to have your way with me. And you tell me to put away my knife, that you're no threat? Sorry if I doubt you." She paused and smiled again. "And I am not called 'Wench.' If you must, call me Carina."

"Carina—hmm, a full name, fitting." With a deft motion, he reached out, grabbed her knife hand and squeezed. Carina gasped and dropped the blade. She tried to step back, but he held on to her hand.

"My name is Morak," he said, picking the knife off the sandy floor, "A Barbarian as you have guessed. And I don't take kindly to having knives flashed in my face." He let go with a gentle push.

"Then you shouldn't burst into people's homes," Carina shot back, rubbing her wrist, "you hurt me."

"You handled that knife like you knew how to use it." He stabbed the blade into the table top and flicked the hilt, watching it vibrate.

"What do you want here, if not fun at my expense?"

"Nothing," he said, still staring at the knife. He looked up and gazed at Carina. "Just a place to rest for a while. A place out of sight," he stood, walked to the wooden door and slammed it closed just as huge raindrops began spattering across the sand. The lightening and thunder continued, and a soft breeze became wind.

Morak looked at Carina and laughed. "I'm here because robbers do not take kindly to having their own plunder stolen." He fingered a bag hanging heavily at his waist. "It's gold, all right, but don't you get any ideas about it."

"And what if your robber friends saw you enter here?" Carina asked. "They'll surround my home, and none of us will get out alive."

"None saw me," Morak said, confidently. "They are still in the village, searching through the dark, poking swords into piles of hay."

Morak began searching the small hut. One sleeping room was empty. When he approached the other, Carina grabbed his arm. "Please, Barbarian, there's nothing in there to interest you." She tugged at him, "come with me, and I'll show you a good time." The intensity of her voice belied the nature of her offer.

Morak looked at the woman. "What's in there you don't want me to see?" He reached for the door skin and drew it back.

"Please, Barbarian..."

Morak looked inside. In the darkness he saw a bed. Upon it, a small indistinct shadow moved. He reached for his sword.

"Draw that blade, lad," a masculine voice said from the hut's front door, "and it'll be your last time."

Morak turned and saw an old man, the blade of a yet another throwing knife held loosely between his thumb and forefinger. Morak let his hand drop to hang twitching at his side.

"Tok!" Carina cried, "am I happy to see you!"

The old man shed his wet outer clothes, keeping his eyes and knife on the Barbarian.

"Kill him, Tok! Kill him. He came in here and tried to attack me. He almost found Meesha. Kill him."

"Nonsense," Tok said. "Tell Meesha to come out."

"What?"

"Just do it."

Hesitantly, Carina went into the second sleeping room and brought out a small girl child. She looked up at the Barbarian with wide, fear-filled eyes. She was thin and delicate and quite beautiful. Morak stepped back as Meesha came further into the room, his eyes never leaving her pale glowing face. She had hair the same golden shade as Carina's, but with what seemed an inner shine. She was seven, perhaps eight, seasons old.

"The two of you," Tok said, "go out and check on the horses. They'll be spooked by all that thunder. My Barbarian friend and I have some things to discuss. Come, my friend, sit." He made his knife disappear and urged Morak into a chair. The Barbarian sat, but did not relax. He angled his sword back, in case he needed to draw it quickly.

Tok ignored the gesture and took another chair. "Tell me, my young friend, what has brought you to our fair abode?"

Morak sighed, looking away from the child as Carina ushered her through the door. "I am on my way to Areban, my home in Barbaricum. When I ran out of gold, I entered a robber's camp as one of them. It worked, too. Long enough for me to get some of their gold and be on my way. But they chased me with their horses to the very edge of this village."

"And how good are you with that blade you carry?" Tok's voice cracked with age and overuse.

"Good enough to last five years in the wilderness, fighting everything from madmen to dragon-beasts. Good enough to run through any man you send against me."

Tok leaned forward, his greasy, whiskered face shining yellow from the lantern. "Good, then you might be the one we've been seeking. This is good, very good. I expect you'll join our quest, then, and have enough adventure for two Barbarian lifetimes."

Morak leaned back and laughed. "What kind of crazy quest do you want me to join? I've a lot of desert to cross, and no need to listen to an old man's mad tales."

"No, no, it's not tales, Morak, but the truth. Just listen, and I'll make you rich beyond your wildest dreams. You'll be king of your kingdom!"

"Keep your imagined kingdom, old man." Morak leaned forward, "just give me some gold and a night or two with Carina."

Tok laughed, a hacking cough. "My friend, I think we can do

business."

"You still haven't told me..."

"Ever hear of the Blood Jewel?" The old man's voice was hoarse and raspy, like the wind through rocks. But there was a quality in that voice which kept Morak from laughing.

"Blood Jewel? Yes, I've heard of it. Years ago, the legend was whispered around a campfire by a dying man from the eastlands. From what he said it's valuable beyond all else. Other than that I know only hints of legends. And listen to me, old man. I put no stock in legends."

"The jewel is no legend, Morak. It's real. How would you like to put it in your pocket?"

"It has been said the jewel is protected by a demon god."

"Yes, yes," Tok said, waving away Morak's implied fear, "such a being lives, I'm told, in a cave on an island's highest mountain." Tok's eyes glowed with madness, "but we need not worry about gods and demons and such."

"Why not?"

He laughed and pointed, "because we have *you*!"

Morak said nothing, but shook his head. "I'm just here to hide for a while. I have no need..."

"Deep within an island called Simathica," the old man continued, "lies the Blood Jewel. As big as a camel's hump, it is said, or even bigger, and worth more than all the gold in Karan."

"Hmm. There's quit a bit of gold in Karan. If you really know something about this jewel, I might be interested. Just—how do I know you tell the truth? Or that you have not been deceived by someone selling fake treasure maps? Perhaps you have nothing better to do with your time than waste the time of others."

"You'll see, my friend, my well-muscled Barbarian friend. You'll see. Soon Dagrag, the sorceress-witch, will be here. Soon. Then you'll believe me!"

"A witch?" Morak said with disgust, "And what has this to do with one of the Dark Realms?"

"Why, it was she who found the island of Simathica, proved it was no legend. She's been there and fathomed its mysteries. Or at least some of them. She says the jewel is real, and she knows where it is. She knows."

Morak snorted an answer, then watched through the open door at the flitting shadows of Carina and Meesha. There was something about that child, something in the way she looked at Morak...and then there was Carina. All the rest may be lies and legends, but she, at least, was real. And that was enough to hold Morak's interest, for a while.

Continuing his non-stop description of the jewel, Tok brought ale and bread for Morak. They ate and drank, awaiting Dagrag's arrival. Carina and Meesha returned, slamming the door to shut out the wind and rain. The desert of Karan seldom received rain, but each was a memorable occasion. Carina ushered Meesha, who walked as if transfixed staring at Morak, into the sleeping room, and drew the skins.

"She is a strange child," Morak commented, "did you buy her?"

"She is not of your concern, Barbarian."

"By strange, I did not mean..."

"I understood your meaning, Morak. She is not your concern." Their eyes locked for a moment, then Morak shrugged and looked away.

When the witch did arrive, it was not through any door. A slight breeze kicked up sand and dust in a corner, became a wind, a swirl of debris and a howl that echoed—and echoed again. And from within the dust, glowing deep blue by an inhuman light, stepped Dagrag. Her face was somber and cruel, as if it had been carved from the hardest stone. Her hair, dark and stringy, ended above her wide, masculine shoulders. And she was tall, almost as tall as Morak. When she spoke, yellow teeth sparkled like gold beneath leathery lips. She wore a flowing robe of the deepest black, like a piece of the universe ripped away and draped over her body, and Morak could feel himself being drawn into that shroud of nothing and night.

The Barbarian had stood at Dagrag's arrival, sword drawn, and her appearance did nothing to relax him.

"Magnificent," Tok muttered, staring openly at the battle-image Morak presented. "You are indeed the one we have been searching for."

"What have you found, old fool?" Dagrag screeched, her

voice dry and raspy, powerful and demanding, and it got on one's nerves. She floated to the table, black-robed feet never touching the ground. She glared at Tok and ignored Morak. "Are you ready? You've had enough time, old man. And it's almost day break."

"Yes, yes, it is he," Tok pointed eagerly at Morak, "his sword shall aid us."

Dagrag stared at Morak, seeming to notice him for the first time. "This? It is scarcely even a man. Look at that scraggly brown hair and those jackal eyes. Better we should have a monkey," she said turning away.

Tok ran around to face her again. "You don't understand. He's a great swordsman," he touched his balding head, "and a thinker beyond all." Tok shook his head, "you shouldn't dismiss him outright. This is a good man. Good."

"You're a fool, old man. This wild one does not have the principles of a goat. If we take him, he will kill you. Or see you dead sooner. And then what would happen?"

Tok flinched and turned away, the words, meaningless to Morak, lashing the old man with a great pain.

"But the jewel," he said finally, plaintively.

"Yes," Dagrag hissed, "there is that." She turned back to Morak, stared into his eyes. "I see you, Barbarian, as a child, with a friend. You're climbing at the base of a mountain, playing your childish games of conquest. But unseen to you, a flying serpent swoops down and your friend is plucked off the mountainside and carried away." She stopped and watched Morak closely. "And..." she whispered.

"And I went after that thrice cursed creature, and slew it."

"You see," she turned away, back to Tok, "it's useless. He's no thief, no cutthroat to be used and discarded. He's a Barbarian. They live for their stupid oaths and their meaningless battles. You've chosen poorly, old man."

"No," Tok said with more forcefulness than Morak had seen since the witch arrived. "All the others were stupid and drunkards. I have a feeling about this one. Ah, yes, a feeling."

"Just what we need," Dagrag threw up her hands, eyes heavenward, "another of your 'feelings.' Am I to be forever cursed with your 'feelings'?"

"You are cursed anyway, Witch," Tok said quietly, "my feelings won't make much difference. Morak is the one. He is my choice."

"Well, then, all right. On your shoulders be it." She turned back to Morak, "you will join us in our quest for the Blood Jewel—but it will not be a joyous association. There will be pain and death. Remember that, Barbarian. Remember that."

Morak, curious, fingered his blade. "I'll remember," he muttered, wishing he were elsewhere.

• • •

For a week, Tok, Carina and Morak prepared for their journey. Morak knew the island, if it truly existed, was a journey of many days, to the northern area of Karan and along the sea coast. They departed while it was still somewhat cool from the rain, as the sun peeked over the horizon and began its six-month journey across the sky.

It was said that no man lived on the isle of Simathica. No city stood opposite it on the northwestern shores of Karan. Ashmond, a city of robbers and thieves, was closest, was the last desert outpost nearest the edge of the sea.

Now Morak, Tok, and Carina rode into Ashmond atop spirited white stallions. Before they left, Tok and Carina had taken Meesha for care to an old cleaning woman they knew, sold all their meager belongings in the marketplace to pay for the service. Of Dagrag, Morak saw nothing after their first meeting in Tok's hut. He was as comforted by her absence as he was pleased to be riding side-by-side with Carina. She had shown Morak little more than passing interest. But there would be time, later. Unlike most of his kind, Morak often practiced the art of patience.

With the coming of day, Karan's inhabitants hurried to plant crops, breed livestock and horses, and cure bricks for construction. Trees and other plants woke from their hibernation, sending leaves eager for a sunlight that would be little more than dusk for several more weeks. During the Long Day, battles were fought, trade increased, and people celebrated.

The three travelers stopped at Ashmond's largest inn, entered the noisy establishment, and took a table near a far wall. This was a place for the unkempt, the dishonest, the murderer and the wayward. They all made too much noise to suit Morak.

He sat nervously, hand on his sword hilt, watching the sweaty, bearded men and the stocky women laughing and eating and taking time for boisterous play.

He also noticed many furtive glances in his direction. Morak could safely pass as a new resident, for he recognized one or two Barbarians in the place. But, by the gods, Tok and Carina were too clean and well kept. And Carina much too winsome for a pirate's wench. She was going to cause trouble, for sure.

A short, fat man with red graying hair made his way toward the three newcomers. He wore a jovial look of one who enjoys eating and noise.

"How may I help you, citizens?"

"We're not citizens," Morak growled, "and a little less noise in this place would do for a start."

"Now, now, my boy," Tok soothed. He turned to the inn-keeper, "we want only hot food, wine, and a good dark place for sleep, for which we will pay in wildlands gold." *My* gold, Morak thought. This quest for legends would not come cheap.

"Gold, you say," the innkeeper muttered, glancing over his shoulder and rubbing his palms together, "gold is always welcome here. But you've got to keep this young pup in his place," he said as he turned and left, taking a finger from Morak's face.

Carina laughed and the Barbarian turned away, muttering.

His eyes lit on a giant bull of a man, who, himself, was intently staring at Carina. Morak saw the intense, hungry look in the giant's eyes as he stood and moved deftly through the cavernous room of men and smoke and noise. He was halfway to the trio before Morak alerted the others.

"Be wary, Tok," he whispered, "there's an ugly giant coming this way."

The "giant" stopped in front of their table, an overbearing odorous mountain of blubber and muscle. Only then did he take his eyes off Carina. He looked at Tok and spoke in a guttural tongue thick with some unknown accent. "How much for the golden one?"

Tok looked up and smiled. "She is my granddaughter, kind

gentleman, I could not bear to part with her."

The giant smiled, exposing rotted teeth. "How much?" He placed the palm of his hand on the table and leaned forward. The wood groaned.

"As I said, she's not for sale." Tok's voice was firm.

"A dead man cannot sell."

"Or buy," Tok replied instantly. Morak noticed how quiet the inn had suddenly become. The three sat woodenly, but the huge thief was not about to let it lie.

He stepped back and drew the biggest sword Morak had ever seen. Morak stood, sending his chair clattering against the wall. Reluctantly, he pulled his sword. The other was larger and weighed more. He was dirty, unkempt, and he smelled bad. All of which added up in Morak's mind to a demon fighter.

"You choose to die for an old man and his skinny wench?" The giant seemed genuinely surprised. Nevertheless, he drew back, and Morak braced for his attack.

But, "wait!" shouted Tok. A knife was suddenly buried in the giant's chest, and another sunk, with a meaty sound, in his neck. Just to be safe, Morak lunged and drove his blade through the other's mid-section. The thief stood for a moment, eyes glazed, blood splattering to the floor. Then he fell loudly amidst a cloud of dust, and lie quiet.

Tok and Carina warily retrieved their blades.

A full silence held the tavern but for a moment. Then swords were drawn, oaths shouted, and three more challenged Morak. Again, blades flung by Tok and Carina sang through the air, and two dropped. Morak lunged, driving a shoulder into the third opponent's gut, then pivoting, swinging his sword with the power of both arms. The attacker's head fairly leapt from his shoulders and landed amongst another group of the inn's customers. Those heading their way stopped, hesitating. More men in the back stopped and gazed at Morak, then quietly returned to their tables. Of the remainder, none seemed willing to continue the attacks.

Again, all was quiet.

Morak looked wildly about the room. "Any more of you want to lose your heads today?" He screamed, "then come on, *do* something!"

"Morak!" Tok shouted. The Barbarian whirled. Tok smiled, "My knife—get it for me, will you?"

A second passed, and Morak relaxed. He bent and pulled the blade from the dead man's throat. As if on signal, everyone turned away from the three intruders. Slowly, talk and eating returned to normal. Men began to go about their business, sometimes stealing glances at the trio who sat, now unmolested.

"I told you he was the right one," Tok whispered to Carina as he wiped his knife on his pants leg, "I told *her*, but *she* didn't believe me."

"It will take more than a severed head to convince Dagrag, Grandfather," Carina whispered back as Morak turned toward them and, after a brief pause, resumed eating.

Later, Morak and Tok prepared for a restful sleep in the upper floor of the tavern. They sat on the edge of their one bed —the best the innkeeper could provide even under threats of pain—removing boots and weapons.

"You think Carina will be all right, alone in the next room?" Morak asked.

Tok laughed. "I would warn you, young friend, if you think to keep her company, you might find a knife planted in your ugly hide. And not by my hand," he grunted as he pulled his other boot off, revealing a well-worn, smelly sock, and the end of a big toe. He grimaced and looked at Morak, "I taught her to use a blade, and by damn if she isn't better than me." He sighed and lay back on the bed, running a hand through his thinning hair, "still, if she finds you interesting, she might..."

"What is all this talk, old man?"

"Carina's happiness matters to me, that's all." He looked at Morak, "it's important to me. Important. I don't want to see her get hurt."

Morak reclined on his half of the bed. "Don't worry about it. I can wait. The promise of a woman to come prompts one to do things he would not normally do, and with caution."

"Ah, we have a philosopher among us. Unfortunately, most philosophers have a habit of eating their words, sooner or later." He was quiet for a time, then said, "Morak, have you ever heard the legends of how Karan came to be settled?"

"Many times, old man, but why speak of them now?" Morak turned on his side to look at Tok, "especially on the eve of our quest?"

"Because there is something about this isle of Simathica, beyond a witch's spell and a Blood Jewel, something different. Legends say Karan was once ice—this desert," Tok laughed, put his hands behind his head to stare up at the ceiling, "and that we are survivors of a war between lightning gods and thunder devils. Simathica has been shunned even by this city of thieves. They say it's possessed by those same thunder devils and other nameless evil things left over from this war. None who have tried reaching it have ever returned."

Morak laughed, "I've not seen a devil yet whose eyes my sword couldn't fill with fear. As for the legends of Karan, I think they are to frighten and amaze old women and little children. Now go to sleep, old man. I'm tired, this has been a long trip. Worry when you see this thunder devil."

"Yes, when I see it," Tok sighed, a sigh that drifted up and mingled with the stale airs of the inn, soon replaced with snores.

A sand storm whirled through Morak's dreams, dreams populated with ethereal and shadowy horrors. Sand stung his skin and made his eyes water. He tried to run, but he was too weak. He woke. His eyes opened and the wind still blew. He reached for his sword, but realized it was across the room, hung behind the door by its belt.

"Up, you dung worms," the growled shout echoed from the bottom of a bottomless pit. Morak sat up with a start, and gazed into the emptiness of Dagrag's black robe. Curtains slid back from the windows of their own accord. The early morning glow of the sun fingered through closed slats of the windows. Tok took a deep breath and groaned with wakefulness.

"It's time to be on our way, fools! I have need of you while you yet live." Dagrag's growl ended in a high pitched scream.

"All right, Witch, you needn't shake the dead's bones with your screeching." Tok grumbled as his feet hit the cold floor.

He and Morak dressed with somberness while the Witch woke Carina. They went down to the tavern for a quick breakfast. Few were about this early hour.

"By the gods," Morak exploded, breathing deep, "there *is* a good feeling when the Long Day begins."

Tok laughed, "and waking up without a great hangover, eh Barbarian?"

Morak laughed also, and slapped the old man's shoulder.

They reclaimed the same table where they had eaten their dinner, and an equally plump, gray-haired old woman had replaced the smelly innkeeper from before.

She smiled a toothless smile. "What'll ye have this fine new day, friends? It's a beautiful beginning, and a full break fast is what you need. It'll be too crowded to eat later."

Dagrag snorted and looked away.

"Never mind her, good woman," Tok said, smiling, "just bring us hot cakes, sausage, and wine. Yes, plenty of wine."

"And be quick about it," Morak added, "or you'll lose yet another tooth." She went, laughing.

"So this is your champion?" Dagrag sneered, "who threatens to remove rotted teeth from old women? The Blood Jewel awaits, and you sit around joking."

"Now, Witch, we can't go killing your dragons and devils on an empty stomach," Morak replied, smiling. But the smile died as his eyes met those of the Witch. Those orbs lived apart from her, it seemed, writhing and pulsing with a hateful life of their own. And like her robe, they were an empty black.

Dagrag turned her attention to Tok. "You saw to Meesha before you left?"

Tok said nothing, nodded.

"Are you sure she will be safe?"

"I'm sure," Tok said angrily, glancing at Morak.

"You know why I am concerned, old man. If you don't come back...."

"She's *okay*," Tok shouted. "She will be fine. Just fine."

Dagrag stared at him, a preoccupied look glazing her eyes. Then she glanced at the door. "Three men are coming—on horses," she said quietly, "they would kill for a woman. Be wary, fools."

And sure enough, three large, brawny men stomped in, bringing with them the clouds of dust, dirt and smell of a long ride. They came in, laughing and slapping dust from their clothes.

"Certain they'll bring us trouble," Dagrag whispered.

"You've a suspicious mind, Witch," Morak said.

"Be quiet, she knows what she's talking about," Carina said, glaring at the Barbarian.

One of the newcomers looked at the table where Carina sat with the others. He grabbed one of his partner's arms. "Look at that wench, hey. I'd like to get that golden haired goddess under me, I would." He made no attempt to hide his voice.

His friends laughed. One said, "she'd rather die than touch your smelly carcass." They slapped each other and laughed.

"She'd not have a choice," the first said quietly, a lusty hoarseness entering his voice. "You two take the Barbarian and the old man, and maybe I'll share her..."

They drew swords and moved toward the table. Morak sighed. "Gods, woman, you get me into more trouble around here." He stood and drew his blade, left hand resting on the back of his chair.

"You three dogs," Morak said, "go back to the dung heap from which you came. Leave us in peace and you'll yet live."

They ignored him. The center one lunged suddenly, but Morak easily met that blade with his, twisting sideways and swinging the chair down on his opponent's head. He heard bones crack and dismissed that one from the fight.

He back-swung his sword and caught the one on his right full in the chest, cutting him almost to the heart. He watched as the man slumped toward Dagrag. The Witch reached out and pulled the dying man into her black robe, his screams of terror echoing, then dying. And watching that, Morak almost died. His sword was knocked from his hand and he faced the third man unarmed. The other drew back for his killing blow.

Carina flung her knife, but the man ducked back. It was the opening Morak needed. He bent low and leapt, coming up under the other's chin. The two wrestled, landing on tables and kicking chairs out of the way.

The outlaw was strong and fast, but he was not a Barbarian. Morak gained the upper hand and was about to crack the man's neck when Carina suddenly thrust her blade deep into his throat just above Morak's forearm. Blood erupted over the Barbarian's arm and Carina's hand. The victim convulsed once, then was still.

Carina looked at Morak with a perverse smile, pulled her knife from the body, and wiped blood on her hide-covered thighs. She took one last look at scattered bodies and blood-slippery parts, flipped hair out of her eyes, then sat back down.

Morak looked up at Tok's smiling face. "Gods, old man, I'll never understand women." He also sat and shook his head. The serving woman brought their breakfast along with hot wet cloths with which to scrub their hands. She carefully stepped over dead bodies, clicking her tongue in disapproval. Three of them ate in silence while Dagrag watched impatiently. She seemed to have no appetite.

After the meal, they mounted their horses. Tok, Carina and Morak rode their white stallions. Dagrag, of course, joined them atop a spirited black mount, dark as night and twice as wild. The sun was half-a-finger above the horizon, just clearing distant hills on its slow journey across the sky.

Once outside the city, desert surrounded them, and hot dry sand opened before them right to the edge of the sea. Morak had never seen so much ocean before, and sat forward in his saddle when he first sighted it, breathless at the endless procession of gently rolling waves, going to where water met the sky. They rode along the edge of waves for hours, enjoying an occasional sea breeze, but saw no other person.

Tok rode up behind Morak. "Legends say men used to sail on those waters as we now cross lakes and rivers."

"Fools they must have been," Morak said. "Fools to challenge the end of the world."

"Well, we've got to sail on it, for a while at least. We're going to an island, after all." The prospect did nothing to comfort the Barbarian.

Tok called them to a halt two sleep periods later." The travelers dismounted and watched gulls soaring overhead, riding the wind and screaming. Morak breathed deep, coming to enjoy the fresh yet organic smell of the sea. A gentle breeze off water cooled the sweat on his body.

"We're here, Morak. Help me find some wood to make a raft."

Morak eyed the old man. "You really mean to sail across that ocean?"

"Yep. It's a fact. A fact." He looked up at the Barbarian. "We must sail, of course, to reach the island." He pointed to the north, along the coast. Out, far out, where mist made it almost as blue as the sky, was a slight rise. "That is Simathica," Tok said, "an island of legends."

Carina and Dagrag had ridden over the next rise and Morak could hear their horses splashing in water as they trotted along the beach.

"What lives on Simathica?" Morak asked, squinting to see that dim isle.

"No man knows for sure. We've only those legends and the words of liars. Dagrag has been there, of course, but she tells what she wishes to tell and nothing more. Whatever does live there, we'll not have a pleasant meeting with, I'm sure. Now, are you going to stand there all day? I can't build this raft myself."

"Yes," Morak said absently, still staring. Slowly he turned and he and Tok bent to the task of gathering enough suitable wood for a raft. Pickings were slim along this desert seacoast. Yet they found several large pieces of driftwood, strangely worked and smooth with age and time, and, it seemed, the hand of some ancient craftsmen.

They labored until Carina called a halt to eat and sleep. Tok used some of the smaller pieces of wood to build a campfire. "I think we have enough wood," he said, stirring the fire. "I'll put together a raft when we wake, one that will," he glanced at Morak, "hold together long enough to get us to Simathica. We'll be ready to sail in two sleep times, maybe three." That last he said to Dagrag.

"Finally," growled the Witch. "You work too slow for me, old man. If I hadn't need of you, I'd have gotten rid of the lot of you long ago." She glared at Morak, "especially him." Then she lifted into the morning sky and disappeared.

"What need does she have of us? She's a witch, and she can do that," Morak raised his hand upward, toward a dark blue sky. "Here one minute, gone somewhere else the next." Morak looked at his companions, then gazed into the flames. He shivered at the cool ocean breeze and watched idly as Carina ignored his question and slid gracefully into her bedroll and relaxed to sleep.

Tok sighed and looked skyward. "The jewel's behind a gate or door or something, so she says—one she can't open."

"She's really been to Simathica?"

"On the island, aye. She's a witch, and has been many places we've not been. But she says her witch powers don't work well on Simathica, and not at all near the jewel's crypt. Strange, wouldn't you say, Morak?" Tok was quiet for a moment, then he said, "And Dagrag has another reason for keeping my tired old bones around. She's my da...my sister."

"What?" Morak was startled. "That ugly hag?"

"Oh, she once looked as normal as you or I. Very attractive, I might say." He shook his head. "It happens that way. It's a witch's fate. No one knows when one will be born. Only the gods know. As children, they are near normal as can be. Only a few hints of their dark abilities show, and at first none of their eventual fate. Later on, as their powers grow, their—appearance—begins to deteriorate. Until..."

It was a chilling thought. To start life bright and beautiful, only to find the witch powers developing within, and outwardly turning all ugly and angry, knowing things and doing things that suck out all the laughter and smiles.

"And Carina," Morak said gruffly, "she's your daughter. She a witch too?"

It was a question, but it didn't get answered. Tok ignored it, lit the night candle, and went to bed.

This close to the sea, and this soon after beginning of the Long Day, the environment was much colder than the inland desert, and the three slept badly. None of them knew where Dagrag spent her sleep time.

They woke to a light mist, with clouds so low they seemed to touch the sea with their weight. No amount of smiles could brighten their mood, so after eating a sparse meal, the three worked at building their raft.

Before they were ready to sleep, a seaworthy craft of sorts lie at their feet. There was about as much hope holding it together as there was wood in it. Morak looked at it skeptically. "Will it float?"

Tok wiped his forehead with the back of a hand, and sighed. "Barbarian, right now, I wouldn't say so or not. My faith in such things is about as tired as my creaking bones."

"You talk too much about your bones, old man," Morak said. He shook his head at the raft, then crawled into his sleeping roll.

A moment later, he felt Carina's warm body recline next to his. "Of course it will float," she whispered, "Tok is a master craftsman."

Then she was silent, unmoving, gazing at the sand. A sea breeze moved golden strands of hair about her face, and the orange glow of the sun gave her eyes a ghostly, feline sheen.

Morak watched her face closely. "Are you cold?" He asked finally, his voice almost a whisper.

She nodded, dropping her eyes in sudden shyness.

Morak raised the flap of his bedroll. Carina smiled and crawled in. Morak glanced over at Tok's bedroll. The old man was sleeping over near his raft, and turned away, huddled against the cold. Morak shrugged and pulled Carina close to him...

• • •

"Let all the gods that roam the skies be damned!" Dagrag's hideous shout woke the other three. They sat up, wondering at the thick whiteness that surrounded them. Morak could barely see Tok through the whiteness just on the other side of the tiny campfire. The Barbarian had not experienced its like before, and he shivered in the bone-cold shroud. His home, Areban, was an inland city of Barbaricum. Even to Carina and Tok, such a sight was rare. It was like being enclosed in an endless, yet tiny room. Carina shuddered and moved closer to Morak for warmth. Tok glanced at the two of them, a wordless argument ensued, the understanding of which escaped Morak, and which was evidently won by Carina for she reached up and pulled Morak's face to hers. Tok turned away.

"Well, are you going to sail now or waste even more time?" The Witch demanded of Tok.

"I don't know!" He shot back. "We could get lost out there, lost, you know."

"Cowardly fool," Dagrag screeched, "the jewel awaits us..."

"And so does death, Witch. I may be a cowardly fool, but not a stupid one."

"You fear for nothing, old man. I'll guide you. My powers ..."

"Start to fade when you get near the island," Tok said.

"You must trust me."

"Trust you?" Tok laughed, "you who can save yourself at any time? You who can leave us abandoned in this," he waved a hand toward the sea, "endless mist?"

"I'll not abandon you, old one." The Witch's voice grew suddenly quiet. "You know why. Aye, more than me, you know why."

Tok was silent for a long moment, then he shrugged. "We'll try it. Try it, I guess."

Morak watched the argument with interest, but also with a growing frustration. He suspected there was something strange about this family, which somehow included Dagrag. Hints were frequent, half-formed, but answers were rare and Morak was getting a little tired of it.

Tok spent an hour checking his raft, stretching the time, hoping for a glint of the dim sunlight. He finally sighed and gave up. Morak and Tok pulled the raft into the gently lapping sea, while Carina freed the horses from their burdens, and sent them off to find their way back to a small outcrop of two or three trees and grass fed by a small bubbling of water. Tok crawled aboard the flimsy craft as it rocked from side to side, and seemed, to Morak at least, about to fall into its many pieces.

"Well, Morak, what are you waiting for?"

"Waiting to wake up from this nightmare," he muttered as he cautiously edged himself onto the raft. He sat near the middle, and held on with both hands. Carina ran and leapt onto the raft, laughing as Morak hissed in fear.

"Relax, Morak," she laughed, "Tok makes better rafts than that."

The Barbarian looked at Carina for a long time, uneasy at her laughing eyes centered on him, yet not quite willing to let go of his handholds. Finally he did so as Tok handed him one of the flat pieces of wood they had chosen for oars. They pushed out into the open sea, the raft swaying gently on soft undulating waves, and Morak took a deep breath. He was suddenly thankful for the thick fog.

Dagrag floated silently down from somewhere in the sky. "Just follow me," she said, "and put muscle into it. You've cost me too much time already." The two men began paddling after the Witch's blackness, a splotch amid the endless fog. That enveloping surrounding white mist rode with them all during their journey. Morak thought later that perhaps it was best so. If he had been able to see the true vastness of the waters upon which they were precariously perched, he might have been even more nervous.

As it was, half of forever seemed to pass before they reached a shallow lagoon at the edge of Simathica. They had been guided unerringly by the Witch, even when they heard the distant sound of water breaking over rocks. She guided them between potential hazards, and into a swamp-like lagoon, calm behind a natural breakwater. They beached the raft and climbed onto a sandy beach of Simathica.

The travelers stood looking around the eerie silence of the place. The fog was here, too, though it seemed to be thinning somewhat. It was an island of tropical jungle, much different than the desert of Karan. Mountains rose out of the sea, and thrust themselves into the sky with a covering of choked growth. Scrawny plants erupted here and there, and Morak decided that the green color of those held much stone greyness, as if they lived off the rock itself. Something of an evil, putrid smell hung thick with the fog, and the dampness left a greasy feel to the skin.

"I don't like this place," Morak proclaimed. "It stinks. And it's too quiet for me." He also did not like the deep shadows; the dim sunlight was still too near Karan's horizon to illuminate those shadows, and the things which hid within them.

"Come along," Dagrag said. Following the Witch, now on foot, they made their way inland. The fog became thinner, and made white wisps to curl about the upper portions of the island. Still, a dimness remained, as if the morning sun was unable to penetrate this far into the unknown.

"Gods," Morak exclaimed, "a herd of dragon could attack and we'd never know."

"Yes we would," Tok shot back, "we'd hear the beat of their wings."

Morak was about to laugh when he heard it. "What was that?" He looked around wildly.

Tok bade the Barbarian's open mouth to be quiet. Everyone stopped and listened. It had the sound of a tent flapping regularly in a desert breeze, distant but moving closer. An ear-splitting cry broke the day into nightmare. Carina dropped to the ground, looking up in fear. Morak drew his sword and stood waiting, eyes roving the empty whiteness.

Tok, too, waited. But Dagrag was nowhere to be seen. The tent grew to a thousand tents flapping in a wind storm. The scream came again and again, growing louder and closer. A dark indistinct shadow flittered down from the mountains and passed overhead.

Then it was upon them, the mist blown away by its incessant flapping. Morak saw only a glimpse of its evil reptilian bird face, a long, tooth-filled beak and dark, glowing red eyes on each side of its alligator head. Its thirty meter wings covered all three of them in a wind storm as it lowered itself to snap at their ducking heads. The talons that grabbed for them could have enclosed a horse with no difficulty. It hovered above Morak's head and squalled, those talons opening and closing, the wind from its wings sweeping dust into the Barbarian's eyes. With another ear-splitting scream, it dipped and attempted to catch Morak. But his sword sung and buried itself in the thing's huge claw. It shrieked in pain and drew back, taking Morak with it—holding onto his sword. He wrenched until it came loose, and fell painfully to the ground, stomach first. Morak lie gasping for breath. Before he could move, the creature again descended, this time to grab at Carina. She screamed as she felt the talons close about her body. Tok flung his knife, to bury itself in the thing's chest. It seemed not to even notice as its endless tent wings flapped another wind storm. It rose into the white sky, still holding the screaming woman in its claw. The pulsating screams grew dimmer, fading into the whiteness that surrounded the mountains.

Morak slowly got to his feet and brushed himself off as the giant creature disappeared into the fog. Both Morak and Tok took hesitant steps toward the mountains.

Dagrag stepped from behind a tree. "You stupid clumsy oaf!" She screamed, "you've failed us all by your bumbling."

"Shut up, Witch," Morak said quietly, and Tok, noticing the cold look in the Barbarian's eyes, wisely said nothing.

"You don't tell me to shut up, Barbarian," she spat, "Carina's gone because of you..."

"I said shut up, Witch."

Dagrag stormed, literally, at those words. "You miserable unspeakable cur, I'll call up your ancestors to haunt you..."

"Powerful Witch," Morak shouted, his face inches from Dagrag's ugly one, "then why didn't you do something to stop that thing? Tell me that." He turned away, his eyes searching.

The Witch was quiet. The wind blew a little less harshly. Her face became a darker shadow. "My powers don't work on it," she said quietly.

Morak turned back. "Then you'd best not be accusing others of failure." He picked up his sword and sheathed it, then strode off.

Dagrag flew in front of him. "Wait," she cried, "that's not the way to the jewel. Where are you going?"

Morak ignored her.

"We're here to get the jewel, nothing more. Forget the girl, she's dead by now anyway."

Morak kept walking. He topped a rocky rise and headed down into a shallow valley choked with the gray-green vegetation. He slashed through it, unheeding of the biting insects and larger, hissing things that slithered from his path. The way began to rise, until finally, he came to a rocky mountain that stretched jagged into the white mist.

Several times, in his youth, Morak had gone after the dragons that lived in the southern mountains of Karan. But those creatures were much smaller than this beast. They could carry away a child, but a grown human would be too much for a dragon.

Morak had heard legends of such creatures as this, but he had never seen one. He'd been told this about such creatures; they always sought the highest point to make their foul nests.

He gazed up at that craggy mountain, his dark eyes searching, narrow and angry. He wiped his hands together and began to climb. Hand and footholds were scarce, and movement became painfully slow. Yet an urgency nipped at his heels, tired and insect-bit though he was. It began to get warm. Sweat rolled down his back and made his hands slick. After a while, Morak looked down, and saw he had not gained much up the steep mountainside. He sighed, flexed his huge arm muscles, and climbed some more.

He concentrated on the sound his body made, scraping against the rock, his hoarse breathing. The fog cleared and the sun appeared over the distant horizon, and his whole world narrowed to that next hand-hold, the next painful pull up a few centimeters. Perhaps another would have given up. But he was Morak, a Barbarian, and Barbarians kept their promises, and delivered vengeance where vengeance was needed.

When a chill wind blew across his shoulders, Morak felt he would die on that forsaken rock. But he saw the vision of Carina's face before him, frightened, crying. He climbed.

It was many hours later when he grabbed the ledge with one large, bleeding hand. Another forever brought the other hand into view, then a face strained with effort no human body was expected to endure, wet and shiny with sweat, covered over with grime and rock dust. Slowly, shaking, too weak to move another meter, he pulled his body over the edge, and lie gasping.

The sun shining in his eyes woke him. Morak tried to remember where he was. His joints were stiff and aching. It took him several minutes to sit up, and more to stand. He viewed his surroundings, the top ledge of a mountain. The space was empty, except for a huge nest made of sticks and branches, and a few life-hungry plants. It stank, too, as if some of the carcasses that flapping horror had brought home for dinner had been left too long. There was no sight of the thing, or of Carina. Morak stepped over bleached white bones lying scattered about the nest. Small scurrying things made way for him, and others hissed from nearby rocks. It was an effort to climb up, and look into the nest.

Carina's head was in there, staring eyeless up at the dark morning sky. Shy scavengers scurried for cover. The rest of the woman was nowhere to be seen. Anger was useless, as was sadness. Yet he felt both. In his Barbarian way, he had loved Carina as much as he had any wench. Now a haze seemed to envelope his short memories of her, blotting out even consciousness.

Carina. Beautiful Carina. What deep, dark secret did she, Tok and the Witch hide? His mind reeled, not even in anger, but in a deep sorrow that came pounding to the surface as the sea did on hard stone rocks. Slowly the rocks became sand, and as such, Morak was swept away into that sea of remembering, swirling through and about him, touching. Touching. And crying out in pain. If only...

The jewel! That incongruous shout echoed through the dream caverns of his mind. A shout—and a scream. The pain! He tried to put his hands over his ears, but they wouldn't move.

Wake up you fool! You fool! The jewel! The jewel!

And pain.

Morak woke. He was bound, could not move. He looked down at what held him tight, and the ultimate fear grabbed his heart and mind, and traded places with his stomach. Land was far below and moving past. He was held fast by talons of the giant dragon. He tried to wiggle loose, but the thing's grip held him tightly. Morak's ribs ached, sending sharp pains through his chest. Visions of Carina's face kept popping into his mind, eyeless and chewed, with Morak's face taking its place.

He tried to quiet his pounding heart and think. He was Morak, a Barbarian. And Barbarians do not fear, instead they kill and conquer and fill the hearts of men and beasts with terror.

With those words from his youth, Morak calmed his mind and began to consider his move. He knew the thing had to land soon, somewhere, high up on rocky cliffs. Then maybe he would have a chance to escape. Maybe. He prayed to all the gods he could remember to give him that chance. He would make the most of it, aye, and more. He'd make that bird pay.

But he knew the gods would not answer. Barbarians made their own way, and gods merely looked on with interest.

The beast lazily circled a craggy peak. Below was lost in the ground mist, and Morak suppressed a shudder of fear. The flapping horror dropped down, and perched at the very tip of that pinnacle, dropping Morak to grasp at small handholds or fall to his death.

Gravel and small pieces of rock broke off in his hands as Morak grabbed wildly. His feet kept slipping on the smooth rock sides. Could this be his time to die?

By the gods, Morak swore, if it was he'd take that beast with him. He grabbed for its left claw, providing him with a handhold. The monster seemed not to notice as it sat preening its scale-like wings.

Hanging by one hand, Morak broke off a piece of rock—and with a growl of rage and anger, smashed it with all his strength against the thing's other claw. The flapping horror screeched in pain, jerked back, and jumped into the sky. Morak hung by one hand, feeling the strength slipping from his arm. And when that huge evil maw snapped at him, he could hold on no longer. He fell, too weak to even scream.

And it seemed he was floating, not falling. Was dying like this? Morak thought. He always expected to die the death of a Barbarian—matching swords against some other rogue or thief and having his head lopped off. He was somewhat sad, dying at the whims of some hideous creature that even now, flapped its tent wings, uncaring into oblivion.

The feeling of floating persisted. Morak wondered when the end would come. Or had it already? He opened his eyes, and found that he actually was floating. This amazed him even more than falling. Seconds later, he softly touched solid earth.

Dagrag stood before him, scowling, arms folded. "Well, are you through with your useless nonsense? We've come here to do a job." She turned from him, then turned back, "and be thankful you were not closer to the center of his island, Barbarian, because my powers fade further on. I would not have been able to save you."

Morak looked at the witch woman's morbid face. "Carina's dead," he said softly, looking again to the ground, unused to such things.

"Yes, I know," the Witch said, "now come."

"You don't even care, do you?" Morak looked again into those night-black eyes of hers. "You don't even care."

Dagrag looked as if she were about to flare with anger again. Then she looked away. "I care," she said in a muffled voice. "But I'm not human, even as you might think yourself. Not any more. Perchance, someday when you've seen most of this land as I have, you'll understand the way a witch mourns the death of her daughter."

"I don't think so," Morak spat. Then, "your daughter?"

But the Witch was no longer talking.

Morak brushed himself off, then followed Dagrag to a small camp Tok had made.

The old man crouched before a fire. He looked up hopefully as the Witch and Morak entered the clearing. Something died in him when he saw only the two of them, that something which fights against the waves of time. Morak could see it in the old man's eyes. Tok seemed to shrink and grow older, his shoulders sagged, and he turned back to the fire with a small, sad smile on his lips. He never asked about Carina. But his eyes never grew young again. And they never held the fire of youth again.

"Hello, Morak," was all he said, stirring the ashes with a charred stick. The fingers holding that stick were grasped tightly, whitening the knuckles.

"It's time to move on," Dagrag said gruffly. "There are many more ways to die on this cursed island."

• • •

The island's interior was much the same as the fringes, except here grew thicker vegetation among swamps created from water trapped in crevices. Some of these crevices had been covered with sand and dust, and grown thick with many types of plants. Sounds filled the air like a rising heat, but each died without echo, as if enclosed. Screams and twitters, rustlings and other ill-defined murmurs assailed their ears. This kept their eyes roving, searching for the lurkers of that rocky, foul-smelling swamp.

"My powers end here," Dagrag said, looking at the dim gray sky intently, as if searching for the means of that mystery. "Ahead about a kilometer from here lies a crypt—and inside, the door to the jewel. But we must be careful, all manner of hell has broken loose in this forsaken land."

"I'll agree with that," Tok said grimly.

They moved on, slowly, warily, circling bogs and depressions choked with vegetation, insects, and small animals.

As they descended into a large valley, a quietness settled over the island. The wind stopped. Morak could hear all three of them breathing. He looked around, over his shoulder, searching, saw Tok's eyes moving, a little frightened.

Nearby something waited. Morak could feel it.

Something godlike in its size and power.

"Something's out there, watching us," Dagrag said softly. Their pace had slowed to a standstill. The silence seemed to become thick, seeping from everywhere until it filled the steamy air, choked it. Yet it was a silence filled with threat, and it pulled fear out of them. The muscles along Morak's back began to ripple.

"Come along, fools," Dagrag growled softly, pushing past them purposefully. But even that seemed small amid the silence. Morak and Tok followed. But their bravado lasted only a few more steps.

Morak felt the ground shudder. Or was it his imagination?

What he saw next he could not define. It was huge. It rose up before them, hideously grinning mouth dripping with slime. Its eyes glowed red-yellow. It had a long, snake-like neck, attached to a green body that disappeared into the swamp.

Its cry was small, but the body moved toward them like oil, pushing aside bushes and swamp plants.

The three had stopped in fear when they first saw the thing, now it loomed over them, coming closer, growing larger. Morak was the first to break that death-spell.

He drew his long knife, and with a scream of defiance, threw it with all his strength. The snake-beast dripped its head to gulp down the bronze blade.

"Run!" Dagrag screamed, looking wildly about for a place to.

"Where?" Tok cried. Morak looked around swiftly. There was only one choice—a rocky rise that led up into the heights of the isle. If they could climb that in time...

"This way," he shouted. They began running, jumping, leaping over and around puddles of mud, swampy bogs, and other living and dead obstructions. Morak looked over his shoulder and saw the creature gaining on them, effortlessly, slithering through the mud and swamps with a speed no running man could match.

Finally, there was a hard rock surface beneath Morak's feet.

He stepped aside and shoved Tok ahead, then Dagrag. He turned and the monster was upon him. The Barbarian drew his sword, swung back and sliced as the creature dived at him. The blade struck and bit in, startling the worm. It drew back to consider this little thing that bit.

Morak turned and scrambled up into the rocks. His pursuer hesitated but for a moment, then crushed rocks with its jaws just behind Morak's foot. The creature pulled back, shaking its hideous head.

Tok reached down and pulled Morak up to a higher position. The Barbarian turned, breathing heavily, to see the worm once again working its way into the rocks. Still, its body stretched back into the swamp, an endless green cable of hell.

"Gods, will nothing stop that beast?"

"Nothing we've got," the old man puffed, then he tapped the Barbarian's shoulder. "Keep going—higher, it's the only way."

"Unh," Morak grunted. They climbed. At this, they were faster than the beast which followed. The rocks were not its home grounds, but it had chased prey into them before—none had ever escaped.

Higher the humans went, an old man, a Barbarian, and a witch with no powers. Their feet scraped and slid on the steep sides of rocks. Progress slowed as their strength waned. The creature kept on, tirelessly, gaining on them.

Finally, Dagrag slumped to rest against a boulder. "Get up Witch," Morak growled, "up or be eaten."

"I hope it gets a bellyache," she replied weakly.

Tok had collapsed near her. Now he stood and looked down at the monster, then back up the heights. "An idea old man?" Morak asked quietly, seeing the gleam in Tok's eyes.

"Maybe," Tok said as he climbed over a small outcropping to search for something.

When Tok returned, Morak looked surprised. "An old piece of wood?" He said, looking down at the fast-approaching worm.

"Leverage, young one. Have you never heard of leverage? You will, when you get old. We can use this piece of wood to move even the largest rocks. Genius, eh, Barbarian?" He smiled as he ran behind one of the boulders, fitted the log under it, and began bearing down.

"Move over, old man. The wood weighs more than you do." He grunted as he added his weight and muscle. The boulder grated, moved slightly, but did not come loose. Both men bore down. "Harder, old man," Morak shouted.

Dagrag peered around at them, fear in her pit-black eyes. "Hurry fools, it approaches."

"Then get your fat body over here and help us," Tok grunted. Dagrag started to shout a retort, then heard the small, baby-like scream just down slope. She hurried to the two men and added her not inconsiderable weight.

She grasped the end of the pole and bore down. The rotted wood splintered and cracked, throwing all three to the ground. But the stone had come loose. It rolled, slowly at first, then began to pick up speed, bringing other boulders with it. In a very short time, an avalanche of boulders, rocks, and dust engulfed the beast. The last Morak saw of it was its open maw. Then the rocks and dust obliterated his view.

The three lie where they had fallen, too exhausted to move.

• • •

"There," Dagrag whispered her foul breath into Morak's ear sometime later, and some distance away from the swamp. "See it, the door to the crypt. Beyond that is the *Tome of the Dark Devices*, which is valuable beyond all meaning. But the jewel—the jewel exceeds even that."

They crouched behind some bushes and a boulder. Before them, beyond scraggly trees and vines, carved out of the side of the living stone, was a door, also made of stone.

The atmosphere had become hot, and insects buzzed about the three, biting and annoying.

"Well, then, let's go," Tok said, pushing between the other two and out into the open.

"No! Wait," Dagrag shouted, reaching for the old man. Tok turned, a questioning look spreading across his face.

"Wha...?"

"The vines, you old fool, they live—on meat..."

Tok looked down at his feet, where thin strands of greenish-gray leaves were silently wrapping around them. He looked up, an amused kind of horror on his face. Before he could utter a sound, a vine dropped from a nearby tree, slapping him on the shoulder like an old friend, but it stuck there, draping itself over his arm and around his chest, small living needles leisurely sucking blood.

Tok choked out a word and tried to move. The jungle floor came alive—and the trees seemed to writhe as vines left their branches to envelope the old man's body with their hypodermic stickers.

"Help...hel—" There came a gurgle, a shifting weight. Morak leapt into the mass of vegetation and began slashing away at the vines.

"Bloodthirsty plants!" He growled, his sword slashing through dozens of the dancing, coiling vines. The air filled with the sound of rustling leaves and the stink of old flesh.

Vines coiled about Morak, wrapping his sword arm and legs. "Barbarian, forget about the old man—forget him," Dagrag shouted from the safety of the rock.

Morak felt the stinging pricks of the vine's needle sharp thorns as they lashed at him and stuck. He tried to move, and fear rose in his throat as the devilish mass of moving vegetation danced toward him. His sword arm kept slashing, cutting. He worked like a machine, chopping the vines that clung to him and slicing at those that moved his way.

His efforts allowed him to free one foot, then the other, and he stumbled back toward the rocks and the Witch. Morak cut the remaining vines and freed himself from their sticking strands. Dagrag grabbed his arm and pulled him out of reach.

The Barbarian collapsed, breathing in ragged gasps. "Tok?" He finally got out. His body, pricked in a hundred places, oozed crimson.

"He is dead, Barbarian. Those vines do not take long to suck their victim dry of blood. He was a fool."

Morak looked. Most of the remaining vines were slowly repositioning themselves in the trees and along the ground. All became still, except for a cocoon-like mass where Tok had stood, still pulsing slightly.

Morak sat up and looked at the Witch. "Then there's just the two of us, eh? Well, it was better for him. Without Carina. Without Carina, he was nothing but an empty hulk of an old man."

"You know nothing," Dagrag growled, "with Tok's death, a great experiment has passed on, uncompleted, unrealized." She shook her head. "Sit, Barbarian, for a moment while you catch your breath. And listen to Tok's real purpose in life. Yes, listen. It's a tale that begins with great daring and some joy and ends in failure."

Puzzled, Morak leaned back against the boulder. Dagrag's face softened a bit as she gazed off into whatever fond memories a witch might have.

"We who are born with dark powers are always the most beautiful of children, Morak. We become winsome wenches, frolicking with young men." She looked at him, "Our powers are weak, Barbarian, until we reach adulthood, and somewhat beyond. And yes, with the rise of our powers, *this* happens," she indicated herself, "we grow ugly and wizened, and foul of breath and temper." She looked around her, "something—something about our powers burns the beauty from our souls, and from our bodies."

"A sad story," Morak agreed, "yet what has this to do with Tok, and his—experiment."

Dagrag's cold eyes met Morak's. "I am his daughter."

Morak sat up. "*You?*"

"Yes. And when I was much younger and beautiful, Carina out of these loins came, fathered by Tok.

"But..."

"Yes, evil in the eyes of our society to inbreed thusly. But there was a purpose, had it reached its conclusion. Tok's original mate was a woman only, not a witch. From their union, I was born. Witch power consumed me when I reached adulthood. Before the ugliness took me, I gave birth to Carina. She had not yet become a witch, herself, but she carried the potential. In a year, maybe two, she would have gained her power and become old and ugly. Our plan was to birth a witch with stronger power, younger. And holding off the ugliness until more years had passed. Yes, a forbidden experiment to be sure. Caught, we would have been put to death. We knew that, but were still willing to try. And from

Carina..."

"Meesha?"

Dagrag nodded. "A forbidden child, perhaps doomed to the curse of witches. She was to have born Tok's child once again when adulthood arrived for her—and that one, Meesha's child, would have had the power in childhood," Dagrag's fist clenched and shook, "but not the hideous fate of the witch as she grew older. But now it's too late. Meesha will be the most powerful witch of all when she is grown. But her fate is sealed. We needed one more generation." Dagrag shook her head sadly.

"If this—experiment—was so important to you," Morak commented, "why subject Tok to these dangers?"

"Because, Barbarian, we also needed the jewel and its power, and knowledge found within the pages of the *Tome*. Would you have followed an ugly witch and an untried girl on this quest? Besides, it was his experiment, after all. The jewel within this island is part of the mystery, and no one so far has been able to claim it. And there is," she paused, looked at Morak, "well, you'll see." She jerked her head toward the door, "but the only way to reach the crypt is to run, and run fast. Understand?"

"Yes, Witch." And a few minutes later, that is just what they did. Dagrag surprised Morak with her speed. The vines moved after the two as they passed by, but most were too slow to snag the fear-spurred humans.

Morak grasped the handle of the crypt door and tried to catch his breath. "Gods, Witch, I haven't run so much since those sand pirates found out I stole their gold."

"Well, you'd best get that door open, thief, or those sand pirates won't have to be concerned." She pressed close to Morak as the vines weaved their way closer.

The stone grated as Morak pulled. Sweat broke out on his brow, yet his efforts were of little effect; almost as if time had welded the door shut. Dagrag hissed as a vine touched her shoulder, and she squeezed closer to the Barbarian.

"Hurry, you fool, hurry!"

"Shut up, Witch. Let me get this door open." Morak planted a foot against the stone casing, grabbed the rusty round handle with both hands, and pulled with all his strength. The door held for a moment, then gave way all at once, knocking them both within reach of the plants.

They pulled vines from each other, then scrambled up and inside the dark corridor. Morak stood and pulled the door shut, locking them in darkness. He waited for his eyes to adjust but there was not much light from which to adjust. Dagrag reached around him and pulled a torch off the wall.

"Got a striker?" she asked. Morak handed over his flint piece. He looked around nervously. He could hear the vines swishing against the door, whispering among themselves it seemed. Ahead there was only the blackness of an unknown corridor. Morak much preferred the open, the desert, where one could see one's opponents, and know whether to fight or run.

Dagrag finally got the torch lit. The flickering light revealed a long, narrow stone passageway, dank and dusty.

"Follow me," Dagrag grunted.

She led the way down to another door. This one opened easier, and Morak peered inside at a small room with several more doors and a dark passage leading from it. And there, among the dust and air of ages, rested the *Tomb of the Dark Devices*.

"There it is," Dagrag hissed, "*that* is what brought Tok to this forsaken place."

It rested on a pedestal made of an unknown metal. They both stood looking down at it for a long time, wonderment filling even the Witch's face. Dust lie as a coating atop the huge book, and cobwebs wove its pages.

"You see, Barbarian," Dagrag said softly, without looking up, "legends sometimes are true. When he was young, Tok had discovered a few paragraphs that he thought were copied from this book, part of a hand-written chapter on how to increase witch power and reduce the evil effects." She looked at him, "but the final pages of that chapter were missing, Morak. He could begin the experiment, but he didn't know how to end it. Except that the fourth generation..." She shrugged, "what? He didn't know. The pages within that," she pointed, "might have told him. Now...it will never be."

She sighed, and the cobwebs moved slightly with that sound. "But come—we must not forget the jewel. That's why *I* am here."

The silence, wonder-filled and ancient, was broken by the Witch's grating voice. Morak looked into her endless eyes.

"Yes, Witch. Your—jewel."

They continued along the passageway, lit a second torch, a flickering comfort among the blackness.

Another turn, and the corridor began to descend, deeper into the island's bowels. The walls became damp and slimy, and clumps of some smelly green growth appeared. The way down steepened. Footing became unstable. Once Morak slipped, reached out a hand to steady himself, then drew it back even more quickly, wiping a green goo from his palm.

He could almost feel the stone pressing in upon him, and had it not been for the Witch ahead of him, Morak would have fled back into the welcome freedom of the surface.

Worse, the air became stale, settling on his skin, damp and greasy. He felt they were on the path to hell itself.

They came, finally, to another door. This door was different, however. It was made not of stone, as the others had been, but of metal, a metal that shined like the steel of his sword. This door had no handle.

"How...?"

"It opens for us," Dagrag whispered. Morak looked at her questioningly as she stomped up to the door and waited. And it did open, with a click and a thunk, then sliding into the wall to leave a dark entrance.

"How did you know...?"

Dagrag shrugged. "I dreamed it in a dream. Perhaps I read it in a legend. Beyond that, I can't tell you."

Musty odors emerged, along with muted noises and hints of a muted glow.

Peering in cautiously, Morak could see more metal, and strange eerie lights that went off and on and glowed softly.

In fact, the entire room seemed to be made of metal, punctuated with lights.

"Well, go on in," Dagrag prodded, pushing at him. The Barbarian held back, almost against his will. "Fool! Are you afraid of your own shadow? There is no Thunder Devil here—age has made him silent. There is only a jewel and some left-over lights."

She dropped the torch and stepped through, urging Morak ahead of her. He stepped into a room filled with an ancient silence.

"Yes," Morak said, "but still, Witch, there is a feeling about this place that I do not like. It's older than us, yet those who built it knew how to bend and mold metal as we do cloth." He turned to the Witch, his eyes aglow. "And what if they come back and find us here, in their magic room of lights and metal. What then Witch?"

"Bah! I'm sick of your weakness and fear. This is a place of gods, not men..."

"You're right, Witch. And if they come back..."

"They're *gone*, Barbarian. They died ages ago; time is their epitaph. So move on, or go back to your blessed morning light. Just get out of my way." She tried to push past him.

He moved further in, stood in the center of the small room, turning slowly, eyes wide in wonder. "This is a Devil's place," he whispered.

Dagrag shoved past him to another door, this one with a metal turning handle. Morak followed her through, sword drawn, as if it could do any good against such that had made this place. Yet, the blade felt good in his hand. He felt less naked with it.

The passageway turned to the right. Dagrag went about halfway, then stopped. "This is the final door, Barbarian," she said, examining it closely. "Beyond is the jewel."

At the center of the door, about halfway up, a square plate held words, and above that, a small window. Morak studied the message, written in words he didn't understand, nor did he care to. He would have left long ago—fled back to the swamps to fight the worm. Except that Carina wasn't here, and Tok wasn't here. And he'd promised them.

He looked at the message again. Most of the unknown writing was meaningless to him, but he sensed a great warning:

Danger
Cosmic-Jewel Amplifier
Laser-Fusion Device
Radiation: Alpha, Beta, Gamma, X-Ray
Enter Only When Apparatus is Inoperative

Protective Clothing Required
s/J. R. Darm, Lt./Cl. Cmdr.
Simathica Antarctic Research Station, USAF

Above the message and the window, a small red light flashed steadily. From the window itself came a bright glow, red with a tint of yellow. An angry red, Morak thought, like the eye of a devil.

"Look in there, Barbarian," the Witch whispered. "Look upon the Blood Jewel of Simathica. See how it glows."

Morak glanced into the window. He saw a tiny room filled with more lights. But it was the center of the room that rooted their attention. A pedestal-like stand rose out of the floor, the height of a man's chest. On it was the source of the glow—a large jewel, glowing red and yellow, pulsing with energy.

"So you have found your jewel, Witch," Morak said.

"Yes, Barbarian, I've found it, the source of all power in Karan. And it's mine." Her voice was thick with triumph, drunk with success. She turned to him, an insane smile on her leathery lips, and a strange glow in her night-black eyes.

"Take the book, Morak, it's yours. It's worth half a kingdom or more. The jewel is all I want." She looked down at her left hand and tugged at a pitted, dull green ring around her index finger. She handed it to Morak. "Here, give this to the one watching Meesha. It will identify you. Take the child to the east, Barbarian, to the cities there, and sell her to a rich family. Tell them of her—of her ancestry, Morak, and she'll bring you a heavy bag of gold." She grabbed a handful of cloth at his chest, "do this not for me, but for Tok and Carina. Do you understand?"

Morak pried her hand loose, and placed the ring in a pocket. "Yes, Witch, I understand. If we escape from this," he looked around, "this pit of hell, I'll do as you say."

"Good," she took a deep breath, "good. Now help me get this door open."

She impatiently fingered the wheels and latches. "Gods and devils," she screamed in rage. Morak joined her, turning a large wheel one way, then another. Suddenly, there came a click, and the wheel began to spin by itself. Another click, and the door popped open slightly. In the distance, a loud noise howled on and off, like a Thunder Devil awakening. Dagrag grasped the edge of the door with leathery hands and pulled it wide enough for her to enter. She slipped in and pulled the door shut behind her before Morak could move to follow. The wheels spun and clicked, and the door was once again locked.

He watched through the window with a feeling that, perhaps somehow, he'd misunderstood about the jewel. He could see the Witch's evil mouth open in a wondering, insane laugh. Dagrag approached the jewel, she stopped, slowly reached out both hands, and moved her fingers to close over the huge, brightly glowing crystal. Morak saw beams of yellow-red emanating between her fingers, flashing in her black eyes.

From somewhere, another loud screeching noise began. It frightened Morak.

Then he realized it was Dagrag, screaming.

The flesh began melting from her face, leaving black orbs of eyes, dripping skin and flesh and blood.

She screamed again, as none have ever screamed before. The walls shook with it. Morak's eyes, already open wide with fear and wonder, opened even wider. The screams became high pitched echoes, and after a time, the echoes died. He glanced back into the room and saw what had once been Dagrag evaporating, becoming mist, floating toward the glassy, shiny surface of the tall ceiling.

With her last bit of substance, Dagrag grasped the jewel, jabbed it against her iridescent breast. The scream echoed and was lost in a thunder of flashing light. Morak, almost blinded, ducked behind the door, dropping his sword and sliding to the floor.

He clasped hands over his ears to hold out, unsuccessfully, the howling noise and a deeper, shaking rumble. To Morak, it seemed like a battle between Thunder Devils and Lightning Gods. He shook in fear and pain.

Sometime later, silence returned. Finally, he dared to rise and peer cautiously into the room. A fine violet mist hung in the air. That, and a few lights. The Witch and the jewel were both gone.

Morak stood there for a long while, afraid to move, and thinking thoughts too deep for his simple mind. He shook his head, then turned and retraced his steps back through the steel door, up the damp passageway, and to the book.

He looked back down that black pit from which he had just emerged, fearing something following him. But there was nothing. Nothing at all.

He carefully examined the book. He blew and brushed the dust from the ancient tome, and cleared away the age-old and new cobwebs. Slowly, he lifted the heavy cover. The words were strange, like those on the door. Yet he found himself almost able to understand them. As if he'd once known, and had then forgotten.

It had taken three lives to get the book. Legends spoken only in whispers had barely mentioned it, yet Morak, a southlands Barbarian now held it in his callused hands. Its value could not be measured in terms of gold, Morak thought. Yet, what would be its value if someone could understand the words? What secrets could be found there among those scratches and lines?

Enough to make a man a king? Morak smiled slightly. Yes, somewhere in Karan would be someone who could understand the words. It would be a new beginning for him, Morak thought, someone to be feared and respected for more than a strong sword arm.

He tucked the book away in his pouch, then walked toward the corridor leading to the outside. Once back in the morning sunlight, he still had to face again the horrors and evil surprises of the isle of Simathica.

It hardly seemed a challenge.

Book Two

Caravan to B'saad

Morak looked outward from the rise upon which he stood. Before him, spread to the horizon, was the largest desert of Karan, the Center Pole Desert. He wore a gray-white robe of the desert dweller, and a hood to protect himself from the heat. At his side, a sword, large by most standards, and sharp. Slung over his left shoulder was a leather bag filled with his few belongings, and a book.

His build and manner proved him to be a Barbarian from the southlands, where, among sand dunes and a few inland lakes and rivers, his people carved out a precarious existence. The rivers provided irrigation for crops and water for livestock, and the lakes held a variety of fish. Barbarians were a wild and untamed people, proud of their warlike customs. They lived one rest time to another, never knowing if food would fill their bellies. Barbarians, for the most part, were quick to laugh, quick to fight; and death too came suddenly more often than not.

Morak was a long way from home now, though. He gazed across the endless desert, toward the east. Behind him, beyond the range of low, sandy hills, and some far unknown distance back down the coast was the isle of Simathica. He shuddered at the thought. Simathica, an island rich in legends and quick ways to die, had required a raft ride there, and back. Three had gone in with him to steal the fabled Blood Jewel of Simathica; Morak was alone coming out, carrying not the jewel, but a book.

Ah, but what a book! One that almost rivaled the jewel in legends, whispered about and dreamed of in camps of thieves. He knew it as *The Tome of the Dark Devices*. Now he had it, here, within his pouch. He fingered it idly, wondering at its meaning, and how it could make him rich. And whether or not he wanted to know its secrets. For as certain as he was of the book's value, his mind could not escape the conviction that the pages therein held many dark and terrible ways to die. And even, perhaps, a horror beyond his capability to comprehend. Considering what he'd seen on Simathica, he could comprehend some significant horrors. He'd already been told of one of the book's secrets, and the resultant child of a forbidden experiment involving the old man named Tok, and witches. The thought of it made him shudder.

Morak stepped off the rise, back down to where his horse waited. And along with the horse, a child named Meesha. He'd left the child holding the animal's reins, but one flick of the horse's head would probably be enough to knock her down, tiny waif that she was.

"It's hot," Meesha commented as Morak came up. Meesha was perhaps eight seasons old, a little tall for her age and whisper thin. She had the soft golden hair of her sister/mother, and the black shining eyes of a witch.

The Barbarian grunted in reply. He helped her into the saddle, then climbed up behind. Privately, Morak wondered if there ever were lands where green grew in more than just patches. He'd heard of such places, some toward the east where they were headed, and others, legends told, of lands across seas. Yes, across seas. He laughed at that. The seas were more endless even than the thrice-cursed desert.

Tok and the Witch, Dagrag, had made him promise to deliver Meesha to the east, sell her to a rich family. A week ago he'd picked up the girl child from her keeper, using the Witch's ring as identification, only because he planned to go east himself. At least as far as B'saad. That might not be far enough east to suit the Witch, but she was dead, and Morak thought he could sell Meesha to a prince of B'saad for almost as much as a wealthy easterner might pay.

The girl was the product of Tok's experiment. And Morak was certain the old man's methods violated the precepts of all the religions on Karan.

The third step in a quadrabred experiment, Meesha would never fulfill her part. Tok, her father, grandfather, and great grandfather, had died on Simathica. Meesha's child, had Tok lived to father it, might have had a unique concentration of witch power without the bodily deterioration all witches faced. So they said. But now...

Meesha, it seemed to Morak, was destined to have little or no witch power, so he wondered if they all were fools. However, he'd make a promise, and he intended to keep it.

Morak and Meesha rode eastward toward the rising sun. It would be weeks still until the orange orb rose higher in the sky and turned yellow. The Long Day was only weeks old on its half-year journey across the horizon. The desert was swept by cool winds and a few stars still pricking the dark blue sky. Legends also talked of a moon, a giant shining round orb in the sky, like the sun only smaller, which shared the heavens with stars. Morak searched the sky, trying to imagine such a thing, but he couldn't. Occasionally, especially during the Long Night, he saw a thin glowing crescent his teachers had called Marama, but that could not be the round Moon that the legends spoke of.

Topping the next sandy rise, the Barbarian sighted distant campfires. He stopped to consider his next move. Meesha turned in the saddle, looking up into his dark eyes. "Why are we stopping? I'm hungry." To Morak's surprise, she'd taken the news of her family's death with quiet solemnity, and she seemed to accept Morak as an adequate if not completely suitable substitute.

"That you probably are, little one" Morak muttered, "but we daren't go bursting into a camp uninvited—it might be a nest of hornets." He thought about it some more, then dismounted, lifted the child down, and ordered her to stay with the horse. "And keep quiet," he implored.

Morak moved in a rapid zig-zag pattern that took him to cover behind every rise in the desert ground. His heart was free of all worry, for this was the kind of action upon which a Barbarian thrived. When he heard voices, he also sighted a guard out beyond campfire glow. Silhouetted against the sun, Morak could not tell whether that one was clothed in the flowing blue robes of a caravan rider or the patched, drab grayness of the Outrider.

He could hear the nickering of horses and the groaning bleat of camels off to his left, where they were penned. From the right came quiet mutters and occasional laughs of the men seated around fires. Morak could discern several dozen such fires, indicating a large camp. Fires illuminated a line of cargo and living wagons. Morak suspected it was a true caravan, but needed to know for sure.

A soft wind picked up, and the horses and camels stirred and voiced opinions of the scents it brought.

The guard looked toward the animals, then wandered off in their direction.

Morak followed, moving in a parallel but intersecting course. When he was just over a sandy rise from the guard, Morak heaved a heavy stone to his right, farther out into the empty sand.

As he had hoped, the guard heard the soft "thump" and went to investigate. "Who's there?" the guard whispered. Which struck Morak as somewhat odd. Guards usually didn't whisper.

Morak tensed and waited. Finally, the other rounded the rise and slid down to the bottom of the sand dune, and Morak struck. The guard fell back with an "oof" of expelled air, finding himself with a chestful of Barbarian.

Too surprised to put up much of a fight, the guard grimaced and moaned.

"Be still or die," Morak whispered, holding a knife at his victim's throat. The other gave up his feeble opposition and relaxed. The Barbarian grabbed a handful of the guard's robe and held it up to what little light reached this place. It was blue.

"Well, go ahead, do what you will and be done with it," the guard grunted.

Morak heaved a sigh and rolled off his opponent. Both sat looking at each other, their faces dim from the now-hidden sun.

"Pardon my method, stranger, but I had no way of knowing if you were rider for a band of thieves, or a caravan's guard."

"And how do I know you're not, yourself, a thief? Maybe I should sound the alarm with my dying breath," the guard said slowly, his eyes glinting in the dim light. Morak brought the point of his knife up and rubbed its tip idly with his thumb. With a swift gesture, he tossed the blade to the guard, hilt first. The other snatched the knife out of the air.

"If I'm a thief," Morak said, "then kill me. Don't bother with the other guards—take all the credit yourself. You'll be a hero, and no doubt catch the eye of some lively wench."

The other looked startled, then laughed. He held Morak's knife by the hilt, turned it over in his hand, examining it. But it was such a clumsy examination that Morak doubted he'd ever handled a throwing knife before.

Finally, the guard handed the knife back. "A fine blade," he said. "You wish?"

"Passage with your caravan for myself and a young child."

The guard frowned. "A strange request from a Barbarian. How far?"

"All the way to B'saad."

The guard stood and started back toward the camp. "You'll have to ask our leader. Tarak does not take kindly to strangers— but he can always use a good sword arm."

The guard waited at the top of the dune while Morak retrieved his horse and Meesha. The Barbarian walked beside the guard, leading the horse upon which the girl rode.

"Your daughter?" The guard asked.

"No."

"I'm Meesha," she said, "and your name is Sumar."

The guard stopped. "Why, child, that's right. How did you know?"

Meesha glanced at Morak, then back to the guard, and shrugged.

Shaking his head, Morak followed the guard into camp.

Suspicious eyes watched him as he followed Sumar between fires and caravan wagons. This was a large caravan. Morak estimated at least 50 or 60 wagons, with several hundred men plus women and children. At the fore of the camp, guarded by two burly men with wide, sweeping swords, stood the largest wagon.

Morak observed women and children peering at him with awe and suspicion from behind many of the wagons and small camp tents. A family caravan rarely traveled these parts; it was one ripe for attack. Outriders needed women—and sons to grow into new thieves. And B'saad was a long way off.

One of the burly guards pounded on the heavy oaken door of the lead wagon. But a scream interrupted that gesture, a high pitched, shrill scream of abject horror. Morak turned and saw Meesha's face contorted in fear. Another scream erupted from her tiny throat.

"Meesha! What is it? What's wrong, child?"

"Don't make me go in there!" She screamed the words through tears of fright. "Don't make me go in there. Please, don't!"

"Go in where?" Morak asked, stepping beside the horse, and grasping the child's arm. "Do you mean the wagon?"

"Don't make me go in there."

The wagon door slammed open.

"What is all of this noise?" The leader, Tarak, stepped out, a tall, thin, imposing figure. "The rest candle is only half done."

Before Morak could speak, Meesha slumped out of the saddle and into Morak's arms. Her eyes were open, but her body lie limply like a doll with no bones. Her skin was cold and clammy, and damp with sweat.

An attractive red-haired woman stepped from the gathered onlookers. "Please, may I be of help?"

"Yes," Morak said, "can you care for her, for a short time."

She curtsied, "of course. I'm over there," she nodded toward a wagon to the left. She took the child from Morak's arms.

Morak turned back to the caravan's leader. Yes, he was tall, taller than Morak even, and thin, dressed in luxurious clothing one seldom saw outside the larger cities of Karan. The man's eyes were gray, small, and held a burning Morak could not quite place. His hair was long, unkempt, and black mixed with gray. A long, pointed beard matched that.

His eyes looked from Morak to the guard. "Well, Sumar, are you going to talk, or stand there staring at me until the Long Night?"

"Forgive me, leader," Sumar said, bowing low.

"Get on with it. What are you bothering me with now? Who is this?"

"He's an excellent swordsman, leader. He could have killed me if he wanted."

"Not much of a challenge there," Tarak muttered.

"I am Morak," the Barbarian said. "All I seek is to travel with your caravan until you reach B'saad. I can work for our passage."

Tarak looked the Barbarian up and down with a gaze bordering on utter contempt. He stroked his beard idly.

"Swordsmen are hard to come by these days; good ones are rare. How good are you?"

"Better than those who've come up against me," Morak growled, meeting the dry gaze of Tarak. "Not many have been foolish enough to try, but I'm alive and the fools are not."

"Hmm, yes." Another moment's close examination. "I can use you as a guard, and as a scout perhaps. You'll receive food and water, a place to sleep. And if we get through to B'saad without a loss—ten pieces of silver."

Morak nodded. "Fair. Yes, that suits me."

"Good, you've got guard duty starting now, south perimeter."

"But," Sumar protested, "that's *my* area."

Tarak turned his eyes to Sumar. "I no longer need you as a guard. Back to the cook's tent with you. That is where your talents lie, easterner. And I do not wish to be disturbed with any more screaming nonsense." He slammed the door shut.

"Well," Sumar said, "it seems I've talked myself out of a job." He shrugged, turned to Morak and grinned. "Well, then, so be it. A guard's life is not always the safest, but perhaps being a cook's helper isn't much better."

"How so?" Morak asked.

"Wait 'till you taste the food here, friend."

They walked back toward the animal compound. "Your leader seems to be lacking in some humor."

Sumar gestured, "Oh, that. Ignore it—he's just worried. This is the first caravan he's led in over 10 years." Sumar looked around then lowered his voice, "and this is a rich one, ripe for the taking, I think." He watched as Morak assumed his post, then shrugged and moved off into the main part of the camp.

The rest candle had passed half its length when another guard appeared at Morak's side. "You may go," he said gruffly.

Morak walked slowly back to camp, where dying embers of campfires provided a bit of welcome warmth. He found the woman's wagon and knocked quietly on the aged door.

She opened it immediately.

"How is Meesha?"

The woman smiled and shook her head. "Gave me quite a time, she did. She's quiet now, though. Her reaction to seeing old

Tarak's wagon was a strange one."

"Yes. I don't understand it."

"Is she your daughter?"

Morak laughed. "She is much too thin to be a Barbarian's daughter. No, some—people—gave her to me, to sell in B'saad, to make sure she's found a good home."

The woman nodded. "She's already asleep. If you don't mind, I'll keep her here until they light the day candle."

"Yes. You are kind to strangers. Thank you."

"She had need, Barbarian..."

"Morak."

The woman stuck out a hand. "I'm Jamet."

Morak took the hand, judged its softness. "You are not a caravan wench..."

Jamet laughed. "Perceptive, Morak. No, I'm but a cleaning woman in the house of a prince. Or was, until he decided I was too old for his eye. Now I'm going home, back to my family in B'saad." She shook her head. "I left there a dozen years ago to make my fortune. Now look at me," she held her hands out, "the wagon I live in is my only fortune, and it's barely holding together. I return home humbled."

"You've life, woman."

"Yes," Jamet said, "there is that. Best now you be off to sleep. We leave in a few hours."

Wandering about the unfamiliar camp, looking for a good sleeping area, Morak realized he was dead tired. He spread his bedroll near one of the smoldering fires and was soon asleep.

• • •

He dreamt of the book, that he had opened its pages, and on them were words he could read and understand. And he was at the edge of understanding the secrets the book held...

...when Meesha began screaming. She appeared before him, terrified, bloody, and convulsing rhythmically, growing before his mind's eyes from beautiful waif into hideous witch.

He felt pain. He saw Carina. He saw Tok. He felt pain.

He woke.

"Up! Get up, I said." The pain was real. He looked through sleep blurred eyes. A foot swung past his vision and violently planted itself in his rib cage. Morak grimaced, rolled away from his attacker, and sat. His assailant stood above him, tall, wide, with a cruel sneer on his unwashed face. An unkempt black beard and bushy eyebrows framed deep-set and sadistic eyes.

"Who be you sleeping in our camp?"

"Your killer if you kick me again," Morak replied coldly, looking about to see them ringed in by guards and other onlookers.

Morak got to his knees as the other's face boiled into an uncontrolled rage. He kicked out again. This time, Morak caught the foot and twisted it to the other's howl of pain, then pushed, throwing him back into a group of guards. They all went down in a tangle of arms and legs.

Now it was Morak who looked down, standing with hands on his hips. "I think I'll let you live, stranger, since I am a stranger in this camp myself, and don't wish to create ill will toward me."

Considering the grins and suppressed laughter, ill-feeling probably wouldn't be a problem.

The other burned his hate into Morak's eyes. He looked around wildly while scrambling to his feet. "Don't just stand there, you fools, kill him!"

A trio of guards reluctantly moved in, swords threatening. Morak looked to the gods, then drew his blade. He backed away a step, crouched in readiness. The first guard attacked, swinging his sword in a death arc. Morak deflected the blow, pivoted as he kicked out, planting a boot in the man's groin. As the other doubled in pain, Morak kicked out again and swept the other's feet out from under him. The victim landed heavily and curled around his pain.

Laughter arose from those gathered and the other two guards hesitated.

"Don't stand there, cowards," the bearded one shouted, "he is only one man. Kill him! Three pieces of silver to the man who runs him through."

"Only three pieces?" Morak asked with raised eyebrows. "Make it ten and I'll stab myself."

More laughter.

With much wariness, the two guards advanced, one on each side of the relaxed and apparently unconcerned Barbarian. The one on the left sought to move in. Morak whirled, shouting, and raised his sword, shaking it. The other guard, now at his back, rushed to attack.

Then, just as suddenly, Morak fell back, levering a leg up, catching the other guard totally unaware. Morak's victim flew through the air and landed, stomach first, in the dirt, sliding almost to the feet of the bearded one.

Morak stood, strode over to the remaining guard and calmly knocked his sword away.

"You fools!" The bearded one screamed, "must I kill him myself?"

"It seems you must," Morak said, crouching, sword ready.

"Why then, I will." He drew a long thin blade, whirled it singing through the air several times, then advanced on the Barbarian.

Morak waited until the last possible moment, then dropped back, causing the other to miss with a swing. The Barbarian stepped in swinging heavily and clanged his broadsword against the other's thinner blade.

Startled and turned half around, the bearded one neglected to notice that his sword had been sheared off near the hilt. "Die!" He shouted, delivering a wicked back swipe. Morak rested on his sword and watched as the remnant broken blade hissed past. Its owner realized his predicament. The beard grew longer as the man's face fell.

Morak joined in the laughter around him.

"Now," he said, suddenly becoming serious, "do you wish to apologize for kicking me awake?"

"Never cur. I'd rather die."

Morak nodded. "If such be your wish." He raised his sword just as two people pushed their way into the crowd.

"Morak!" Meesha shouted. "Don't hurt him." She ran to the Barbarian and grabbed his free arm.

"Halt!" That command of authority cracked like a whip as Tarak followed the child into the circle. "Bram Sud, what is the meaning of this?"

The bearded man took his eyes off Morak. "I found this—Barbarian thing—asleep in camp. He has no right to be here. I sought only to kill him and leave his carcass for vultures."

"You are a fool, Bram Sud. This man I hired last night—as you would have known had you but asked him. He is a guard, one of your own men, you ass!"

"Are you okay, Morak?" Meesha asked, concern showing in her large eyes.

"Yes, child. Oh, a bruised rib or two, but..."

Tarak glared at the three guards, two still resting in the dust. "One man did this to three of you?"

He waited. The guards looked at each other. Finally, the one standing nodded. "But he is a Barbarian, lord."

"That is not excuse enough. You will not be paid for this day; you are of no value to me. Now go, I'm tired of looking at you. Go somewhere and practice your craft until you are worthy of your pay."

"Yes lord."

Tarak turned his attention to Morak. "You have a good sword arm, and you know when to stay your blows."

"Truly, lord Tarak, these are not worthy opponents against any trained fighter..."

Bram Sud stepped forward. "You lie, cur, I hired those men myself, I paid—"

"Enough. Bram Sud, go to your duties, prepare for our departure. As for this one, I think I'll keep him for a personal bodyguard." Tarak gazed at Morak. "Can you be trusted, Barbarian?"

Morak returned the gaze. He saw no humor in Tarak's eyes—only coldness and emptiness. No hate, no cruelty. "Yes," he said quietly.

Tarak kept his eyes fixed on the Barbarian's for another long moment. Then, without a word, he turned his attention to other matters.

"Let's be off," he said briskly, clapping his hands, "we're late as it is. We lit the day candle an hour ago."

Morak sheathed his sword, picked up his bedroll, slung it over a shoulder and followed Tarak toward the lead wagon,

Meesha firmly holding a large hand.

"He doesn't like you," she said softly.

"Tarak?"

"No, the other one. He wants to kill you some night when you are asleep. But he won't do it himself, he'll pay someone else to do it."

"Hmm, interesting. Thank you child, I'll beware of it. Now tell me, how do you see these things?"

Meesha shrugged. "The same way you see another person, I guess. But your eyes only see part of them, and only this moment. My..."

"You're a violent man, Barbarian," Tarak said over his shoulder. The caravan camp bustled with activity.

"Only when I need to be," he replied, "and when I'm waked from a peaceful sleep."

As they reached the leader's wagon, Tarak turned to look up and down Morak's well-muscled frame. "Be sure you know where that violence is pledged for this trip," he said quietly. "I think you'll drive my wagon today. Just follow the lead scout." He turned away, then turned back, "and one more thing—that child, I don't want to see her around you."

"But you can't..." Meesha began, but Tarak had opened the door of his wagon, and the child stared silently, unable to speak further. Both her hands grasped Morak's in a death grip.

"What is it, child? What is it about Tarak's wagon that frightens you so?"

Meesha shook her head and turned away. "Nothing," she said unconvincingly, "I'd better go back to Jamet's wagon." She extricated her hand from Morak's and ran off. She turned to wave at him, then disappeared into the woman's much smaller wagon.

It was a rough and sometimes nonexistent trail he followed. Morak had to keep a constant vigil to prevent the horses from dragging the heavy vehicle into deep ruts and holes. Morak wondered why this route had not been maintained. He could think of several answers, none of which he liked.

Their progress was done in a sweltering heat, and by the time they reached camp, Morak was bone tired. He rested against the wagon's rear wheel as the camp fires were made, and meals prepared. Sumar dropped down beside him, bearing two plates of steaming food.

"And how well does fortune shine upon you my friend?" Sumar asked, breaking the dry hard-crusted bread in two and handing half to Morak.

"Whoever built this road must have been drunk."

Sumar laughed at that. "Surely, to be used by fools like us to cross a desert. This is not a well-traveled route."

"Oh."

"Lord Tarak chose it in hopes of avoiding an attack."

"Hmm. There is something about this caravan that seems out of place."

"I agree," Sumar said, "but what am I but a lowly cook?" They ate in silence for a while, then Sumar lowered his bread to look at the Barbarian.

"What are you staring at?" Morak said.

"Oh, nothing. It's just that I've never seen one man face three before—and remain alive to eat supper afterward. Not only alive but unharmed. Without killing anyone in return. You must have great confidence in your abilities. We don't have such warriors where I come from." His voice was filled with awe, and perhaps just a little fear. And much respect. He took another bite.

"Where *do* you come from, Sumar?"

"Me?" The other sighed, then looked into the burning flame of a campfire. "I come from the east—the civilized lands of Naog, where green things grow, and there are cool lakes and rushing rivers, and noblemen have large houses and lawns and gardens." Sumar's voice held a breathless quality, then he blinked and smiled. "I guess it's different than the world you've seen, eh Barbarian?"

"Call me Morak. Where I come from, there are lakes and rivers, too, yet the land is untamed, mostly desert, and the beasts that roam it, more so. The men and women who live there are rightly called Barbarians—and proudly." Morak paused and took a sip of wine.

"But tell me, easterner, why do you now ride with a strange caravan in this barren land? Most of Karan is desert, one cannot help but see it sometime—but to leave a life such as you describe, for this?"

"Just so, friend. There are no dragons to slay in Naog—few thieves, no battles. I had a need to find out about myself. Am I a fighter or a coward?"

"And...?"

"I..." Sumar looked away and said nothing. "I'm sorry, Morak, I must go now. I have—cooking—duties to perform." He stood and was soon lost in the darkness.

"I didn't think he'd *ever* leave," said a feminine voice. A swirling cloth blocked Morak's view until the woman seated herself beside him. "It is a good work-day's end, eh Barbarian?"

"Aye it is, Jamet. Have you eaten?"

She nodded, bouncing red hair about her shoulders. Morak studied her between bites of food. She seemed healthy enough, though somewhat thin compared to a Barbarian wench. She appeared to be close to his own age. Very comely with red hair framing her face and green eyes dancing in the sun's weak light.

"How is Meesha?" He asked.

Jamet looked worried. "She's fine, only—there is something bothering her. I can't tell what, and she won't talk about it. She's a very beautiful child, yet she seems to have lost a child's happiness."

Morak told Jamet an edited version of how Meesha lost her family. He omitted the quadrabred experiment and Simathica and a few other details.

"I do hope you find her a good home," Jamet commented, "I would consider buying her myself had I the wealth."

Morak nodded. He liked this wench. She was intelligent and confident, unlike the frail females that were the general rule outside Barbaricum.

"What are you thinking, Morak?" She paused, then laughed. "No, don't bother to answer. Your thoughts are no different than those of any man."

He took a swig of wine, then wiped his mouth with the back of a hand. "I am a Barbarian, and you might find some of my thoughts different. Though, when it comes to wenches, aye, I have the same thoughts as others." He lifted her chin with a finger, "and why not? You're a pleasant eyeful."

"And you are more than any man in this camp," she said softly, lowering her eyes in invitation.

"Morak!" Came a high pitched voice. "Where are you?"

"I'm over here, Meesha," he grumbled, idly stroking Jamet's jaw, disappointment in his eyes.

"What are you doing?" She asked, joining them and glancing from Morak to Jamet.

"Just talking. Jamet said she'd continue to look after you during our trip, if that's okay."

Meesha nodded. "Yes, that would be nice. I'd like that." She gave the woman a hesitant smile.

"A pleasure for me, as well, child."

Tarak opened the door of his wagon and stood on the steps, breathing deeply. Then he glanced down and noticed Morak, Jamet, and Meesha around the wagon wheel. His look reeked of disapproval.

"I thought I told you to stay away from that child," he told Morak. "And you, wench, get away from here."

Jamet gave an angry, defiant look, grasped Meesha's hand. "It's true that I'm nothing more than a wench now, but once I was a Lady of a Lord of B'saad."

"Out of here with you, drunken liar. And you, Barbarian, come in here. There's work to be done." Tarak turned and entered his wagon, leaving the door open. Morak climbed the four steps and peered into an opulent room. He saw small but luxurious furnishings, with fabrics of many colors hanging from the ceiling and walls. A square wooden table, supported by one oak trunk, occupied the center of the room. On it rested a lantern, giving off shadowy light and pungent smoke. Four chairs with plush coverings were placed around the table. At the back of the wagon was the leader's bed, concealed by a thick curtain.

"Don't stand there gawking, come in. Leave the door open; others will arrive soon." Morak entered the room, felt his feet sink into a thick, soft carpet. He had not seen such richness even in large homes. "Sit there," Tarak said, indicating one of the chairs. Morak sat, somewhat self-consciously, idly studying some charts and maps on the table.

Presently, two others came in. Morak noted with a rush of

anger that one of them was Bram Sud—the captain of the guard, apparently. Bram's eyes met Morak's and they glowed with a red hate. Morak glanced at the third man, but did not recognize him.

Tarak seated himself after the others and looked at the men gathered around his table. A delicate smile crossed his lips, then was gone. He nodded at Bram Sud. "You've, eh, met Morak before. Morak, this," indicating the other, a tall, quietly dressed man, "is Trag, head scout for the caravan."

Trag inclined his head slightly and Morak returned it. Morak was impressed by the reticent scout, more so than with anyone else he'd met so far on this strange caravan. Apparently, Tarak had managed to hire at least one competent man.

"Soon we will reach the Santar Oasis. We'll camp there for three rest periods before going on to B'saad. Your report, Trag."

The tall scout cleared his throat. "The Santar Oasis is not presently occupied. But we must be wary of outlaws; their signs are all about."

"Strange. This is such a seldom-traveled route." Tarak looked at the three men. "I've recently had two caravans attacked on the main route," he said, "The losses were significant. I do not intend to lose another single wagon to thieves. That's why I'm leading this one myself."

"We should not stop," Bram Sud said, the anger of an old argument heating his voice, "I say we go straight on to B'saad."

"B'saad is at least 72 hours of hard travel beyond the oasis," Tarak replied. "We'll need the rest—we're at the greatest danger of attack when we are at our weakest, you know that. We rest at the oasis. We are all tired, and tired men make mistakes."

"Old men and women get tired, you mean," Bram Sud muttered.

"We stay for three rest candles," Tarak said firmly. "If there are thieves about, there can't be many of them. Not this far off the well-traveled routes."

Bram Sud snorted in anger. "This is not going to end well," he said.

Tarak ignored the remark. "You may leave now. Trag, I remind you of your duty to warn us of any kind of attack."

"It shall be done, lord Tarak." He stood and adjusted his thin sword.

"Be off with you then, and may the gods be about your work."

"May they be with us all, lord Tarak." The Scout stood, bowed, then left.

"Lord Tarak?" Contempt in that voice.

"What do you wish, my brother?" Tarak said gently, sadly. Morak looked sharply at Bram Sud—yes, there was a slight resemblance there he hadn't noticed before.

"Our sister was on the last caravan you sent to B'saad."

"Yes," Tarak said, head erect, yet seeing nothing.

"And she was killed—because they stopped to rest..."

"Enough! I have heard enough. You talk as if I had killed her myself." He was silent for a moment, then waved a hand at his guard captain. "Go now, I would sleep."

Bram Sud paused at the steps, took one last hateful look at Morak, then stormed away. As the door slammed shut, Morak could see that Tarak's face held a haunted look. It lasted but an instant, then the hardness of leadership returned. But the Barbarian knew—the leader *did* blame himself for his sister's death.

"It's hard for a stranger to tell that we were once a close family," he told Morak briskly. "You go also, my Barbarian friend. Sleep at my doorstep. Kill anyone who attempts to enter."

"Yes lord Tarak," Morak said, looking deeply into the eyes of the leader. He saw a tired old man turning toward his bed, his shoulders bowed under a great weight. It seemed he had stumbled into a complex situation, with sides to be taken. Well, at least Morak knew which side he was on.

Quietly he stepped out of the wagon. He prepared his sleeping area at the foot of Tarak's wagon, working slowly in the hope that Jamet might pay him another visit. He lie down, sighed, and fell asleep.

Morak was awakened by the sound of horses being harnessed. The ground beneath Tarak's wagon had become hard and cold, and he ached. He stood, stretched protesting muscles, and walked in circles to help life flow back into his limbs.

Just then Sumar arrived with a smile and Morak's breakfast. Grateful but curious, Morak talked as he ate. "Not that I mind," he laughed, "but why do you keep bringing me food?"

"You are one of lord Tarak's bodyguards, and favored thusly with personal service. They don't seem to last long, these body guards of Tarak. Your predecessor was killed in a drunken brawl just outside of Opes."

Morak paid scarce attention, his mouth full of food and no longer curious. After the break fast, the caravan packed up and headed once again toward B'saad.

As they approached the end of their travel time, Morak could just see the Santar Oasis, a rather large cluster of trees and a thick band of green surrounded by endless sand. The horses and other animals became restless, smelling water. Morak thought he saw a sparkle of blue and silver—a small, clear, cool lake—so Sumar had told him, fed by an underground river. His parched mouth and scorched body longed for its refreshment.

An hour later, the caravan had arrived and set up their camp. For most of the travelers, it was a time for relaxation and merriment. The campfires burned high, water splashed, wine and other spirits flowed freely and a feast of culinary delights kept coming to all who would eat.

Morak stood on the sandy bank of the lake, looking down at the night-black water which bubbled furiously with the arms and legs of men, boys, children, and wenches. Meesha waved at him, then dove under again.

Jamet climbed ashore, wet clothes clinging to her full body, giving Morak's eyes more than they alone could handle. She slipped and fell back into the water, giggling. Morak broke out in a laugh—the first of genuine humor since he could recall. Jamet raised up a hand to him, a sparkle in her dark eyes.

"Well man, are you going to just stand there and laugh, or will you give a lady a hand?"

He stepped forward, grasped her soft hand and pulled Jamet to her feet. She came into his arms, a squirming, soft, wet armful of fragrant woman. Her body felt good next to his, and ideas other than more swimming came to his head. He bent down and kissed her softly. She moaned and pulled him tighter to her. Jamet's mouth parted and her fingers quested in his hair.

When they separated and gazed at each other, her eyes swam,

two dancing orbs reflecting torchlight. She drew him away, toward a dark part of the oasis. Soon they lie behind a group of rocks, on a bed of soft green grass. She cradled her head against his arm and looked up, past the trees, to a dark blue sky sparkling with only the brightest of stars. Morak idly stroked her cheek.

"Treat me," she said softly, "like you would a Barbarian woman."

Morak said not a word, but turned to her and unbuttoned her dress. It slid off her smooth shoulders, and she lifted up to allow the Barbarian to draw it past her thighs and down her legs.

He gazed down at her nakedness, and they came together hard, and began touching, moving against each other almost as with anger. His mouth growled against hers, as he gave himself and she gave herself, and they were one for a moment, two wanderers in the desert.

For Morak, it had been a long time, much, much too long...

When time began to pass once again, Morak found himself lying beside Jamet, breathing deeply. He smiled contentedly. His mind slowly came back to him.

"Thank you," she said, not looking at him. Suddenly, she sat upright, looking deeply into Morak's eyes. Silently for a moment, they searched each other. Then she sighed and lie back, her head pillowed on his shoulder.

"What was that all about?"

"I was wondering how much of the wild man dwelled within you," her voice, though soft, held a strange wistful quality.

"And?"

"You are too much of a Barbarian to be married..."

"Married!" He sat up, twisting around to look at her again. She smiled shyly. "How do you talk such, woman. We've shared a roll in the grass together, not a wedding."

"Aye," she murmured, "and a right nice roll it was, too. Want to do it again?"

Morak was about to reply when he heard his name called.

"Over here, Meesha," he said, draping the dress across Jamet, and quickly clothing himself.

Meesha came to them, breathless. "Please, Morak, you need to come with me."

"What is it, darling?" Jamet said, gathering the child in her arms.

"Something, over there," she pointed. She looked at Morak. "Someone needs you. Now."

"I'd better go have a look," Morak said, "come on, child, show me."

Meesha took his hand and pulled him away, to the edge of the oasis. "I know what you and Jamet were doing," she whispered.

"You're too young to worry about such things."

"Yes, but Morak," she paused, a hesitant pause, and glanced over her shoulder. "Morak," a deep breath and a sad still voice, "she's going to die here. I'm sorry. I feel very sad for her. I like Jamet and I want things to be different. But..."

The Barbarian stopped and dropped to one knee. "Meesha, you're young. Someday you'll have witch powers, but now you have dreams. They may seem real, but don't take them too seriously."

She looked at him for a moment, then buried her head in his shoulder, trembling. "Please Morak, please," her muffled voice sobbing into his shoulder, "let's leave this place. Let's leave right now. It's going to be awful."

"What is? What, child?" He held her at arm's length. Tears streaked her cheeks, but she suddenly became alert.

She turned to the left. "Over there," she whispered, "it's happening over there."

Morak listened and heard the sounds of a scuffle. The noise came from beyond camp, out in the dim morning of the desert. He stood, motioned for Meesha to remain where she was, and quiet.

The Barbarian stalked up to a tree and peered beyond it. In the pale sunlight, he saw a man struggling with a girl. He, trying to undress her, and she, struggling against it.

"Please," her voice was strained, frightened, "leave me alone, please."

"Lori!" Another voice demanded behind and to the left of where Morak hid. He saw light from a torch moving toward the struggle.

"Mik!" The girl screamed, "help me!" Morak watched the torch bobbing as its carrier broke into a run.

"What is it, Lori?" He burst into the clearing and saw. Morak saw too. The girl was young, only a season or two past her teen years, and now half undressed. She was a sight of beauty, having long, dark hair and flashing eyes, and the softest face Morak had ever seen.

Her adversary was none other than Bram Sud, an evil leer on his face as he looked down at Lori's small, pointed breasts.

When Mik arrived, Bram Sud shoved Lori to the ground and turned to face the young man. Mik stood a full head shorter than Bram Sud, but was amazingly wide and stocky. His hair was blond and curly, cut close to the scalp, and offset by a dark, bronzed body. His face twisted in anger.

"You! Bram Sud, you slimy dog, what are you doing? Lori, are you all right? Did he hurt you? By all the gods..."

"Shut up, boy. You talk too much for someone about to die." Lori screamed. Bram Sud glared down at her. "Shut up, bitch. I'll take care of you after I kill this foolish young pup. You'll be a woman afore this night's done."

He strode toward Mik, drawing a long, pointed dagger from his belt. Mik stepped back and brought the torch down in a poor defense. He did not seem to be otherwise armed. The two came together at the edge of the desert.

It soon became apparent that Bram Sud was the more adept, a master at close-in fighting. Again and again, he lunged out with cat-like quickness, scratching Mik and letting blood. The torch, while aptly wielded, was no match for the guard captain's blade.

Bram Sud toyed with Mik a while longer, obviously trying to impress the girl. Lori sat, small fist to her mouth, as she saw Bram Sud wearing down her young champion.

Suddenly, Mik tripped and fell, the torch slipping from his grasp. The other stood over him, a cruel smile on his lips. He kept twitching the dagger back and forth.

"Well be done with it," Mik growled. Lori screamed as Bram Sud lowered the dagger toward Mik's throat.

"Hold!" Morak shouted, stepping out of the trees. Bram Sud whirled, his face livid with anger.

"What do you want, Barbarian pig? This isn't your affair. Begone with you. Go change your baby's cloth."

"You talk too much as well," Morak growled, stopping in front of Bram Sud. Suddenly the other lunged. Morak sidestepped, grabbed the knife-wrist, and brought his knee up in a powerful blow to Bram Sud's ribcage. Air exploded from his lungs and he bent double.

Morak wrenched the dagger free and threw it from him. Then he brought his other fist down hard to the back of Bram Sud's neck. The guard captain went limp, except for a soft groan and ragged breathing.

Morak helped Mik to his feet. Lori ran over, oblivious to her exposed breasts, and smothered her young friend with kisses and tears.

Mik, breathing hard, looked at Morak. "Thank you friend—"

"Morak."

Mik smiled, "friend Morak." He held Lori tightly to his side, with she biting his earlobe and murmuring softly in his ear.

"Think nothing of it."

"Leave us now, friend Morak," Lori said softly, "the cur was right about one thing. I'll be a woman afore this night is over." She giggled.

Morak smiled, turned and walked back toward camp.

He returned Meesha to the wagon and put her down to sleep. Then he found Jamet, took her to his bedroll, and found something to do until breakfast.

• • •

"Thieves!" the cry was shouted throughout the camp. "Arm yourselves! Thieves attack!" Men woke slowly—but hearing the cry, scrambled to don their weapons and armor.

Morak raised his head from the pillow of Jamet's red hair. The sun had risen clear of the desert dunes on its six-month journey, creating long shadows. The Barbarian checked his weapons and hurried to the outer perimeter. Once beyond oasis trees, he could see the rising dust, glowing yellow in the sun.

"There must be hundreds of them," a man next to Morak said.

Sumar rushed up, a grim look on his face. He shoved a longbow and a handful of arrows into the Barbarian's hands. "Use this," he said, "until they get close enough for your sword—and we'll find out how good you are with it. Gods, I've never seen such a dust cloud made by men."

They watched until individual riders came into sight.

Morak looked into Sumar's frightened eyes and wondered.

Suddenly an arrow sang past his head. He and Sumar dropped behind a large rock. When Morak peered around it, he could see a line of thieves on horseback riding toward them, firing arrows. They were a huge stain against the desert lightness.

"Fire your arrows, man!" Sumar cried, fitting a shaft to his own bow and letting fly.

Morak rose slightly from behind his rock, sighted and let the shaft slip through his fingers. One of the approaching riders fell off his horse. A lucky shot, thought Morak. He rarely used a bow, but he knew how, having practiced for hours as a child. By the time he loosed his second arrow, many arrows were being exchanged, and the air sang with them. Morak heard cries from nearby, and knew the thieves had hit their targets as well.

The attack became personal just as Morak let fly his last arrow. A horseman came riding up to him, sword held high in readiness. Morak threw his bow, then ducked as the outlaw's blade struck rock. Morak grabbed that sword arm and pulled the rider from his horse, slamming him to the ground. The Barbarian pulled his knife and slit the outrider's throat.

All around him, the sounds of battle echoed; the clanging of steel, the screaming of injured and dying men, the occasional hiss of an arrow. And still more thieves came. One jumped his horse over the rock Morak guarded. The Barbarian leapt to the side, swinging his blade, and caught the thief full in the belly as the horse landed.

He turned and ducked as another enemy swung his sword at the place where Morak's head had been, then rode on past toward camp. Morak saw one of his fellows being beaten back by a horseman. He ran up behind the thief, grabbed him by the seat of his breeches and yanked with all his strength. The outlaw shouted in surprise as he was jerked from his horse, and hit the ground with a dull thud. He looked up, pain and fear in his eyes, as Morak separated that head from its body with a backhanded swipe of his blade.

"Many thanks Barbarian," the other breathed heavily, then stumbled off to engage another of the enemy.

On the battle went. It seemed to Morak that hours had passed, and still he kept chopping away. He wondered if Meesha was safe. And Jamet. Heads and parts of bodies were everywhere under foot. The peaceful oasis ran red with blood. The small lake thrashed and bubbled with wounded and calmly floated the dead. Horsemen kept coming at Morak, and he kept chopping them down, rushing occasionally to the aid of his fellows. Sometimes too late. Once he saw Tarak. The caravan leader only smiled grimly while boring his sword through an enemy's neck. He stopped for a moment and saluted Morak with his sword.

There came a time, weeks later it seemed, when he was too weary to raise his sword arm, and Morak found himself leaning up against the rough bark of a tree. Blood covered him from head to foot, not a little of it his own. And he was so bone-tired that he knew if a thief raised sword against him now, he would die.

But it was so strangely silent. That seemed odd. Heavy weights were pulling him down into sleep, clouding his thoughts. There was blackness, only blackness...

"Hah! Raise your weary head, Barbarian," the blood-stained thoughts faded from Morak's mind as he opened his eyes. He saw the blond head of Mik in front of him, shouting, smiling. "We've beaten them—sent them home with their bony tails between their legs."

Morak looked at Mik for a long time, trying to remember, then he struggled to his feet, finding that a painful process indeed. He leaned back against the tree gingerly and let out a long sigh. Again he looked at Mik's smiling face.

Suddenly that face was pushed aside, and Jamet stared down at him. "Phew, you smell like death itself. Come to the lake and I'll wash you." She bent and helped Morak to his feet. His muscles were so stiff, he could barely walk. He felt support on his other side, and looked to see Meesha helping.

"Are you okay, Morak?" She asked anxiously.

He reached out a hand and stroked her silky hair. "Okay, little one."

By the gods, he must be getting old, he thought, stumbling in their grasp. He knelt by the shore, pushing away a stiff white hand that had no body attached. Jamet dipped a cloth into the water and gently washed Morak's body.

"I've never seen so many thieves in one band," Sumar said, kneeling down beside them, breathless.

"Ah! Man, you still live! So, have you found the answer to your question? Are you fighter or coward?" Morak asked, rising his dripping head from between Jamet's hands.

Sumar's eyes dropped. "This is not the time for such tellings," he murmured, "we have much else to discuss."

"Yes, friend Sumar," Morak said gently, "but remember, 'tis a fool who fights without fear or kills without grief."

Later, the four walked slowly back to the main camp. Along the way, they passed pallets filled with wounded. Their thin, mournful cries filled the oasis.

Before the great wagon, Tarak and Bram Sud stood at the center of a crowd, anger flowing heavily.

"Seventy of us now lie dead, more wounded, because we stopped," Bram Sud shouted.

"And more would be dead if they had met us in open desert," Tarak shot back in a tired voice.

"That is your thinking, it is the thinking of a fool." Bram Sud half turned away, then whirled back, an accusing finger pointed at his brother. "I say you are no longer fit to lead!"

A deep murmur went through the crowd. Morak clearly heard some in agreement.

"And *you* are fit to lead?" Tarak returned, rising to his full height and looking down at the other.

"I am."

The two faced each other, red with anger.

"This has gone far enough," Morak said, stepping into the center of the argument. "If we fight among ourselves, we shall certainly all die."

"He speaks the truth," Trag said, joining them. "There are at least two more groups of thieves camped nearby—a thousand of them at least. There is something odd here, and this is not a time for quarrels. We number less than five hundred, counting women and children. We are almost helpless before them. If we are to survive, we must find a way out of his place."

A tremble of hysteria ran through the gathered caravan.

Over a thousand thieves in one place! Even in the Dark Years such a band of outlaws was unheard of. They each roamed the desert in their own small groups, rarely joining together. Why the sudden cooperation?

"They are here for some reason," Sumar whispered to Morak, "They must think there's something of great value, beyond the cargo we carry. I wonder what it could be?"

For the first time in days, Morak thought of the book in his pack. It was valuable beyond measure, which was why he hadn't mentioned it. But no one could know of it, least of all outriders. Morak alone had left Simathica alive—something no one else had ever done—so he was the only living person who could know about the book. It couldn't be possible...

And yet, the thieves were here for something more than women and plunder.

He knotted his brow in deep thought. He knew outriders were well organized, with spies in all the great kingdoms. They knew where the richest caravans traveled, and where the most valuable treasures were stored. It was a constant vigil for soldiers and guards to keep their kings and lords safe from a thief's touch. They had a Karan-wide organization, admittedly loose-knit, but an advantage no kingdom had. This massive cooperation, out here in the middle of the desert far away from any rich city or kingdom, however, was unheard of.

The confrontation broke up. Both Tarak and Bram Sud realized that their survival depended upon working together and maintaining control over their people.

As the time for sleep approached, a meeting of war took place in Tarak's wagon. Trag, Bram Sud, and Morak attended.

"I hear you accounted for a large number of the enemy dead today, Morak," the leader said briskly, a hand on the Barbarian's shoulder.

"When I am attacked, I fight back," he replied, looking at Bram Sud with accusing eyes.

"You may have to fight more before we're out of this."

Morak inclined his head slightly in reply.

The lantern's light flickered, causing shadows to ripple across their faces. Tarak sighed wearily. "Now we face a critical question before us—and one we must decide rapidly—is how to get away."

Bram Sud stood. "I say we load all our wagons and run for it now."

"Perhaps it would be best to head back the way we came," Trag said quietly, "make our escape, leaving campfires burning. Later, we can circle around them and continue on our way."

Tarak nodded. "That might work. Any comments?"

"Yes."

Bram Sud glared at Morak. "What is it, Barbarian?"

"Leave a small group of swordsmen here, along with a couple of wagons, to meet their next attack. The diversion will delay them longer, and give the rest more time to escape."

"And who shall lead such a group?" Bram Sud asked with suspicion.

"I will, if needs be," Morak replied.

"Good," said Tarak, "and Trag shall lead an advance party to eliminate any who guard the west road."

"Why go back?" Bram Sud asked, "head east, on toward B'saad—it's much closer."

"Just as our adversaries will expect us to do, my brother. No, Trag's right, we head back west." He looked at the faces made yellow by the lantern. "Then it is agreed?" Bram Sud opened his mouth, but said nothing. Their final decision was made. No voice disputed it.

Tarak dismissed them with his usual abruptness. But the plan never had a chance to be implemented. When they stepped out of the wagon, their people stood in small groups talking quietly and pointing.

A quick look in all directions confirmed their fear. While they were planning their escape, the thieves had surrounded the oasis. A ring of glowing campfires now encircled them. There would be no escape.

"Gods," Trag muttered, "they must have an entire army assembled out there."

Morak left the group. He wanted to find Jamet and Meesha.

"Well, Barbarian, what do we do now?" Mik asked, joining the Barbarian as he strode purposefully through camp.

"We wait."

"Wait? Wait for what—to die?" The anger in the young man's voice was deep.

"Yes, if needs be."

"I can't believe we came all this way, just to be cut down," Mik said sourly.

"Morak! Man Morak!" A guard shouted and came running up, breathless.

"Here," the Barbarian answered.

"You're wanted by lord Tarak and Trag, the scout."

Morak sighed and turned back, following the runner to the north edge of camp, opposite the lake. He saw four figures there, features hidden by shadows. When Morak reached them, he recognized Trag and Tarak. The other two, he was startled to note, were dressed in the garb of their enemy.

"You sent for me?" He asked, curiosity knitting his brow.

Tarak looked at Morak with suspicion. "They say they want you—alive."

"What?"

"That is right," one of the thieves spoke up. "You are the one—the Barbarian—called Morak?"

"I am."

"Then come with us and we'll let you live. Your life has been purchased with ten pieces of gold—though I'll not understand why."

"Who would be so foolish to pay for the life of a Barbarian," Morak mused, "and ten pieces of gold? He's not only a fool, but a madman, too."

The outrider shrugged. "We're only interested in the gold, dog, not in who pays it. Come with us."

"What about the caravan?"

"They will die, of course, except for the wenches and boys."

"Then I'll stay here, to kill more of you."

"'tis your choice, fool—you can come with us now, or we'll deliver your mangy head later."

"Go back to your leader and tell him I'll dance on his bones.

I am a Barbarian, not a man, and I'll listen to no more of these dog droppings." With that Morak turned and went back to the camp. His thoughts troubled him. Someone was offering ten pieces of gold to get him. Since he wasn't worth ten pieces of gold, that meant someone knew of the book. That made him even more curious, and being curious, he desired to live to fathom the mystery.

So he sat down at his favorite resting place, the wagon's wheel, and considered ways by which he might survive the coming attack. To save the caravan, he knew, was a hopeless task. It was himself, and the mystery surrounding the book that he must concern himself with now. The book was important, he knew that, though he knew not why.

Deepening the mystery was the apparent fact that someone knew he had the book, and they wanted it badly. He had to find out who and why, and learn what priceless knowledge was contained in the *Tome of the Dark Devices*.

"Sumar!" Morak hailed his friend. The other came and sat beside him.

"The night doesn't look too good for us, eh, friend Morak?"

"It can if we make plans," Morak said quietly, "Gather Mik and his wench, Lori, along with Jamet, and Meesha. Meet me on the far side of the lake. There we'll discuss my plan. And hurry," he added, "I fear those curs will not wait much longer before they decide to attack."

Morak glanced at a bank of clouds obscuring the faint glow of the sun, and wished it were even darker.

Soon, the small group was gathered together in a quiet place away from the main camp. In the background, the enemy's campfires burned ominously. Morak outlined his plan, a risky one, one that could very well bring them a death more terrible than by a thief's sword. Yet, they were all willing to try it. The two women knew what would happen to them if they fell into the hands of outlaws. The men knew they would die fighting, or be killed for sport later.

Yet some doubt still remained in Sumar's mind. "We're abandoning all the rest."

"That is so," Morak answered slowly, "were there but a

chance to win victory, I would take it. And it is my destiny to die at the hands of a swordsman, and had I no other purpose, I would gladly die here, killing as many of those," he nodded toward the campfires, "as I could."

"Of what purpose do you speak?" Lori asked softly.

"I can't tell you, now. Perhaps someday, if we live, you will come to know. What you must know now is that even if my plan works, we may not be better off than our doomed fellows. The desert kills just as dead as a man with a sword."

• • •

Back at camp, at that very moment, Bram Sud and Tarak glared at each other over the meeting table. Hate, like a muggy heat, filled the room—though Trag sat between them.

"Because of you, we are all dead, my brother," the last word was spat by Bram Sud with a jerk of his head.

Tarak lowered his eyes and looked deeply and longingly at his gnarled hands. "Perhaps—perhaps you were right, perhaps I am not fit to lead." His voice faltered, cracked, and with difficulty, carried on. "I'm sorry, I don't know any more." He looked up, an incongruous softness in his eyes. "My brother, I didn't mean for it to end this way. I know you hate me because of what happened to our sister. Poor Mara. She was so innocent to the world. What I did to her..."

Even a tear now crept, unbidden, to the edge of Tarak's eye. His weary head lowered again.

While he stared at the table, he spoke one more time, in a voice barely audible. "Do what must be done, brother."

Bram Sud stood and in a long step, went to his brother's side. For a moment—a second in time—the hate in his eyes turned to a softer, inward anger, and he placed his hand on Tarak's shoulder. His other hand drew a long, pointed dagger. And as Trag watched in a horrible fascination, and before he realized fully what was transpiring, Bram Sud plunged the knife into his brother's chest.

The older man jerked, every muscle taut. His left hand grasped Bram Sud's free hand and held on tightly. He opened his mouth to speak, but blood gushed out instead. Bram Sud pulled the knife out and buried it again, then again. Tarak slumped in his chair and was still. After a time, his hand slipped from Bram Sud's.

"I now lead this caravan," Bram Sud said gruffly. "It is my duty to die with it," his voice was cold, and he gazed straight ahead at nothing.

There came a pounding at the door. One of the guards rushed in. "They attack!"

• • •

Morak selected five reeds from the edge of the lake and made sure they were hollow. He gave one to each of his companions, who stood beside a cluster of large boulders. A trembling Meesha held Jamet's hand. Silently and quickly, they knelt and began scooping out the sand and dirt at the base of the rocks. They had little time, and worked like demons possessed until they had each carved out a deep cut next to and slightly beneath each of the rocks. One by one they wrapped a coarse cloth around their heads and faces, with the reed exposed for breathing.

Sounds of the impending attack could be heard all around them. Those in the caravan were arranging their meager defenses, while the hooves of half-a-thousand horses drummed toward them in the dusk.

Lying down as close to their rock as they could get, each of Morak's friends held the reeds in their mouths. Morak buried them with the sand and dirt. He tried to make each hiding place look natural, but there was scarcely time for that. He buried Mik and Lori at the base of one rock, Sumar against another. Finally, he began scooping handfuls of sand over Meesha and Jamet.

"I'm scared, Morak," Meesha said in a hoarse whisper. "It's going to happen, I can feel it."

"What's going to happen, child?" Morak asked.

But whatever "it" was, Meesha apparently had no words to describe it. She looked terrified and began shaking.

"You'll be okay," he said reassuringly, holding her hand tightly. "Stay where you are until I come for you, understand?"

"Be careful, my Barbarian," Jamet said, her face peering out through the cloth, "and don't worry, I'll take care of Meesha."

"Thank you," he said. He kissed them both, wrapped their faces in the cloth, then buried them against the base of the largest stone. He checked their reeds to make sure they were clear of sand.

His friends were all covered, buried, hidden. If they held very still, they might escape notice. Now he must save himself. As the shouts and noises of battle reached his ears, he ran back toward camp—to where the palm trees grew thickest. He found his target, but before he could climb the tree, a group of horsemen broke through headed right for him.

Morak drew his sword and steel sang as he cut one rider down, ducked under another's attack, and buried his blade into a third.

Sounds of battle broke out all around. He chopped his way toward the tree. The gods were with him when he reached it. He dispatched one last thief and for the moment, no one else was nearby.

He leapt and grasped the trunk as high up as he could reach. Using hands and feet, and his not inconsiderable strength, Morak climbed the tree to the very top where the flat fronds were thickest. Carefully, trying not to disturb the fronds, he worked his way between the rippled leaves, and up until he rested at the very top of the tree—hidden from anyone directly below him on the ground. Other trees nearby obscured him from the sides. Now all he had to do was wait until the band of thieves departed, and pray to whatever gods might be looking down upon him.

And that, it turned out, was the hardest of all. He was forced to but lie silent and listen as an army of thieves raided the camp. He had to listen to the screams of men dying, the women and children living. His own battle lust coursed through him; he wanted to kill.

He couldn't see, and for that he was thankful. In the heat of battle, he scarcely noticed the cries and screams, but waiting and listening was another matter.

He rested atop the tree, his dark eyes looking up at a few persistent stars, still wondering if he had done the right thing. As he watched, he noticed that one of those bright stars was slowly moving. As it passed over the oasis, it stopped and became one more star in a heaven filled with stars. Most of those stars would soon be invisible until the Long Day began its sleep months from now, and the Long Night began. Morak wondered if its movement had been only in his imagination.

Finally, after an eternity, it was all over. All he could hear were the sounds of horses moving about, and the excited laughter of the victors. Occasionally, he heard the cry of a child, or a woman's scream. Hate flowed up from within him—a boiling hate that made him shake. But he knew he could not—must not—do anything.

He had to escape, for in B'saad there lived a priest he had once known near his homeland in the south. His childhood friend would know what to do, how to discover the knowledge contained in the Tome Morak carried with him. And this friend would help Morak hide from those who would pay ten pieces of gold for his head.

Suddenly, voices came closer, and the restless sound of hooves. "Search the entire area, the Barbarian was not among the bodies. He's here, somewhere. He must be found, and soon. A bar of silver to the one who finds his body."

A flurry of activity and excited voices answered that as the searchers took off in all directions. Morak dared hardly to move, yet his muscles ached with stiffness. And the desert heat would rise once the clouds burned off. It was his hope that the outriders would have moved on by then.

They did not. In fact, they seemed prepared to remain for a time. They were still going through their plunder and assaulting the wenches they'd captured. It was not often thieves had their way with women, and these would be used until they could no longer respond. Then most would be killed and left to rot. The boys? Well, another generation of thieves to raise up and train.

Sun in his eyes woke him. That and some voices. "Over here!"

"There she is!" Said another.

"I've got her." Morak heard a child's scream. He caught himself from sitting up—it almost sounded like Meesha's voice. But then he remembered, Meesha was safe, buried at the base of a large stone with Jamet.

Morak knew that if he were forced to remain in the tree long enough, he would be dead from the heat or someone would see him.

He tensed as the tree swayed with an unexpected weight. Morak jerked almost to a sitting position, then slowly lowered himself.

"Carak, what are you doing up there?" A voice from the ground challenged.

Another, closer voice answered. "These coconuts will go well with our meal, Chakka. Do you want one?" Morak held his breath as he felt a hand fumbling directly beneath him.

"You'll break your fool neck," was the reply, then there was a hollow cracking sound, a shouted exclamation.

"Why you dog, you dropped that on me on purpose."

Laughter. The tree shook as the thief climbed down. There came sounds of a mock scuffle, then silence except for the distant sounds of others in the camp. Morak relaxed and lie back down, trying to ignore the heat, the hunger, the thirst. Gods! It would almost be easier to die. His thoughts returned to the book. It held more secrets than words between its crumbling covers, of that he was sure. And Morak was going to discover those secrets. By the gods he was.

As the endless hours passed, he lie in a half-stupor, unable to move even if he had wanted to. His tongue filled his mouth; a thick, dry desert of its own.

Sounds came and went. Sounds that had no meaning to him. The sun was high enough to hurt his eyes, the desert heat soaked up his energy. He thought of Meesha, thought of her fully grown, the quadrabred's mother that would never be. A quadrabred had never been born in Karan, Morak felt sure. Such experiments were forbidden, and Tok's reasoning would never be known.

Why was Meesha so frightened of Tarak's wagon? Well, no matter. Soon they'd be away from this place and never see it again.

Once, Morak heard singing, then discovered it was he, himself, singing softly. He stopped and listened for indications that someone had heard.

• • •

Some unknown time later, clouds again moved across the sun, and a cool breeze rippled over Morak's sweat-shiny body. Thoughts came to him slowly—reason slower still. When he was able to remember where he was, who he was, he knew it was time to make a move, or die.

Morak sat up. It was quiet and he worked his cramped muscles as well as he could to relieve some of the stiffness and pain. It was a while before he could climb down from the tree, and even then, every movement was an agony of stiff muscles.

He stood, crouched low, at the base of the tree, listening. Yes, the thieves were still here. He heard snores and the sounds of horses at rest. Probably guards about, too. But he couldn't stay any longer in that tree—he *couldn't*! And his buried friends were probably in worse condition, if not dead.

The Barbarian silently made his way to the edge of the lake, where he refreshed himself. Then he quietly went to where Sumar had been buried. He tapped the rock three times and felt an answering movement. With a flurry of sand, Sumar sat up. Or tried to. He fell back with each attempt. Morak grasped Sumar's hand and pulled him to his feet. But Sumar was unable to stand by himself, so they sat.

"Gods Morak," he whispered weakly, "I thought that was my grave. Gods."

"Quiet, the thieves are still here. You must walk..."

Morak left Sumar behind and went to where Jamet and Meesha were buried. But this time there was no answering movement. Morak's heart quickened as he dug into the sand frantically, stopping once at the sound of someone nearby.

Jamet was there, cold and stiff. Morak realized immediately what had happened. They had dug too deeply to make room for Meesha, and the rock had rolled slightly, crushing Jamet.

But where was Meesha? Morak groped around in the sand and found the small wrapping cloth, empty. So Meesha had escaped—then that scream he'd heard earlier was—*gods*!

He pivoted on his knee to gaze toward the main camp. His face held an assortment of expressions.

"Morak, hurry, dig up your two wenches...oh." Sumar rushed up. He watched with an embarrassed silence as Morak replaced the sandy dirt.

"Meesha has been taken prisoner," Morak said quietly, "and Jamet is dead."

"I did not know her well, friend Morak, but Jamet had great love within."

"Aye," Morak whispered, "love and—understanding. Let's go."

Mik and Lori were alive, weak and unable to stand at first, but alive. Morak and Sumar helped them to the edge of the oasis, then went back to get supplies of water and food—and Meesha if possible.

Many long hours of hard desert travel faced them before reaching B'saad. That was a task of no little achievement even for a horseman and the best of supplies.

The desert does not choose its victims, but takes gladly what it can get, and leaves in return only bleached bones and a death-white skull to warn others.

Morak and Sumar made their way to the main camp. The Barbarian dove behind a rock as one of the guards appeared around a wagon. Sumar's hot breath curled about his neck as they watched the guard spit into the smoldering embers of a dying campfire, gaze for a long moment into the distance, then disappear again behind the wagon.

"Come on," Morak whispered. They moved again, out into the open, with a death-like silence. Almost as one, they came alongside one of the wagons, flattening themselves against it as if they might blend into the canvas and wood of its sides. There were many sounds and the smell of death still permeated the air. At any time a guard might see them and raise the alarm.

Morak motioned Sumar to keep watch the other way while he crept slowly to the front of the wagon. He was in luck! They had found one of the supply wagons. The Barbarian stepped onto the sideboard—and the wagon creaked like a witch in pain—or so it seemed to Morak as he froze, waiting for a challenge, a call from the guard. His hand rested on his throwing knife but after long seconds no sounds came except for a wandering breeze, and the sounds of sleeping thieves and restless horses.

Once inside the Wagon, Morak noticed it was almost

stripped. It must have already been raided. He fumbled around in the darkness, not daring to strike a flint. Somehow he was able to locate some of the dried meat and grain cakes they used to break fast on long trips through the desert. He stuffed his bag full of them, hoping it would be enough.

Then he heard a knock at the side of the wagon, soft yet insistent. He lifted the canvas to see Sumar staring out, searching the camp.

"I heard a noise..."

Morak nodded, patted the bag and two full canteens he'd found. He slipped out of the wagon and the two retraced their steps toward the edge of camp.

Then they froze. A muffled scream came from somewhere to the right. Morak looked and noticed Tarak's huge wagon.

"Wait here," he whispered to Sumar.

"No, Morak. We can't. You'll be seen..."

But Morak was already gone. The Barbarian crept between wagons, ducked beneath one when he sighted a guard. The sound came again, and he was right, it had come from inside the wagon. He came up beside it and carefully looked in the tiny window.

Meesha! Yes, he was certain. And what he saw made him tremble with anger. There was a man, a tall thin man with a pointed beard. He stood before Meesha. She was trembling and trying to push herself into the bedding and the corner of the sleep area, and the man was doing things to her. He held a knife in one hand, and while Morak watched, horrified, he began using it.

The thief did terrible things. Unspeakable things. Morak looked away, his head buzzing. His lips curled in rage—nothing living should have to bear what Meesha was bearing right now.

She screamed again.

Morak pulled his knife and reached up for the latch. To his left came a scuffle and a shout, and a faint cry of "Morak."

He turned toward the door again, reached out a trembling hand.

Then he dropped and ran off toward the left. His mind was blank, he dared not think. He saw Sumar grappling with a guard, one hand over the guard's mouth the other holding off a knife attack. Morak came up behind and broke the thief's neck.

Both men ducked into the brush and ran. "What was in the wagon, Barbarian?" Sumar breathed.

"Nothing," Morak said, grinding teeth. "We need to hurry."

They almost made it, too. Morak saw Lori raise her head to look at them as they ran up.

Then: "Halt! Do not move. Guards, to me at once. I've found the Barbarian!" The guard held a torch up high, its signal damning them all in its yellow light. He looked from one to the other.

Unfortunately for him, Morak was in no mood to be challenged. He whipped out his knife and threw it. He heard the meaty chunk as the blade found its mark, and saw the outlaw fall to the sand, the torch igniting his robe.

"Quick," Morak hissed, "this way."

He led them, not into the desert, but around back to the camp. They used every bush and tree for cover, and they saw many men, rushing almost parallel to them in the direction from which they had come.

Morak guided his small band to where the horses were kept. Because of the excitement at the other end of the camp, only one guard was left with the animals. Morak motioned for the others to stay hidden while he crept around behind the guard. His progress was like that of a jungle cat—silent and swift. And he was a man moved by anger. He leapt upon the thief, his legs wrapping around the man's middle, his hands grasping the eyes and mouth. The guard's cries were cut off as Morak twisted the head in his hands. He heard the bone snap, the other go stiff, then limp in his arms. Finally, he let go and the guard's body slipped to the ground.

"Come on, come on," he hissed sharply. The others ran from their cover. They made haste to saddle and mount four horses. Morak led them out, toward the desert, holding the gate open so the rest of the animals could follow.

Sumar rode up beside him. "By the gods, Morak, I would hate to have you for an enemy."

Morak kept his eyes ahead. He kept seeing the tortured look on Meesha's face in Tarak's conquered wagon. Her face—and the other man's evil smile.

"Shut up," he told Sumar, and rode on.

Meesha had been right to fear that wagon, Morak thought,

somehow she'd known—not the words—but the horror that awaited her there.

And he did nothing.

He did *nothing*.

They rode out, into the desert and beyond the horrors of the caravan. Morak scattered horses and a few camels as they went, hoping to keep them out of the thieves' hands long enough for them to reach B'saad.

• • •

They traveled until the desert heat tired the horses. They stopped atop a sandy rise and checked for signs of pursuit. Seeing none, Morak then led them down into a depression. There they spread a tarp from one of the saddlebags over them to provide protection from the heat and hide them from searching eyes.

"Gods, Morak," Sumar gasped, his face shiny with sweat, "it would have been better to let them take us. At least now we would be standing at the doors of the gods."

"Ha! Us?" Mik laughed. "We'd be cooling in the fires of hell."

Morak said nothing. If only he'd had time to kill the man and free Meesha. If only he could go back and finish the work. His right hand grasped air, his left rested on the pouch containing the book. He'd abandoned Meesha for this cursed *book!* He hated the choices he'd been forced to make. *Forced!*

They rested and ate some of their rations. The wait seemed almost as bad as the one Morak had endured in the tree. He swore that if he ever got out of this desert, he'd never enter it again, not even for gold.

Sumar agreed with him. "Yet, where in Karan would one find a land with no desert? Even my home land is bordered by desert, cool and green though it is even during the peak of the Long Day."

"I don't know," Morak said, "yet I feel this is not the nature of man. He was not meant to live as such. There must be a place where green trees cover tall mountains, and cool lakes rest in the palms of valleys. Our legends..."

"Still the believer in legends, eh, Morak? Don't you know

those are for old woman and small children?"

Morak looked out from under the tarp, out over the shimmering sand. "Once I did," he said quietly.

Eventually a few clouds obscured the sun. They had slept a few fitful hours, but it was time to move on. The four mounted their exhausted horses and began their race to B'saad. Morak thought the horses might not make it. They'd had nothing to eat and very little of their precious water. They moved listlessly and foam dripped from their mouths.

Just as they reached the location of their next camp, one of the horses died, and another dropped to lie unmoving before their camp was made. The humans ate sparingly of the dried meat and grain cakes, and drank the water of which they had little.

"Those two horses still live," Sumar said, "but they are useless to us. They could never carry two." His voice was dull and lifeless.

Morak swallowed a mouthful of water. "You've got two legs, we'll walk on after we've had a few hours of rest."

Lori sighed as she dragged her head from Mik's shoulder, for even in the heat the two sat together. "I don't think I can walk at all," she murmured.

Mik looked at her with scorn. "Of course you'll walk—or I'll carry you. We'll get to B'saad together or not at all."

"Bold words," Sumar muttered, "let us hope they will remain true ones."

They almost did. The four continued on foot when they woke from a brief, restless sleep. They were within sight of B'saad's walls when they heard the sound of many horses coming out of the desert behind them.

"*Run!*" Sumar shouted.

"I can't," Lori screamed.

They stopped and looked behind, trying to see beyond the rolling dunes. "We'll never make it," Morak said checking his sword. "But they can't be in much better shape than we are," he mused. "Maybe one of us can delay them."

Then Sumar's hand was on the Barbarian's wrist. Morak looked up, a challenge in his eyes. Sumar smiled. "It is mine for the doing, friend Morak. You got us out of camp, kept us going through the desert. I will delay them here—long enough for you to reach the city."

"You don't have to do this, my friend" Morak said.

"One of us has to," Sumar replied. "Those two," he indicated Mik and Lori, "have their lives before them. And you, Barbarian, are driven with the need to fulfill an oath and some other things you won't talk about. So go on, live, and remember me."

Morak nodded and re-sheathed his sword as Sumar drew his. The blade gleamed dimly in the sunlight. He turned to them with an evil grin on his face. "Now run, you stupid fools, run!"

They ran.

Morak could see the shining tower lights of B'saad. He and Mik and Lori pushed on through the soft yielding sand. It held a dreamlike quality, this madness, this trying to run through sand.

Behind them, the noise of pursuit stopped, the horses had quit running; the thieves had found Sumar.

"Faster," Mik whispered hoarsely, grasping Lori's arm as she stumbled and almost fell.

Morak could see the gate lights, the twin towers of B'saad, with their ever-burning torches. They flickered and beckoned. There was safety behind those towers, and places to hide.

Morak heard distant screams. They echoed across the wasteland, and died slowly only to be followed by another and yet another. Sumar's or...?

They did not pause to look back, for they again heard the dull thudding of horses beating their hooves on sand. This time, they could see that too near cloud of dust.

Ahead were the walls of the city, growing larger. Behind them, the tiny men on horses grew larger. But which grew faster?

"I can't—no farther—no more," Lori murmured. Then she collapsed. Mik stopped and stood beside her. Morak, who was in the lead, turned to look back at them. If he stopped...

"Please Lori, get up—please!"

"I'm...sorry, Mik. Kill me," she whispered, "don't let them get me."

Not this time, Morak thought, *not this time*. He ran back, pushed Mik out of the way, picked Lori up and tossed her over his left shoulder. "All you have to do is hold on—understand me, girl?"

She nodded and grasped Morak's neck. Again they ran. The thieves were almost on them, Morak could hear their shouts.

"Look," Mik shouted, "we've made it!" Suddenly an arrow grew out of his shoulder, and he went down, rolling and crying in pain.

"Gods," Morak demanded as he pulled Mik to his feet.

"That arrow, get it out," Lori cried in his ear.

"No time. Come on man." Pulled along by the Barbarian, Mik was able to stumble forward. Arrows sang about them and men shouted.

Then they were inside the city walls, past startled guards before they could react. The long market street of B'saad lie before them, filled with people doing their break fast shopping.

Morak dropped left, pulling Mik with him, into an alley which was dark and narrow. He hoped the thieves would first search the marketplace, giving them enough time to hide.

They came to a stable at the rear of a large building. It held two goats, a horse—and several large piles of hay. Morak threw Mik at one of the piles, then dumped Lori beside him.

Reaching over, Morak pulled the arrow out of Mik's shoulder with a quick wrench. With no warning, the young man answered with a yelp of pain.

"Gods, it hurts," he hissed weakly. Lori soothed him with her voice and soft fingers.

"Quiet," Morak growled, tearing Lori's dress and applying the strips to staunch the flow of blood from Mik's shoulder.

They worked quickly getting themselves buried in the hay. And just in time, for they heard the sound of voices echoing down the alley, and the click-clop of horses on pavement.

"Nothing here but rats and garbage," one of the outlaws sniffed.

"We still have to check it; that Barbarian is a crafty one."

"Aye," his partner replied, "Kam would be displeased if he escaped again."

The two thieves rode slowly down the alley, checking into corners and shadows. Morak remembered the name they'd used, Kam. He attached it to the bearded one he saw momentarily through the window of Tarak's wagon, standing before a terrified, tortured Meesha.

He would remember that name, and that face. And someday...

The alley was quiet except for the shuffling feet of horses and goats, and a pig or two further along. The thieves rode on through, to check other alleys.

Mik let out a shuddered sigh. "They're gone. Perhaps we'll live after all."

"What of Sumar?" Lori said.

"He was a brave man," Mik said gravely.

Morak turned toward them, taking his eyes from the alley. "Or a fool. In either case, his death has given us our lives, and for that we should be thankful."

"Then we are safe?"

"You, girl, and your man friend there, you are safe." Morak looked back out to the alley. "As for me, well, as long as I've got my sword, I'm safer than they are."

"Aye, I'll agree to that," Mik said, leaning up on his good shoulder. "So *you* are the object of their searching."

"Me, or something I've got."

They dug their way out of the hay and parted ways. Mik and Lori went to find a healer, and Morak to begin his furtive search for the priest he once knew.

And to find the one named Kam and pay him the vengeance of a Barbarian.

"You will need the help of the gods," Mik had said.

Morak agreed.

Book Three

Jaksim and the Book

T he Barbarian known as Morak stood before an old wooden door, his wild, brown-hued hair surrounding the dust and whiskers of many days. The tall door was an entrance to a temple where he hoped to find answers.

He pounded a huge fist against the pitted wood and listened past the hollow echoed booming.

He glanced over his shoulder nervously. The city of B'saad was full of outriders—all of them, he knew, were after him.

There was no sound, but the door opened a crack.

"You wish?" A small man, clothed in a hooded black robe, asked in a soft voice.

"I wish to see Jaksim, the priest." Morak's words seemed shouted next to the little man's voice.

"Brother Jaksim is in isolation. He cannot be disturbed."

Morak impatiently pushed his hand against the door. "I must see him—lives depend upon it."

The door resisted his efforts. "I am sorry."

"Not as sorry as you will be if you don't let me in there," Morak growled. He started to shove his way in, but found the door jerked from his grasp. As the Barbarian stumbled into the dark temple, the little man pivoted and kicked out with a heel that landed in Morak's mid-section. With an "oof" of expelled breath, he went falling, off-balance, to the deeply carpeted floor.

Morak slowly regained his feet. The small priest stood quietly facing him. "You are not allowed here, you must leave." The voice was quiet but insistent.

Ignoring the priest, Morak looked around. The room was huge, supported by large, round carved pillars. Hundreds, if not thousands of flickering candles provided what little light there was. At the other end of the room, a temple deity rested on a platform and was surrounded by larger colored candles. It looked vaguely familiar to Morak, but he did not have time to dwell upon it.

"Please go, we do not wish violence."

"Then take me to Jaksim."

"As I said, that is not possible." To that Morak laughed. He turned toward a dark corridor on his left. He took a step toward it when another black-robed man moved out to guard its entrance.

Morak smiled grimly. He drew a short, pointed dagger instead of his sword—for these were small men. He advanced confidently upon the silent, waiting monk. When Morak stood before the priest, the other raised a hand.

"Halt, Barbarian, we can not allow you to go further."

"And how will you stop me, little man?" Morak growled, still grinning.

"Like this," the hooded one said quietly. He turned sideways to the Barbarian and lashed out with one black-clothed hand. Instinctively Morak swung the knife up. The priest grabbed Morak's wrist, and the little man's fingers probed between the tendons and muscles until they found the proper nerve. With a howl of pain, Morak dropped the blade, his hand opening against his will.

Morak reached for the priest's hand, but it wasn't there anymore. Out of the corner of his eye, the Barbarian saw the other priest glide silently toward him. He began to duck as he saw two feet, one from each priest, one on each side, cutting in an arc toward his head. But he found he had misjudged them again as pain exploded in a whirlpool of stars and colors. Slowly, he melted to the floor, and all became black and night. And he hadn't even landed one blow.

• • •

Pain! Gods, how his head ached. Morak opened his eyes and watched the flickering colors dance. Soon, the pin-points of light became candles. He groaned and tried to sit up, then bent over holding his head.

"So," a soft voice addressed him from the dimness. Yet another black-robed priest watched as Morak levered himself to a sitting position. "You have come back to life, my Barbarian friend."

He recognized the voice. Perhaps it was a little better controlled, and a bit less shrill than the one he'd known from his childhood, but he knew it was the same one.

He looked around, saw he rested in a small, candle-lit room, a room with no furnishings other than pillows spilled about the floor.

He watched as the speaker calmly and silently gazed at him. He wore the black robes of a Nakish priest. He sat quietly, legs folded, contemplating the Barbarian.

Morak said, "Jaksim."

The other bowed his head slightly. "And you, Morak. How large you've grown over the years. But you always were big for your age."

"That was long ago..."

"Too long, eh, Morak, for anything but memories?"

"In the heat of the desert, even memories may be forgotten. But those of Jaksim are ever fresh."

"I am flattered, and I scarce believe you. Yet memories are always of what we once were, as you and I were once impetuous children; a Barbarian's son and a nobleman's son who dared friendship..."

The priest paused, the hidden, hooded face not moving from its measured gaze of Morak. "Memories..." He paused. "We are not..."

"Not what we once were?" Morak finished.

"Why have you come to me?"

"I need your help," Morak rumbled, leaning back against a wall and rubbing his head. "They're after me, trying to kill me."

"What has a priest to do with the affairs of a Barbarian?" Jaksim asked, though his voice sometimes hesitated. Perhaps in fear of offending—memories.

"You won't help me?" Morak stared unbelieving. Jaksim of all people...

Jaksim said nothing.

"There is a child; I have given my oath before all the gods to save her or avenge her."

The hooded head bowed, the soft voice filled with regret. "I have my own gods to pray to, duties to perform. The affairs of men are not those of a Nakish."

"Once I could have asked you for help. Once we were..."

"Were, Morak," Jaksim said, leaning forward, "were. Not now, we are different now. Time changes us all." He sat back, and there was silence for a long minute. Finally, "you must go."

"I have nowhere to go. B'saad is filled with thieves looking for me."

"I cannot help you, Morak. Please. I know it is difficult, but there are no choices to be made here."

Morak got to his feet, feeling somewhat like the time a large flying serpent carried off another friend of his. The Barbarian slapped his pack over a shoulder and turned toward the curtained door. Then he stopped and turned back.

"I have a book..." He began.

"A book?"

"I got it on the isle of Simathica." Morak thought he heard a gasp of breath. "I think that's why they're after me. Somehow they found out I had it." He reached into his pack and brought out the tome.

Jaksim reached out both hands, eagerly. "Please! May I see it?" There was a contained excitement in the Nakish monk's voice. Morak handed him the scarlet-edged book.

"*By the gods!*" Jaksim hissed. With delicate, yet trembling hands, he opened the cover and stared at the title page. "*Tome of the Dark Devices*," he whispered, "written in the Old Language." He looked up at the Barbarian. "This is thought to be legend..."

"Yet you hold it in your hands."

"Yes," he looked down at the book, "I hold it in my hands."

The priest leafed through the book, taking great care not to tear any of the yellowed, almost brittle pages. Reluctantly, he closed the cover and looked again at the Barbarian. "Legend tells us also that this entire land was once covered in ice."

Morak snorted. He'd heard that legend too often to take it seriously.

"A land of ice," Jaksim persisted, "and one day, the old gods picked up this book, or one like it, and it taught them to defy the new gods who had come to conquer the world. There came a war of thunder and fire, which fell from the sky and melted the ice, and underneath was—desert."

"You believe that?" Asked Morak.

"I did not—until now." They both looked back down at the book. "This must be kept and safeguarded, until we can study it and learn its secrets."

Suddenly the candle flames wavered, flickering first one way then back. Morak felt another presence in the room. He turned as another priest silently glided past him.

"You have heard?" Jaksim asked.

"We have heard," the other Nakish nodded. "We have also heard that within the city walls are many strangers who want that book, and he who wields it. They have already killed many in their searching."

"Thieves," Morak spat, "and worse."

"...and they would kill more, even priests, to get it. They have been well paid, and are willing to face odds, and breach taboos they would not normally dare."

"Whoever pays them must want this book more than his life," Jaksim said, hefting the book in his hand. "But then, what is a legend worth?"

"Just so," the other priest answered, then turned to Morak. "You got this book from the isle of Simathica?"

The Barbarian nodded.

"It has been said that no man may go there and return alive. None have done so, until you."

"Yet I am not a man, but a Barbarian, from Barbaricum, the son of Barbarians. I had to hack my way through half the things you see in your nightmares to get it."

"You will help us guard the book." It was not a question, but a statement of fact.

"I would rather leave it with you. Just give me a sack of gold and I'll be on my way, done with it."

"That is not possible."

"You don't have the gold?"

"We have gold. But it is your destiny to follow where this tome leads. You have a fate in store, my friend, like none of your kind ever have."

Morak frowned. "I would prefer the gold." He paused and the room was silent for a time. He thought back to those who had died because he had foolishly taken the book. He saw Meesha, her tortured cries echoing in his mind. Morak had abandoned her at the oasis so that he could escape with the book. Was her torture worth only a sack of gold?

"There is vengeance to be wrought," he said quietly, "But for now, I will help you guard the book."

"Then come." The Nakish turned and whisked through the dark curtains across the door. Morak and Jaksim followed.

They went down a long, dark corridor, past where the candles burned. There was no thick carpet on this floor, only cold rough stone. The two priests still glided silently, and the click of Morak's sandals echoed loudly. Eventually, they came to a stone wall. The priest adjusted an iron knob set in a nearby wall. The stone slid aside, revealing an iron door, pitted and rusty with age. The two priests stood to one side.

"This is a secret door to the outside. In all our years of priesthood, we have never had occasion to use it. Nor those before us, and those before them. We must use it now."

"Open it," Jaksim said to Morak. The Barbarian went to the door, turned the latch, and pulled. It grated loudly, moved half a finger's width, then stuck. Morak cursed his recent luck with doors, and pulled with all his strength.

This time it came loose and slid open silently. When it reached its stop, it clanged like a bell, echoing again and again.

Morak looked at the damp stone stairway that led down into darkness. A smell oozed out, of old things and wet things, and things that perhaps no longer lived. Jaksim lit a torch, brushed past Morak and started down.

Morak was ready to follow when he turned back to the other priest. "What of you?" He asked.

"I..." he paused as a third priest hurried up and whispered something. "Your enemies are even now breaking down our door. Go, we will remain here and delay them. Go, go with Jaksim and the book. Safeguard it, do not let it fall into the hands of those who would use the book's secrets to gain only power."

The door clanged shut behind him, and he heard the covering

wall rumble across it. He turned and followed Jaksim down a dark stone corridor. "How does this lead to the outside?" Morak asked.

"I'm not sure," Jaksim replied, "the old one didn't know either. None within memory has had the need to use this escape route."

On down they went. Morak felt they must be well under the city by now. The air became damper, slimier, and small trickles of ooze flowed down the stone walls. Somewhere, water dripped, echoing. There was a smell also, the smell of damp, old air that had been closed up for a long time. The gently descending corridor turned into steeper steps, slippery and uneven. Morak began to wonder if there was an end to the stairway.

Deep shadows flickered as Jaksim held the torch high, yet its light always ended in the blackness below.

Quietly it came to them, the sound. A gentle lapping of water. Morak and Jaksim reached the bottom of the stairs and stood gazing at a vast underground lake. Its waves disappeared into the gloom. The water was inky black, and had an oily sheen to it. Giant pillars held up a stone roof, for this was a man-made cavern, though there was no way to tell how long ago men had made it.

"It is strange," Jaksim said quietly, his voice filled with a hushed whisper, "we have no records of an underground waterway. No one knows of this, I think." Jaksim looked at the ceiling, studied it for a moment, "I think above us are the ruins of the old city. Hmm..."

"We'll have to turn back," Morak said, feeling some slight relief. He didn't like this place. It was too filled with darkness and quiet for his blood. Better a war shout and a thunder of hooves. He turned to climb back up the stairs, to face whatever awaited him there.

Jaksim's hand closed on Morak's arm. "Wait. Here, hold the torch." The priest leaned out over the water. "There's a rope here. Perhaps..." Jaksim began pulling at the rope. Fifty feet of the rotting, slime-covered stuff was piled at his feet when a small boat slid into view. It was old and gray, and it creaked with rust and rot.

Jaksim looked at Morak. "It is our only escape."

"Yes," Morak said simply, glancing back up the stairway. He remembered the raft ride he'd had across the sea to the isle of

Simathica. This time it was either a creaky boat or turn back and face an army of thieves tearing B'saad apart looking for him.

Carefully the two climbed aboard; a feat in itself, for the boat had a tendency to sway and rock. Once they were seated inside, Jaksim reached into his robe and pulled out a folded, thin pouch. "Here, my friend, put your book in this. It will protect the pages if this boat sinks."

The Barbarian thought that good advice. He pulled the book from his satchel and placed it in Jaksim's pouch, then returned it to the satchel opposite his sword.

Each man then grabbed an oar, and Morak pushed them out away from the platform. Jaksim jammed the torch in the boat's bow, but it had eaten more than halfway down its length. Morak wondered if it would last until they found their way out. With quiet, machine-like strokes, they rowed with a small current, and into the blackness ahead. Eventually, the pillars were replaced by stone as they entered a large natural underground cavern. But still there was no light.

Time passed, and Morak wondered how many hours—how many eternities—did that journey into nightmare last? He had no way of telling, except to note that he became hungry and thirsty. He had no food and did not trust drinking the water through which they rowed. The boat began leaking, slowly.

The only indications of their progress at first were the huge, crusted pillars that came out of the gloom ahead, passed by them, and were swallowed up behind. After that, stone walls made it even harder to determine progress.

Somewhere along the way, the torch burned out. Morak felt fear clutching at his chest, welling up inside him, wanting to burst forth in a scream. The blackness came over them like the worst time of the Long Night. Morak heard his own rasped breathing, and that of Jaksim. He wanted to be able to run—as fast and as far as he could. Yet he could only sit in the middle of this cursed boat and paddle.

"Morak" Jaksim whispered, "I think I can see something."

Morak could barely bring himself to grunt a reply. He looked around and finally saw it out of the corners of his eyes. Yes, there was something—a soft greenish glow.

"Yes, yes, I can see it," the Nakish said, his voice filled with relief.

"You're sure?" Morak whispered.

"Yes."

Slowly, sight came to the Barbarian also. He could see a faint greenish glow coming from everywhere—the ceiling high above, the stone walls, even floating in the water. Wait! That glow wasn't floating, it was moving under the waves, turning now to follow the boat.

"Morak, I see a light ahead—a real light."

Dead voiced, Morak replied, "There's something in the water, following us."

The priest was silent as they put their backs into rowing toward that distant clean yellow glow.

Morak glanced behind them. Whatever that cursed thing was it had to be huge, he thought, looking down into the murky water. The green glow was at least twice as long as the boat.

"We're coming to it, Morak," Jaksim shouted. The Barbarian glanced forward. It was true, there was an opening ahead. It grew larger as he watched.

"We're going to make it!" Jaksim shouted.

Something bumped the boat, and they felt a shudder course through the old wood.

Something splashed to their right. Morak saw a huge, snake-like thing rise out of the water.

"Oh, gods!" Jaksim cried, "protect us." Rising at the front of the boat, between them and light, was a gigantic tentacle, and with it, a red-eyed creature that lived in the depths of this forgotten lake of hell. More arms writhed in the water about them, bumping into the boat. The tree-trunk shapes were all around them, splashing. Jaksim stared straight ahead, unmoving, into those insane red eyes.

"Row, man, row," Morak shouted, but Jaksim sat immobile.

"Gods, gods, gods," the priest murmured. Yet the beast did not attack. Instead it slid silently and smoothly under the boat and came up behind them. Morak grabbed Jaksim's oar, seated himself in the middle of the boat—facing that thing and its arms—and rowed. The Barbarian watched as it came closer, effortlessly. One of the great arms came over the side of the boat, those red glowing eyes edged closer. The back of the boat was ripped away. Morak struck at a tentacle with an oar, but it had already slipped beneath the water.

Morak rowed. He glanced over his shoulder. Water flowed over his feet as the boat began to sink. The opening was large, perhaps fifty strokes away.

Then the boat splintered and Morak felt it being lifted out of the water. He struck out with an oar again, uselessly. They fell out of the boat, tentacles writhing all around them in the water. Jaksim screamed when he struck water.

Morak grabbed a piece of the boat and pushed it before him. Jaksim screamed again. Morak looked around him, saw the priest to his left, beating at a tentacle with a feeble hand. Jaksim screamed again and again, high pitched, hysterical screams. Something in the inky-black water bumped against Morak's leg. Whatever it was stuck to his skin and began pulling him under. He had no time to take a breath before the water closed over him.

Then, suddenly, miraculously, they were out in the open. A mountain receded behind them, and the creature was gone, afraid to leave its lair during the period of light. Two exhausted humans floated down the river, its swift current carrying them away from the dark cavern.

Morak swam over to where Jaksim floated, unconscious. With his last ounce of strength, he got them ashore. He lay gasping for breath, unfeeling of the sharp rocks cutting into his back. There was a lot of blood, but he couldn't tell if it came from his body or Jaksim's. He drew in lungfuls of air, his eyes closed tightly. They were safe from that thing in the lake; away from B'saad and the thieves. They could rest, relax, sleep.

There was the sound of someone walking on gravel. Morak lifted his head weakly. "Jaksim?" He asked. He heard laughter. He opened his eyes and above him stood three men dressed as outriders.

"You've given us quite a chase, Barbarian," growled one, punctuating it with a kick to Morak's head. He lost consciousness wondering why? Why?

• • •

Sometime later, Morak regained consciousness. He heard the crackling of flames, and smelled the pungent odor of raw burning wood mixed with a crisp breeze. And there were men nearby, too. Though he kept his eyes closed, Morak could hear them moving about, talking and laughing, scuffling in the sand and dirt.

As the gods would have it, that underground lake must have emptied into the river just at the point where the outlaws chose to make their main camp. The city was too small to hold a thousand thieves or more.

Morak heard a groan beside him. He opened his eyes and tried to turn toward that sound. He discovered that he could not move, his hands and feet were tied behind him.

Suddenly there was an explosion of pain in his back. Morak grimaced and heard the loud bellowing laughter of the man who'd kicked him. He was rolled over to face his assailant.

"You son of an ass," Morak growled, "I'll have your head for this."

The large thief grinned and prepared for another kick. He was pushed away by a tall, thin man. The newcomer gazed down at Morak with a curious, intelligent stare. This, Morak thought, was no common thief.

The other smiled, hands on his hips. "Him, the son of an ass? Not so, friend. You insult the ass."

"And who are you?" Morak growled. "Just another dog? Cut me loose and I'll feed you my sword, slowly."

The man laughed. "Me? I was only the offspring of a thief, and nothing more, until you showed up. My father was Kam, and he gave me rule over this band of useless jackals before he died. My name is also Kam, and you are Morak, a Barbarian. We watched you pretend to sleep when we all knew quite well that you were awake." He glanced around at several heavily-armed guards. "There is no escape for you. Not this time."

Kam was tall and thin, his hair light and long, which framed a sharp-boned face, finished with an elaborate mustache and a pointed, almost dainty beard. He smiled often, with a boyish enthusiasm, but his eyes, Morak noted, were granite cold.

Morak, of course, recognized him as the man he glimpsed in Tarak's wagon. Kam swept his arm in the general direction of the camp. "They've had quite a problem catching you. We had to surround the city and torture a few priests, all to no avail. It was some strange fate that brought you almost into the midst of us." He paused and smiled again. "I've heard Barbarians are an unruly lot—and crafty as well—but I must say, I've not met one until now. I thought you would be...hairier."

"Must you blather on so?" Morak said, and looked away. He kept seeing Meesha's face, and it made him ill. She must be dead by now, or...

"Yet we've much to talk about, you and I." Kam and one of his men reached down and together hauled Morak to his feet. The Barbarian groaned, and the world spun for a moment, then settled. Kam ordered his feet untied, then led the Barbarian through the camp. Morak wondered as they wove their way between campfires and the hundreds upon hundreds of thieves crouched around them; who would be powerful enough—wealthy enough—to hire this many outlaws? He did not know of a city king who had such a fortune to waste. Such wealth did not exist to his knowing. Yet someone had hired these hundreds, paid them good silver or gold. Someone who knew he'd been to Simathica—and returned alive with the book.

Morak felt the pouch at his side. The book was still there, maybe a little damp from the water, but at least he hadn't yet been searched. Someone had taken his sword and knives, though.

Kam halted before a huge ornate tent and held the flap open for Morak to enter. Many small candles and several lanterns flickered dimly, but there was sufficient light to show lavish furnishings. Morak looked around while Kam brought him to a small table at the rear of the tent.

"Sit, Morak, sit," Kam said, indicating one of the ornate chairs. Kam sat opposite the Barbarian, his granite eyes staring deeply into Morak's. "This truly has been the strangest adventure of my life, Barbarian. A stranger, the likes of which I have never seen before, with odd mannerisms and dress, and a small, tiny, elfin shape, comes to me and says, 'find for me this Barbarian, called Morak, capture him and bring him hither to me and the book which he carries.'" Kam paused and lighted one of the smoking sticks favored by the wealthy. The sickly-sweet odor of it quickly filled the tent. "He paid me with gold, Morak, lots of it, and promised more..."

"So give me to them, thief."

Kam smiled, tapped ashes onto the carpeted floor. "Not just yet—that book you carry; it interests me. Why should this stranger pay so much for a mangy Barbarian and an old book?"

"That I would like to know myself," Morak muttered, "I would rather be rid of it than have you chasing me all over hell."

"Then give me the book now, and I promise to kill you swiftly."

"You can take it any time you want. Why ask?"

"I always ask, Barbarian. Always." He gazed absently at his smoke, "I like to give one a choice of deaths, when I can, when they have something that interests me." His voice was soft, pleasant. "Your priest friend, now, he has no book, nothing to interest me. My men will dispose of him as they wish."

"And what of Meesha?"

"Who?"

"The girl child, from the caravan."

"Ah," his eyes got a faraway look, and the edges of his mouth turned up. "Such a sweet child. Yes. What of her?"

"Did you kill her, too?"

Kam leaned forward, "what is your interest in her?"

Morak looked away. "I'm responsible for her."

"Oh, too bad," Kam clucked, "such a poor guardian. Tell you what, Morak. Give me the book and I'll return the child; you can spend your last hour together."

"Meesha? She's still...?"

"She pleasures me, Morak. But I'm willing to end her life quickly if you do as I say. Give me the book."

"No."

"I'll let her go free after you're dead."

"No."

Kam jammed out his smoke. "Then she'll die before you, slowly. And you'll watch." He paused. "The book!"

Morak stood and heaved at his bound wrists, breathing anger at Kam. "I'll see you in the fires of hell."

"Almost certainly." He reached out a hand, "The book.

Morak, you're beginning to bore me. My men will enjoy killing you."

Morak gazed steadily at the leader of thieves. Suddenly he smiled. "Well, we Barbarians are sometimes hard to kill."

"So I've heard," Kam said. Again Morak was struck with the coldness that exuded from Kam. He tensed, waiting for the next move, and perhaps win a slender chance for freedom.

He had more reason now, knowing that perhaps Meesha still lived.

Kam stood, looking past Morak to the opening of the tent. "Rodness, Garant, come in here," he called. Immediately the flap opened and two giants entered. They were dressed in leather armor and carried huge swords. They stood a good head above Morak, and their shoulders were wide and thick boned. Thick heads, too, Morak thought, judging from the empty looks on their faces. They filled the tent with a foul odor.

"You see, friend Morak, I have no need of Barbarians. I have giants instead."

"Monkeys," Morak commented.

"This man is to be taken and tortured to death, in any manner you please," Kam shouted. The two idiot giants giggled and slobbered. There would be no reasoning with them. They flanked Morak, each grabbing an arm in an iron grip. They smelled of sweat, filth, and alcohol.

They lifted Morak off the ground and carried him out of the tent, but not before Kam had snatched Morak's bag, and with it, the book.

"We've games," Rodness giggled.

"Fun games," his brother said, tightening his grip on Morak's arm.

They went out past the campfires, out toward the river among the trees and dim shadowed sunlight. Morak strained against the giants' grip, but they only laughed and held on tighter.

"Down, brother," Rodness tittered. They dropped Morak on a sandy spot near the river. Rodness grabbed a handful of Morak's dark hair while his brother held the Barbarian's arms pinned behind him.

Morak looked into those stupid yet malevolent eyes, he felt

putrid breath brush across his cheek as the other laughed and brought his face closer, the slobbering lips pressing against Morak's. The Barbarian had faced many evils, not a few of them horrid beyond belief. But this, this thing touching him, was too much. Morak's stomach turned, and Rodness stepped back as Morak vomited uncontrollably. The Barbarian was pulled to his feet, Rodness stepped close and brought his knee up into Morak's groin. Again and again, the knee pounded home, like some huge log piston.

Morak screamed, ground his teeth, bit his tongue, clamped his eyes tightly shut, and finally passed out of that world of nameless pain into benevolent unconsciousness. He was glad he was not awake to see and feel what else the giants did to him that night. Where he was, there was nothing.

· · ·

But the giants made one mistake in their fun and games; by a tiny margin, they failed to kill Morak. They left him for dead, and he came back.

Water dripped on his head from somewhere. It took him a senseless nameless eternity to realize that it was raining. But mostly, there was just pain.

He lay not moving, seeming to float, not knowing if his eyes were shut or open. He could only see the red film of pain that blocked out all else.

Yes, it was raining, and he was floating. A pitiful groan escaped his lips. He floated in the river, his head resting on the bank. Slowly a lighter pink showed through the red blind of pain. The lighter color moved and twisted and took on a shape—the shape of leaves on the tree above him, whispering at him in and out, between sky and their shadow. After a few moments of staring, he once again lost consciousness.

Some amount of time later, he was able to move his head. The rain helped revive him, helped bring him back to the pain of awareness. He blinked, trying to clear away the haze. He realized someone was there, standing to his left, watching him. At first, it was only a shadow, a strange glinting shadow. Then it became clear, and Morak saw a tiny smile, a bald head, and blue skin, wearing shiny silver. A small man, the size of a child, standing two meters above the river—on thin air. Morak blinked and shook his head. When he looked back, the creature was gone, there was nothing to see. He must have imagined it.

He folded his legs up close to him, trying to stop some of the pain. His left arm seemed to be broken, and that of himself which he could see was covered with blood. The dog-brothers had done their job well. He wondered grimly how long they had been with their "games." He couldn't even feel anger.

The Barbarian brought his right arm up to wipe his mouth. That told him his lips were ragged and torn, and he'd probably lost several teeth. Gods! If only the pain would go away, he'd lie down and sleep 'till the river picked his bones clean.

He passed out or fell asleep. When he woke, the elf was kneeling beside him, holding a small vial of liquid. Morak felt his head raise, and the sparkling liquid poured between his torn lips, burning a cold path down his throat. He fell asleep, but when he woke later, the pain was only a dull throb.

And something made him try to sit up. He had remembered the book. And the smoky whisper of a vision that wouldn't quite come clear...

But the book. Ah, the book was something he could hang his anger on. He had to get it or die in the attempt. Thinking that, he was able to sit. Red stabs of pain shot through his body. He dug his working hand into the sand and mud at the river's edge, trying to make it stop hurting.

Morak rolled onto his side and gathered his legs beneath him. He tried to stand, but the dizziness overcame, and he fell. Thoughts of the book kept him trying, and presently he stood at the edge of the river. His right knee was stiff and swollen and he swayed as with exhaustion.

Still the rain dripped down upon him. It seldom rained anywhere within the desert land of Karan, yet when it did, it was a steady thing, swelling rivers and bringing brief green life to the lands.

The Barbarian staggered through the thin, river-edged forest, gasping through his mouth because his nose didn't work anymore.

He had one thought in his mind—he must get the book. He *must* get the book.

He must get the book and destroy it!

Destroy it? No! He must safeguard it. Now, why had he thought of destroying it? He frowned and staggered on, using trunks of trees and boulders to steady himself.

As he went, Morak gained strength, yet his mind retained a dream-like sensation. The pain of his body had subsided to a dull throb, and he wondered somewhere deep in his mind, how he was still alive.

The glow of campfires finally registered on Morak's brain. Nearby men sat talking, laughing, fondling wenches; this would be no time for him to stagger through. He had to wait until the camp was dead with sleep. So he retraced some of his labored steps and sat against the base of a tree, well away from the fires of camp, his hands in his lap, head resting against the rough bark, eyes staring listlessly. The liquid given him by the strange elf seemed to have dulled his pain. He was able to drop off into a dream-riddled sleep.

Sometime later, the camp was silent of men-voices. Morak slowly crept into the midst of sleeping thieves. Most of the fires were deep red and glowing dimly. Here and there, a small fire spread flickering shadows around.

Morak moved cautiously, limping from tent to shadow, crouching behind trees. His body still hurt, and occasional jabs of pain made him wince, but finally he knelt across from Kam's tent, and his mind did not dwell upon the pain.

Rodness and Garant, spears crossed, stood before the door-flap, silent and unmoving. Morak scarcely recognized them; they were just obstacles between him and the book. He felt around for a good-sized rock. His groping found one that fit neatly in his palm. He tensed in readiness, eyeing Garant, the largest of the two. He drew back and flung the stone.

It struck Garant in the face with a loud pop, smashing the giant's nose and mouth to a bloody pulp. His ruined lips prevented him from calling out as he slumped to the ground. Rodness watched in slow-witted amazement, then turned back and readied his spear. But it was too late—Morak landed on him, the useless arm across the other's mouth, and the good hand smashing

Rodness' head with another well-sized stone, over and over.

The pounding gave way to a soft, mushy feel; Rodness convulsed and went limp. Morak lowered his body to the ground, then turned to face Kam's tent. The book was in there. He'd faced death and monsters, and nameless things to get it—and keep it. No one was going to take it from him.

He brushed the flap out of his way and stepped into the dark tent. A small candle flickered as Morak eased inside. He looked toward the bed and saw the humped sheets that must be Kam.

Morak took a deep, shuddering breath, and the pain in his body seemed to distract him for a moment as he stood gazing down at the bed.

"Kam," Morak whispered harshly, "leader of thieves, I've come for the book—and to kill you."

There was no answer. The sheets moved imperceptibly. Morak reached down and pulled them off. He stepped back in shock. Looking up at him, eyes wide with terror, was Meesha, mouth gagged. Her trembling, naked body was tied with a fine cord. Bloody marks covered her, and one cheek was swollen and dark-colored.

"That's right, Barbarian. Although I had hoped you would try to kill me before removing the covers. I would have taken much pleasure when you discovered you'd killed our little friend."

Morak whirled. Kam stood behind him, stepping out from a dark corner of the tent, a sword's point preceding him. He smiled slightly. "She was quite insistent that you would be here tonight, so I waited. You see, Morak, I've discovered that not only does she provide excellent entertainment, but with the proper stimulus, she foretells the future."

"You most foul slime..."

"No, Morak. I am a leader of thieves. I am a law unto myself. And thanks to you, and a strange small friend with lots of gold, I am a king, Morak—a king!"

"I'll crown you king of hell!"

Kam only widened his smile. "It seems my men did a poor job of killing you. They'll have to be punished."

"Don't bother," Morak growled. Anger gave way to pain in Morak's head. Kam seemed to shimmer and fade.

"As for the book, Morak, should you by some chance kill me and steal it, you'll never get to keep it. Someone wants it, someone with more power than you or me or anyone in Karan."

Morak barely heard him, and his eyes again looked through a red haze.

"It's too bad we can't come to terms, Morak. You and I would have made a great team." He strode to a desk and calmly picked up the book, splitting his attention between it and the Barbarian. Suddenly, Morak's pain was forgotten.

"You fool! Destroy the book!" The words came shouted from Morak's mouth, but not from his mind. He was paralyzed with a strange peacefulness. And something, something else spoke words through his mouth.

"Destroy it?" Kam asked, stunned. His sword wavered a bit.

"Yes you fool! It will do you no good," the voice using Morak's mouth shouted, "destroy it—now, before it's too late. Before it's too late!"

"That is a most un-Morak-like voice I hear," Kam said, bringing his free hand up to stroke his beard, a thing he did not do often. "I think perhaps you are possessed by demons." Kam looked thoughtful for a moment, trying to decide. "Still, it seems that if I run you through, I'll not have Barbarians or demons to worry about."

Suddenly, Morak leapt forward and snatched the book before Kam could react. He tucked it away in his pouch.

"That was not a very smart move, my friend." He raised his blade to strike.

A whisper of wind through the tent got both of their attention. And it became dark. Morak heard the sound of scuffling, a shout. He was unable to move, yet the pain returned manyfold. He tried to step back, back out into the open air, but his body refused to obey. He hurt! Something crashed into him and he gasped in pain. He heard Kam grunt, and a sword clattered to the floor. Something touched Morak, clamped itself around his waist. He tried to struggle as he felt himself rising off the floor. And it seemed—yes! He was being lifted, lying on his back, yet seeming to float. How?

At another time, he might have been frightened, but his mind and body were so near exhaustion that he could not bring himself to fear. Something was flung violently about the tent. Kam grunted a muffled oath.

Morak's only coherent thought was of Meesha. "Child!" He shouted, "I shall come back to this place and take you away. I swear it!" His words echoed through the camp. Then he was outside, breathing cool, humid air, still strangely floating. The camp came to startled life.

It was still dark, and he couldn't tell whether it was because his eyes were closed or some witchcraft had blinded him.

He was moved away from the camp. He heard voices, some far away, some near his ears.

"Did you get him?" Far away.

"Yes," close by.

"Good," tittering laughter, closer. "And the book?"

"Yes, yes, just help us get him aboard. We don't want *them* to catch us." It sounded like a female voice.

Morak felt hands touching him, pulling him. He felt the coldness of steel beneath him, and the smell of an enclosed place came to him even through his battered nose. And with it, another odor, a strange odor, yet he knew it. From where? His exhausted mind could not remember.

He was dragged and pulled, and finally left alone with but four words addressed to him: "Go to sleep, Barbarian." Yes, it was a feminine voice, soft and soothing. It made him sleepy.

• • •

Sometime later, Morak woke with a start. He was at once aware of movement. He felt a vibration, a dull muted persistent humming. Yet when he opened his eyes, Morak found himself lying on cushions in a small, metal cubicle. He looked warily about him. This was a strange place, and he did not like being enclosed. The metal walls and floor reminded him of Simathica, and the crazy Witch Dagrag who there found her jewel and became something—else.

Morak sat and took a deep breath, wondering at his lack of pain. This room held no door that he could see, and the room's illumination came not from torches or candles, or from any source that he could tell.

While the isle of Simathica, and its metal buildings, held a dead feeling of ancientness, this place was alive. And Morak did not wish to come face-to-face with the gods who had built it.

Yet, he remembered that woman's voice.

He rolled over and stood, then noticed another cushion against the far wall. A bundle was heaped atop it, and Morak stepped over, his stomach complaining about perceived motion. He rolled the pile of cloth over with his toe.

It was Jaksim.

The priest opened his eyes, blinked a few times. "Oh, hello, Morak."

The Barbarian dropped down and sat next to Jaksim. "I thought you were dead."

Jaksim smiled faintly, in the quiet manner of his teaching. "So did I, friend. I was quite ready to begin my walk across the sky in the hands of the gods. Yet, here I sit, alive, and quite amazed by it."

"I am not too certain that we aren't in the hands of some kind of gods," Morak murmured, looking about him. He turned to Jaksim, "Tell me, Nakish, how you came to be here." His huge hand indicated the tiny cubicle.

Jaksim turned partly away from Morak, looking down at his knees. His voice was strained, as if it were painful—and frightful—to remember.

"When that godless beast smashed our boat, it came after me. It grabbed hold of me, Morak," he shook his head.

"That much I saw."

"Yes, yes, but it began to eat at my legs. I could see blood in the water and it burned, it burned." He stopped and drew in a long, shuddering breath. "It was like nothing I've ever felt before. Then we were out in the open and it was gone. I blacked out and when I came around, two thieves had hold of me and they threw me back into the river. They thought I was dead, and I, too weak to call out for mercy."

"You wouldn't have gotten any..." Morak stopped short. "Your legs!"

Jaksim smiled again, glanced down at his legs, then back up

at the Barbarian. "Yes, they are healed. I do not know how, for when I woke again, I was in this room. I've been here ever since, but don't ask me how long. There seems to be no division of time. Sometimes, a being dressed in strange clothes brings me food. And I press buttons for other—needs."

For the first time, Morak fully realized his own hands, legs, and body were also healed. "I was beaten, bones broken, scarred, and my face..."

"Your face is as ugly as it has always been, my friend," Jaksim said quietly. "It is a miracle. Perhaps we are truly in the domain of those mysterious gods you spoke of."

"Not quite gods," a new voice said; a voice filled with laughter and lightness. Both turned to look.

She was a woman all right, no doubt about that, despite her strange clothing. Morak examined her most carefully; she stood in a doorway where none had existed before, legs spread, hands on her hips, and a smile that seemed, somehow, to flow from her face and eyes and fill the room.

Yet her face was not beautiful and light-skinned and soft as one who had heard her voice might imagine. Oh, it had a rugged beauty, her glowing skin dark with small lines around her mouth when she smiled or frowned. Her face was framed by black hair that tumbled down her back.

Her shoulders were wide, almost as a man's—almost, but not quite. They fit the rest of her—large, but not out of proportion. And not unattractive.

Taken as a whole, she was the most beautiful woman Morak had ever laid his Barbarian eyes on.

She wore clothing as strange as her beauty. It was a one-piece garment, leather, which covered her shoulders and breasts minutely, curved around her neck at the top, and ended in a small kilt that hid almost none of her tanned, shapely legs.

A belt at her hips held an object Morak judged to be a weapon.

"I am known as Isha to my friends," she said with bold confidence in her voice. She smiled again, "and you are Morak, a Barbarian, and Jaksim, a priest. I would hope that we can be friends."

Both men gazed back in awe. Her eyes, Morak noticed in his examination, were as black as her hair, but not the deep, empty black of a witch. No, these were jewels, bright and polished, and silver in their blackness. Morak realized his mouth was open. He closed it, licked his lips, and continued to stare.

"You have many questions, I know, but please, hold them for now." Isha paused, looking at the two men closely, seeing mostly open mouths and wide eyes, "You will have understanding in time. Now come with me, if you will."

Her voice held just the touch of an accent, which showed itself only with certain words. Morak decided he would not mind listening to her talk all day.

She led them down a short, narrow corridor. This emptied into a busy control room. At the front of the room, a large window displayed blue-grey water all the way to a far distant horizon, reminding Morak of the sea surrounding Simathica.

Just behind the windows were consoles at which sat dark-haired men watching instruments and lights. They conversed in a rapid, sing-song gibberish Morak could not understand.

Isha nodded to one of the men. He turned to his controls and Morak felt a sensation of movement. The floor tilted slightly, and from somewhere, a humming deepened its pitch.

"This place reminds me of Simathica," Morak said.

"We have recently departed from that island, Morak." She smiled, her eyes alive and shining. "Our ancestors were the ones who built Simathica. We've been hiding there the past few days, while machines in that facility healed the two of you."

Morak touched Jaksim's arm. "Gods," he murmured, "this is a place of gods—I told you! Only gods can return men from the dead."

"Not gods," Isha said firmly, "only people, like you, with knowledge and powers you have not dreamed of. Power enough to take you away from Karan and over the oceans."

"Away?" Morak muttered to himself. He gazed out the window; clouds slowly moved by. Away from Karan? Over oceans? Maybe it wasn't too late.

"Take us back," he said, looking from the window to Isha.

"That's quite impossible, my friend."

"Within the tent of Kam there lies a child to whom I have given my oath. Take us back!"

"Morak, you don't understand..."

"The door, wench, there must be a door out of this place." Isha did not reply, but the Barbarian watched her eyes. They flicked momentarily over his shoulder, to his left. Yes, there it was, a man-sized square with a small window.

"No, Morak, please. You don't understand."

He ignored her, turned to the door and smashed his shoulder into it. He felt around, searching for a lever, something to make the cursed thing open.

His hand brushed the edge, a small section depressed into the metal beneath his hand. He pushed and pulled. The door slid open, and an ear-splitting sound reverberated through the craft. Wind, such as he had never felt before, sucked at him.

"Morak!" Isha screamed. The Barbarian leaned out and looked down. And down. The wind tore at him as he held on with one hand, hanging out of the opening, deciding whether or not to let go. A firm hand grasped his free one and pulled him back inside. He didn't struggle as Isha pushed him away from the opening and pressed the lever that closed the door.

"In the distance, I saw Karan," Morak murmured, his eyes glazed, "below me, surrounded by ocean. It looked tiny—so far away..."

"Not tiny, Morak. It only looks so."

"We're flying," Jaksim said, "we're high in the air."

"That is so, priest," Isha said, "we are in a machine that flies."

"I gave my oath," Morak said. "I *must* return."

"There are more important things than the life of one person."

Morak looked at her, at those eyes which had been so alive only moments before. Now they burned, a black coal in each. "Karan is my home. You have no right..."

"You have the book, Barbarian."

Again the book! That cursed book! If only...

There was a long interval of silence. Then Jaksim asked uneasily, "To where do we fly in this god machine?"

Isha sighed and her gaze dropped to the floor. "We are going to the land I call home. It is called Brazel by my people, and within that land is a place where we may be free and go about our affairs without fear."

"Fear?" Morak asked, "whom would the gods fear?"

"As I said before, Morak, we are not gods—and we have much to fear."

She motioned them to seats where they could see out the large view ports and the crewmen operating the machine in which they flew. "We have been fighting a long and terrible war, and perhaps it now has a chance of coming to an end."

"You say your ancestors built the isle of Simathica?" Jaksim said.

"Yes, or rather, the buildings within it."

"And you are the ones who hired thieves to kill me," Morak said, a wave of dull anger thickening his voice. His eyes looked away, at nothing.

Isha's smile tightened. "It was not us, Barbarian, it was the Brotherhood of Zartan Morf. They are our enemies, as well as yours. They are the ones who tried to kill you, who tried to destroy the book. They are the ones who hired the thieves. And that was all made possible thanks to your witch."

"Dagrag? What has she to do with this?"

Isha gazed at the Barbarian. "That you will learn..."

"Zartan Morf," Jaksim said slowly, trying the word out on his tongue. "I know them not."

"Of course. You have never seen their likes before. They couldn't come to the continent of Karan until the jewel was discharged. Then it was a race between them and us, to see who would capture the book. We had been working for decades, preparing to do just that. When the jewel was discharged just recently, we were forced to act without being fully prepared. I pray we get away with it."

"Who are these Zartan Morf?" Jaksim asked.

"They came from beyond the stars many, many years ago, and attacked Earth. Now," Isha paused, "Now they practically own our world."

"Beyond the stars?" Morak asked. Weren't stars only holes in the sky where warriors entered their place of honor beyond this life? For every warrior who died in battle, there shined a star as a monument to his valor. That's what he'd been taught from his youth. But stars were to honor those who did not break their oaths, so there would be no stars honoring *him*!

"The Zartan Morf are small, insidious creatures, with blue skin, bald heads and silver uniforms," Isha was saying.

Morak's head jerked up. "Small, silvery?" He asked. That sounded like the creature he had seen while floating, half-dead, in the river. Could it be...

But Isha was speaking. "...there was a war, a fierce and destructive war. Many of our people died, for the Zartan Morf are powerful, and had weapons my father's father's father knew nothing about. Many of our people were forced to take refuge in underground caverns, there to hide and live out their lives as moles instead of men."

She stopped, her eyes burning hate. "They could not destroy us, but we were powerless also. Thus it has been for these last centuries."

"Then it's true, there are other lands across oceans, as our legends have spoken," Jaksim said.

Isha smiled. "Many lands, with more people than could live on all of Karan..."

Morak snorted.

"It is true," Isha said, "Or it once was, and there were cities of such size your imagination could not conceive. But it's all gone, taken over or destroyed by the Brotherhood of Zartan Morf. They've redesigned other cities to house human captives, slaves that do their work. They are much too evil to tell," Isha said, "it must be seen."

"Why is this book so important?" Morak asked, just as a buzzer sounded above his head. He heard the pilot's voice, small and metallic.

"We have a Morf ship on our tail."

Isha sighed and activated her communicator. "We didn't get far, did we?" She spoke into the communicator, "range?"

"About twenty kilometers and closing fast. Two more joining it."

Isha turned to Morak and Jaksim. "This is our only flying craft, if those animals down it, we will have no chance to get the book back to Brazel."

She again spoke into her communicator. This time, her voice sounded all around them. "Red alert, activate all defenses, prepare for evasive action."

Even when giving orders he did not understand, Morak noticed that her voice was almost songlike.

"Come," she said. They stepped down into the control area. "The Zartan Morf craft are faster and better equipped than this one, but if we can reach land before they catch us, we may have a slight chance."

She paused and glanced at a radar screen, then at the man before it. "Chequita," she said, "strap our friends in the observation seats. They'll be safe there."

Chequita turned. "As you wish, my Lady."

She turned to Morak and Jaksim. "Do as he says," she ordered, then left.

The man called Chequita giggled as he rose and addressed the two Karanians. "Plenty of fun we have now, eh?" He talked with a strange accent, and Morak had trouble understanding him. Chequita was a man of medium height, thin, with skin almost as brown as Isha's, and black hair. His eyes danced with mischief. He quickly secured Morak and Jaksim into seats with shoulder straps and one across their waists. They sat behind and a little above Chequita's station, who went back to gazing at his screen.

Thereafter, the airship began diving and turning. Morak watched, every muscle in his body taut, as they seemed almost to touch the ocean on one occasion. It went on far too long, this wild ride through the air. Morak's stomach felt none too steady, while Jaksim was outright green.

The ship gave a lurch, followed by shudders and vibrations. "They've fired on us," the pilot shouted, "closing in fast."

"Left two degrees," Chequita sang out.

"Can we reach the mainland?" Isha's voice asked over the intercom.

"Don't—know," the pilot said through gritted teeth as he fought the controls and guided the ship around another explosion.

"A war between lightning gods and thunder devils," Morak whispered to Jaksim, remembering the ancient legends of Karan.

"Firing missiles," Isha's voice sang throughout the ship. "Deploying chaff and decoys on my mark," she counted, then said, "mark." The ship lurched again.

Their craft was shoved violently to the right. Morak grabbed his straps.

"We just lost our starboard stabilizer," Chequita shouted, "compensating."

"Increase altitude to 750 kilometers, continue evasive action. Firing heat seekers." Isha gave her orders quickly, without emotion, and with a bell-clear voice. She would make an excellent general, Morak thought.

If the two Karanians could have read the radar screen, they would have seen Isha's attempts at fighting back to be miserable failures. Of the three Morf ships closing, one was very slightly damaged by missile fire; all three were delayed and somewhat confused by the decoys, but only for moments.

The Morf ships followed their ascent, and matched their movement with fluid ease.

"Why don't they shoot?" Chequita asked.

"They want to make sure of the book," another said.

Isha moved in close to the co-pilot's station and strapped herself in.

"Land ho!" Shouted Chequita. Morak looked out the window, and indeed, land rushed toward them. But it was land as he'd never seen, many islands, lush and green. Off to the left was a desert to rival Karan. As they rushed over the land, Morak saw ahead land that was flat and green. In the far distance, Isha pointed out a mountain range that continued all the way up the continent to her home. A range of mountains that ran almost the entire length of the continent.

They burst into cloud cover and immediately changed direction. Isha pressed a button and sent her last remaining drone straight ahead. Radar indicated two of the three Morf ships followed it.

They dipped down, out of the clouds, skimming treetops, dancing along shallow valleys and over hilltops. The sea was far behind them as their ordeal went on and on. Using clouds and flying low into valleys, they managed to elude their pursuers for more than an hour. Then, abruptly, it was over.

"He's closing," Chequita said.

They all heard a "shoosh" followed by an explosion. The airship shuddered. Another nearby explosion followed almost immediately, then another. The pilot tried to gain altitude.

Suddenly, the ship was slapped through the air, flipped on its back and over again. Isha's straps broke and she was flung almost into Morak's lap. The Barbarian reached out and caught one of her arms as the ship groaned and flipped again.

"We're crashing," she yelled. It was the last thing Morak heard.

• • •

It came down almost silently out of the noonday sky. It passed close to a rise, frightening a dog-like animal, and on down toward a narrow, shallow river valley. It hit the ground, bounced, then skidded into the jungle undergrowth, collecting dents and scattering trees in its path.

It came to rest with a final lurch, upside down, with parts missing, and scarcely resembling the sleek, powerful airship of a few moments before.

While a thin stream of smoke rose into the air, the craft did not catch fire. Morak groaned and opened his eyes. Everything was upside down. And it all seemed to be spinning slowly. The craft was silent except for a distant hiss and a few items falling.

Morak looked down—or rather up—and saw Isha lying at his feet, or head rather. He saw an oozing cut on her forehead, and a jagged wound along her right arm. A lot of blood, but nothing that seemed serious. He could see her chest rise and fall evenly.

The Barbarian was still held tight by his straps, and he could not by the gods fathom how they were loosened. He saw movement and watched as Isha slowly climbed to her feet, shake her head, and try to focus on Morak. She looked away, her gaze examining the torn machine. She staggered over and examined her crew, then returned to Morak and fumbled with his straps. They came loose suddenly and he tumbled head first to the floor. He crawled to his feet, shook his head, and stared dumbly at Isha for a few seconds.

"Gods," he sputtered weakly, "what happened?"

"We were shot down," Isha replied coolly, "and we must get out of here. Can you stand? The Morfs must not know exactly where we hit or we would already be dead. But you can be certain they will know soon. You can always be certain about Morfs."

Morak stood and flexed his muscles. "Give me a sword and a sharp dagger and you'll not have trouble with those small creatures," he said.

Isha laughed and turned away. She went to Jaksim and undid his straps. The Nakish fell to the floor with a loud thump. "Help me get him out of here," Isha grunted, pulling the priest toward the opening. Morak stepped over to help and together they got Jaksim and the navigator, Chequita Moya, out of the airship. Isha's strength surprised Morak at first, then he decided she was a being of strength, and showed itself in all ways about her, including the physical.

While Morak stayed to revive the two men, Isha went back inside to see about the rest of the crew, and to collect supplies.

Outside was warm and humid, the air so filled with moisture Morak had trouble breathing. The land was choked with green vegetation and vibrated with strange sounds. The jungle growth would hide their location, Morak thought, until he looked back the way they had come and saw broken limbs and burned leaves making a quite effective arrow pointing right to them.

And it was full day, like the Long Day at noon. They couldn't have been traveling for that long. Morak dismissed the idea for the time being; they had other worries at the moment.

"Aye!" Came a voice at his feet. Chequita Moya was awake and rubbing his head. "Flying is dangerous," he said as to himself, "only to those who crash." He looked at Morak and smiled. "You live also, Barbarian. Good, we need strong men who live when others would die." His eyes examined the craft and he shook his head. "This will be one to tell them about back home," he muttered. His characteristic giggle erupted, followed by a groan as he cradled his head.

Just then, Isha returned. Chequita looked up. "The crew?"

The woman shook her head. "Three were dead; the other—his neck was broken." She glanced down at her knife, "he joined his brothers."

Chequita nodded solemnly.

Jaksim regained consciousness just as Isha handed out packs to each of them. "Hurry," she urged, "we must be away into the jungle, toward the river."

Morak helped Jaksim to his feet. The priest was dazed, with an ugly gash on his cheek, but otherwise seemed uninjured.

They started north and east, toward the Brazel place Isha called home.

The jungle noises Morak heard at first frightened him. His imagination gave hideous life to the chitterings and roars going on all about him. He had never heard such a chorus of living things. They came from near and far. Birds flew between the trees above them, and shadowy shapes darted among the branches. Once or twice, he sighted a serpent draped across tree limbs or slithering away into the undergrowth. Isha and Chequita ignored all this activity going on about them, so he tried to as well.

The climate was not as easy to take. The warm air quickly became sticky as the sun moved across the sky, enveloped them with its humid, energy-sapping presence.

Soon a warm drizzle oozed from the clouds and covered their bodies, and mixed with the sweat and dried blood, doing nothing to relieve the heat. The going was rough, as they had only the small knives Isha had found in the aircraft. They were forced to cast about, searching for a clear path.

Suddenly, Isha, who was in the lead, stopped and tilted her head. She turned south. "Listen," she whispered. Morak and the others became aware of a "swooshing" sound; a Morf ship darted overhead, heading south, back toward their downed flier.

The jungle became still, then there was a shrill scream. The humans were thrown to the moist earth; and that earth heaved and shuddered with the force of a massive explosion. Cries and screams went up around them, then silence. Only the dripping of the rain reached their ears as they slowly regained their feet. "That was the destruction of our ship," Isha said. "Morfs like to make sure."

Morak brushed himself off. "I guess they're finished with us now," he said, picking Jaksim from the moldy leaves.

"Not so, my friend," Chequita said, "not by any means, my Barbarian friend. They will search the wreckage. When they do not find you, and more importantly the book you carry, they will again search for us, relentlessly. They must be assured of its destruction, that book; they will sift the ashes for its remains."

"So we've got to hide from them," Morak said, "like cowardly animals?" He disliked this constant hiding. He wanted someone, something to fight, something he could get a sword point into. Then he remembered; he no longer carried a sword.

Isha pointed to the north. "Across thousands of kilometers of this cursed jungle lies our homeland. We not only need to hide, but we must also be wary. The Zartan Morf can sense our thoughts to some extent, if they're close enough. They can make us see things that are not real. They can aptly control the minds of lesser beasts, or humans who have gone too long without rest." She shook her head, "we don't know enough about them or their abilities. It seems an impossible task. Though the range of their mental powers is thought to be limited, they are relentless, and they will send after us thousands of their kind—or anyone else they can get to fight for them. Because they know, Barbarian, if we get the book back to our home, and make use of its secrets, we, the humans of this defeated planet, can still wrest victory from those ancient ashes." Her voice rose as she spoke, and her eyes looked through him, seeing something beyond Morak's understanding.

She glanced at him shyly. "I talk too much. Let's move on."

• • •

The day passed quickly, but their progress was slow. There were small animals here unlike any on Karan. Morak and Jaksim looked about them eagerly, remarking on the strange and wondrous things they saw, the jungle odors and sounds. Morak wished for his sword, which lie somewhere between Kam's camp and the river on a land he used to call home.

They came to a small stream and followed it for a time. They stopped to drink at a tiny, trickling waterfall. Morak wondered how his life might have been different had he been born in a place such as this.

As the sun began to set, they made camp in a narrow, grassy depression, hidden by thick jungle growth. A small campfire cooked the minute, furry creatures they had caught before sundown. To Morak's mind, the vermin tasted foul and greasy, although Jaksim seemed to like them, and the two inhabitants of this land regarded them as a rare treat.

They talked of things time had not permitted before.

"I do not understand the sun," Jaksim said to Chequita, "it moves across the sky and disappears into night in just a few hours. How can that be?"

Isha looked confused, but Chequita nodded. "Karan is at the very bottom of the Earth. At each end of the planet, the sun responds differently than everywhere else." He giggled. "Yes, it must seem strange to you, this dividing of light and dark in a single day."

Morak grunted. "In Karan," he said, "the Long Day and the Long Nigh are equally divided and do not intermix."

Jaksim agreed. "During the Long Day we must work hard to grow food and increase our livestock. The desert becomes much hotter and everything is active. It is also a time for celebration."

"And during the Long Night," Morak added, "we live by the light of fire. Candles burn to tell us when to wake and sleep. The Night is also the time we increase our own numbers." He smiled wanly.

Isha shook her head. "Your lives are so much different than ours," she said softly. "Where we live, there is no sun at all. Yet our illumination mimics its daily passing, night and day."

"You tell us you are not gods," Jaksim said, "yet you can heal and you can fly great metal machines."

Isha spread her fingers. "Do we not look alike? Do we not eat the same foods? Do we not even speak somewhat the same language?"

"Do you speak the language of mortals," Jaksim said, "or do we mortals speak the language of the gods?"

Isha laughed, her dark eyes flashing in the firelight. "It's an old language, older even than your homeland or mine. Back when their histories intertwined, it was a tongue spoken by some of earth's military. It is not native to many, but understood by most.

Earth is home to many people with many languages, and none of them are gods."

Morak considered this. A common language was spoken throughout Karan, though with various accents and crudeness. Then there were the people near Sumar's homeland who spoke an entirely different tongue.

Suddenly he changed the subject. "Why haven't the Zartan Morf attacked your people? They destroyed the world, you say, yet you are alive."

Isha frowned for a time, gazing into the fire, then looked away. "There are many millions of humans on this earth," she said sadly, "slaves and work animals for the Zartan Morf. And then there are the free ones, few in number, such as ourselves. We live underground, where their sensors and mind tricks and weapons cannot reach." She paused, her eyes glowed into Morak's warmly. "Wait until you see our home, Barbarian, the sight will suck the air from your lungs. The Golden City lies underground below a deep, narrow river canyon. It's hidden from above, and there are many such canyons in the area. The weather is poor for flying, and wind currents make exploration tricky. The entrances are protected by many traps."

She laughed, "each year, they search, sometimes with random attacks in vain attempts to draw return fire. They know we are there somewhere, but they can't reach us." Her eyes bored into his, "if they ever do find a way to get at us, Barbarian, it will mean the end of our world."

"You are only a few out of those millions?" Jaksim said.

"Yes, but we have the only scientific laboratories that are still operating. At least we have been unable to contact others so endowed."

Morak shook his head. It was too much for him, too many unfamiliar words. He tossed a stick into the fire, then climbed into the equally unfamiliar bedroll from the ship.

The night was dark, but without clouds. He listened to the others' breathing and the night jungle sounds. He brushed an insect from the side of his face and tried not to think. Despite his efforts, his thoughts drifted to Meesha, and anger and frustration flared within him. He did not sleep well, his body attuned to sleeping half his year in sunlight during the Long Day.

They were packed and moving before the morn sun broke between the trees. Morak caught up with Isha. "You said these Zartan Morf, they use the power of their minds. Tell me, do they have other powers?"

Isha swept a branch out of her path. "It is said they can float upon the air, and make other things move without touching them." She paused and turned to look at Morak, wiping sweat from her forehead with the back of an arm. "It is said, too, but also not proven, that they may disappear and reappear a short distance away."

"They sound like the witches."

"Yes, the witches of Karan," her smile returned, grimly, "I'll tell you about them, about those witches, should we ever get back to Brazel."

Morak watched Isha's lithe body moving easily through the jungle. "Describe again what a Morf looks like." He said to her back.

"They are small runts of men, with no hair. They wear clothes of shiny silver. They see with large orange eyes. Their skin is blue. They do not look evil..."

"As I thought," the Barbarian said, nodding. He told Isha about the strange creature he'd seen while floating in the river half dead. And how he'd been given the strange liquid and compelled, almost against his will, to forget his broken bones and return to Kam's tent. And how he'd tried to convince that leader of thieves to destroy the book.

"Yes," Isha commented, "they got to Karan faster than we thought. You were lucky. Had it not been for the pain in your body, they might have gotten you to destroy the book. And thank goodness, we arrived in time to snatch you and the book from their grasp."

"The book!" Morak shouted, "always the book. Curse the book!" He looked skyward, then back at Jaksim and Chequita. He sighed, "what secrets are hidden within this precious book?"

Isha glanced quickly at the pouch at Morak's side.

"You will know, Barbarian, if we survive this march through hell, you will know."

The days following, they avoided heading true north, knowing the Morfs would be looking for them along that line. Isha led them in a twisting pattern, sometimes following a river, other times an animal path. They made camps. They killed snakes and strange creatures, eating some of them, and frightened off larger animals. Insects swarmed about their sweaty bodies.

"Gods!" Morak exclaimed on the tenth day, "does this jungle go on forever?"

He stopped and shared his water skin with Jaksim, both of them looking over the endless green that made the jungle. He never thought he'd wish for the hot sands of Karan...

"Thanks," the Nakish said, wiping the back of his hand across his mouth and handing the skin back. "Life in Karan did not prepare us for this, eh, Morak?"

The Barbarian shook his head, frowning.

"And, being not prepared for it, perhaps we shall die," Jaksim murmured.

"That is for time to tell," Morak said, starting off again.

• • •

Something woke Morak the morning of the eleventh day. He lay in his bedroll wondering what it was. Then he knew: Silence. A total silence of not even wind. Not even insects. The mad chorus of morning birds was gone. His heart began pounding and he moved slowly to sit up.

Surrounding them, on the ground like a furry carpet, in the trees and underbrush, covering every available space, were countless numbers of the small, furry, manlike creatures Chequita had called "monkeys." He saw a mixture of colors and sizes. Some had long tails, others none at all.

All of those tiny eyes were fixed on Morak. All of the tiny heads riveted to his. And not one made a sound.

Not one moved. The Barbarian slowly reached out and shook Chequita's bedroll. The navigator turned to Morak and opened a blurry eye. "Well, friend, what causes you to wake me from such pleasant dreams?"

"A nightmare, I'm afraid," Morak said quietly. Chequita

frowned, then saw the Barbarian's eyes. He sat up and looked around.

"Holy...Isha!" He shouted, scrambling to his feet.

That triggered action. As the woman and Jaksim came awake, the monkeys moved, as if they were one, screaming an horrendous sound.

The humans pulled knives and threw stones. Isha used her ray weapon to cut down scores of the creatures with its lightning, until that sputtered and died.

"Damn," she said, tossing the weapon at the closest monkey. The animals were upon them, scratching, biting, tearing at them in a screaming rage.

Morak slashed with his knife, crushed tiny skulls in his huge hands. Yet they still came on, mindless, more and more of them, piling atop each other and the dead bodies of their kind.

Morak was dragged to the ground, under the sheer weight of monkeys, his skin torn and bleeding from countless bites. They kept trying to tear his eyes out. When he opened them he saw nothing but frenzied, biting mouths full of razor teeth. His hand fumbled around as he fought to keep his balance. That hand grasped a thick tree branch left partially unburnt from the previous night's fire.

He grabbed it, pulled it to him, and began swinging it, smashing monkeys aside, crushing them as the club gained speed and strength. Morak scrambled to his feet and continued swinging the club, back and forth, with all the power of his body. "Die, you beasts of hell," he shouted, overjoyed finally to have something to kill.

He began working his way to the others, who were by now buried under solid layers of monkeys trying to smother them with their numbers.

Like a machine, Morak smashed the small, furry forms until the club ran with blood and splattered brains. The monkeys screamed and attacked him with hysterical ferocity. And the Barbarian, knowing battle once again, feeling the blood course through his body, met that charge with more and harder swings of the club, until monkey bodies were piled high around him.

Sometime beyond his ability to judge, there were no more

monkeys. Only broken-stick things, some still moving feebly. His companions were buried under the crumbled heaps of bodies.

Morak leaned against the club and rested for a moment. He wiped sweat and blood from his eyes, then moved over to the others.

Isha was first. An unusually large pile of monkeys surrounded her unconscious body. "Some fighter," Morak muttered as he shook her. Isha's eyelids fluttered, then opened wide in fear.

"Oh!" She said, "they're gone."

"Not gone," Morak replied, "dead. Smashed."

Together, they tended to Chequita and Jaksim. The priest had been severely bitten on the face and arms. Chequita was too covered with blood to determine his injuries, but his pile of dead monkeys rivaled Isha's.

After a time, all four were revived. "So we survive to fight again, another day, some other vision from hell?" Chequita said, gingerly surveying his torn and bloody skin.

"That, Morak, is how the Zartan Morf do battle," Isha informed him quietly.

"Evil creatures," the Barbarian agreed, gazing about him, "Someday, I'll run my sword through the heart of their king."

This time, Isha did not laugh.

"Quickly," she said, "They obviously know we're in this area. While they can see through the eyes of their puppets, they may be some distance away. Let us hope the jungle can swallow our signs of passage."

After a time, they found a stream uninfested with vermin, and washed their wounds. Isha gave them pills to swallow that would, if they were lucky, prevent any sickness and disease carried by the monkeys.

"Cowardly creatures," Morak spat as he dabbed at a stubborn wound, "why don't they fight their own battles?"

"A Morf is not cowardly, my friend," Chequita replied, "but he will have others fight in his place, if it were possible." They quickly moved on, following the stream and keeping the canopy of jungle above them.

That evening, just before dark, they discovered an old abandoned and ruined city, largely made of worn stones among the creeping undergrowth. They decided to camp at its edge. The nameless place had been reclaimed by the jungle, and the only sounds that reached their ears from the cavernous, crumbling buildings were those of birds and animals.

"Abandoned how many years ago? How many centuries?" Isha asked.

"Who knows, lady," Chequita said. He sighed, "but someday, we'll come back and find out. We'll live in the open again, that we will." He lie down, clasping his hands behind his head. "These Zartan Morf, now," he said to no one in particular, "are not made for this earth." He glanced over at the Barbarian, "when we throw them off it, I fancy they'll be secretly happy."

"Eh?" Morak asked, "of what did you speak?"

"You seem to be preoccupied this night, my friend. What fills your thoughts?"

"Those of a child, and my oath. I swore to return to the tent of Kam and take her away from that demon. Yet each day I tread farther away from keeping my oath."

"As that may be true, Barbarian, sometimes circumstances force us to fail in our oaths through no fault of our own."

"A Barbarian does not fail. Someday I will keep my oath, just as you vow to rid Earth of the blue skins. Though it seems they are not so easy to discourage."

"Oh, but they will leave willingly, Morak, once we learn how to make the jewels—once we have the book..."

"Chequita," Isha demanded, "why don't you gather some firewood. We can talk of this later." Her voice was firm, and Chequita, looking sheepish, quickly complied.

The next morning, they surveyed the ancient ruins from a distance, hidden, they hoped, by the jungle. "Old, very old," Isha breathed into Morak's ear.

"A river at the far edge of the city runs north," Chequita said, returning from a scouting trip. "If we built a raft, perhaps we could speed our journey."

Isha considered this. "We'd be exposed to attack while on the river. And we'd have to forage around the city to gather materials. That could be dangerous."

"It looks dead to me," Jaksim said, "old crumbling buildings, a few snakes and vermin."

"Yes, woman," Morak agreed, pointing, "there's not even ghosts in those shadows. Let's go."

She shrugged. "All right." She looked at Morak and Jaksim, "but on your heads be this judgment."

Quietly, they entered the ruins and started along the remains of a cobbled street, taking the most direct path to the river. Ruined buildings surrounded them. Some were mostly intact, but empty. Others suffered collapsed walls, and the jungle had done a good job reclaiming the land. They weren't yet to the city's center when Morak's back began to crawl. Suddenly he didn't want to be anywhere near this cursed place.

He looked around him, feeling a dread fullness to the silence. There were things watching him, he could almost see them, in the shadows. And the shadows were moving.

"Rats," Isha murmured, giving a name to the undulating shadows, "behind us and on each side."

"Snakes in the trees over that way," Chequita added softly.

In avoiding the silent, watchful animals, the four found themselves being herded away from the river. The buildings and shadows skittered with dark movement, the trees swayed with reptilian bodies. There were other noises, too, wet, sucking noises, hissing, and Chequita suspected alligators.

They stopped, and silence again fell over the city. A waiting, expectant silence. An intelligent, directed silence. The four glanced here and there, watching the dark corners.

"Let's try to get near one of the buildings," Isha whispered, "we can climb one and make our way on rooftops, if we're lucky. We might even make it to the river."

"It's a slight chance," Chequita said, frowning.

"Better than where they want us to go," Morak said in hushed tones.

They started off again, edging toward one of the buildings. With each step, they feared an attack from the rats and snakes, and whatever else the Morfs were using to fight their battles.

They drew near to one of the buildings, as if seeking shade. Morak leaned against the crumbling wall and reached behind him to feel out possible handholds and cracks.

"Should be easy to climb," he muttered. "Here, grasp my hand. Climb to my shoulder and onto the roof." He reached out a hand. Chequita grasped it, and the Barbarian lifted him up. The navigator's feet bit into Morak's shoulder, then he was gone.

"Hurry," Chequita called from above, "it's clear." Jaksim went next, slipping and clawing, but finally reaching Chequita's outstretched hand.

Isha reached for Morak's hand when the rats attacked, filling the streets with pulsing bodies, all headed for, or climbing upon Isha and Morak. The animals attacked with vicious abandon, teeth biting into the two as Isha lifted herself along Morak's body and up.

Two hands grasped each of her outreached ones and pulled her to the roof. Rats were detached and tossed over the side.

Then it was the Barbarian's turn. But the rats were massing on his legs, climbing his body. He shrugged a shoulder to dislodge one that was biting at his neck. He kicked with one leg, then the other, throwing rats away from him. He reached behind and pulled himself up the wall.

His reaching hands were grasped by Chequita and Jaksim and they pulled him up just as wide, teeth-filled jaws opened up in the midst of the rats and snapped at his feet.

Morak scrambled and finally gained the roof, dodging the snakes in nearby trees.

"Let's move!" Isha shouted, "toward the river."

The buildings were close together, most with flat roofs or remnants, which was fortunate because the streets were filled with angry beasts following from block to block. The four bounded from one roof to the other with wild abandon, knowing that now only speed and recklessness would give them an opportunity and the time to escape.

As Morak made one far leap, he glimpsed something silver out of the corner of his eye, crouching in the corner of the roof.

Without stopping, he turned, grabbed Chequita Moya who had followed the Barbarian's leap, swung him around and tossed him at the silver in the corner. Chequita shouted in surprise and landed with an "oof" of pain.

Isha landed beside Morak, followed by Jaksim. Another

silver flashed in the opposite corner. Jaksim swung around in a fluid motion, kicked out, then calmly watched as the Morf cracked its head on the corner stone of the roof, then disappeared over the edge.

"What happened?" Isha asked, turning quickly from Morak to Jaksim, "what did you do to Chequita?"

"I'm all right, lady," the navigator's voice came weakly from the corner. "He caused me pain, all right, but we landed ourselves a Morf." He moved to reveal the small, crumpled form beneath him.

"Took them completely by surprise," Jaksim said quietly.

"They didn't expect us to escape," Morak added, "when we did, they were caught—they had to stop us and couldn't hide fast enough."

"But you acted so quickly," Isha said in awe.

"In Karan," Jaksim said quietly, "those who move slowly in times of trouble cease to move at all."

Isha gazed at the priest. "You're both full of little surprises, aren't you? Karan, in its short span, with its unoriginal names and storybook creatures, managed to produce warriors of note."

Morak knelt beside the small, bald, elfin man. He noticed the skin was a pale blue, and a small tube ran from behind the Morf into its left nostril. The eyes were closed.

"This is the dreaded Zartan Morf?" Morak asked.

"Their bodies are small," Isha warned, "because they have given them up in favor of intelligence and mental power. Be warned, Barbarian, you touch fire—a fire that may burn you before you know of its heat." Despite her words, she too knelt beside the Morf and examined him closely.

"Perhaps, my friends," Chequita said, "this one has an airship nearby. Perhaps, if we persuade him with the proper motivation, he'll show us where it is."

"And we can fly back to the Golden City?" Isha finished. She looked thoughtful, "but there is one problem—we might lead his kind there, too. But what choice have we? Our journey afoot would take several more weeks, even if the Morfs didn't throw every living thing at us along the way."

They watched their captive for several more minutes. Finally, the Morf's small eyelids fluttered open. Morak grasped the alien's shoulders and helped him to sit. "Do you understand my words?" The Morf remained silent until Morak brought the tip of his knife and pressed it against the alien's throat.

"Yes," the Morf croaked, "I understand you."

"Do you have an airship near here?" Jaksim asked.

"Answer him," Morak growled, pressing the knife.

The alien looked surly, but nodded.

"Take us to it, friend," Chequita said, smiling.

"You are a fool," the Morf said in a small, yet deadly sharp voice. The small eyes looked directly at Morak. "You ally yourself with these creatures of Earth. They are not your kind."

"Take us to your airship, dog," Isha snapped, "or would you rather die slowly and painfully?"

The Morf shrugged. "That way," he nodded toward the river. Following his directions, in Morak's grasp, knife pressed to his throat, he led the humans to his machine, hidden among jungle growth slightly upriver from the center of the ancient city.

They made him open the craft and everyone scrambled inside. Chequita Moya headed for the control room. "Now, my friends, we shall see how this thing works." Five minutes later, a baffled look ruled his dark face. "I'm no pilot, I'll confess, but I know how to fly airships. This one—I can't even open a window to see out."

"Show us how this works," Morak said, shaking the Morf.

"Of course. If I didn't, you'd kill me." With short, precise statements, he gave Chequita Moya the basics of operating the alien aircraft.

"He is too cooperative," Isha whispered to Morak, "his kind will follow."

A few minutes later, they were in the air, heading north. "Its speed is a bit faster than that of our aircraft," Chequita said, studying the controls and the view ahead.

Jaksim, meanwhile, studied the Morf captive closely. "You are the strangest creature I've seen, yet there is something—"

The Morf merely stared back.

Jaksim felt a growing unease, a bit of fear. Suddenly, he was afraid of the Morf, he feared crashing in this strange craft, the possibility of dying clutched his heart. His eyes darted about for a way to escape. He opened his mouth to scream...

But no—he suddenly realized that his fear was induced by the Morf. He looked back and noticed disappointment in the eyes of the alien. He began to pray, putting himself into a meditative state, and ignored the Morf. His silent chants calmed his fear.

Chequita kept the captured ship near to the ground, in the hopes of avoiding detection by other aliens. The jungle slammed past as the ship slithered along, clearing treetops by less than its own height, dropping into ravines, and following river canyons. Morak became dizzy trying to take it all in, and decided to watch, instead, the woman, Isha. Her dark eyes never left the Morf, except for once, when she glanced up at the Barbarian.

"They are never truly prisoners," she told Morak, "their minds are too dangerous, too powerful. He could escape before we might react, or he might bring his pig-brothers down on us. But I don't think this one will sacrifice himself, he is too cowardly."

"You will never have the jewels," the Morf said suddenly, smiling, revealing small, pointed, carnivorous teeth, "you no longer have the knowledge. The book is useless to you. The formulas are gone, the methods..."

"Silence, you creature of death and darkness," Isha said between clenched teeth.

"What connection is there between the book and this jewel you keep talking about?" Morak asked the alien.

"The jewel," Isha answered quickly, "is our hope for freedom. Its radiation destroys the Zartan Morf's mental powers, slows their thinking process, and eventually will kill. If we had enough jewels, we could reclaim our earth."

The Morf laughed. "It would be a simple thing to shield its radiation."

Isha sighed, "jewel radiation on a laser carrier would penetrate any shielding. A large enough jewel powered by a fusion reactor would render half the Earth useless to your kind. You see, we know more about Simathica than you thought."

The Morf laughed again, but no longer smiled.

Morak was too busy thinking to notice. Thinking of the witch, Dagrag, and the jewel—the Blood Jewel of Simathica—of how she had taken the jewel, and yet it, in the end, took her. She was transformed into a strange mist. But that transformation had also destroyed the jewel. "The Blood Jewel of Simathica," he muttered.

"Yes, that jewel," Isha's eyes flashed, dark with anger, "that was the first and only jewel created by man, and that which led to the creation of your Karan and all which dwelt upon it. Its creation resulted in a giant chess game, Barbarian, and a stalemate until now."

"No stalemate, Earthian," the Morf said, "not even close."

Suddenly, the Morf gurgled, stiffened, and slumped forward, revealing a thin knife in Isha's hand, stained now with a metallic blue blood.

"Why?" Jaksim asked.

"It was necessary. His fellows are closing in on us, and they can communicate mentally short distances," Isha replied, "and if our legends are true, he could have escaped, gone from here," she snapped her fingers, "and somewhere else like that. Now his kind know he is dead, and perhaps they have lost the thread that connects them to us. And we may have gained, perhaps, our chance to reach the Golden City."

Chequita shot a look over his shoulder. "So you've done it, eh, my Isha. Well done, except for one thing."

"What?"

"He neglected to tell me how to land this thing. Oh well, none of us lives forever. We shall experiment."

Several silent hours passed. Soon Morak and Jaksim, both exhausted, tried to get some sleep. Later, Isha followed suit, leaving Chequita to pilot the strange ship alone.

There was a lurch. Morak came awake and saw Chequita struggling with a small, silvery figure. The Morf? "It didn't die!" He shouted.

"Not so, Barbarian," Isha said, lunging toward the pilot's station, but too late. The Morf was gone, leaving only a small thunderclap of air. Chequita had both hands on his head as a thin trickle of blood streaked down his right cheek.

"It was a different Morf," Jaksim said from the rear of the airship.

"Are you all right?" Isha asked Chequita, prying his hands from the wound and examining it closely.

"Yes, yes," the navigator said, "he just caught me by surprise, that's all."

"You're sure?"

"Yes—the ship!"

The four turned to the view screen. It was morning, and the aircraft was moving ahead slowly. As they watched, it settled to the ground, gently, with not so much as a bump.

"Wonder of wonders," Chequita mumbled through gritted teeth, "their ships land themselves."

"Can you make it?"

"Yes, but they now know where we are."

"All the more reason we make haste to leave this craft," Isha snapped. They exited the alien vessel and plunged into the jungle with reckless urgency.

• • •

And none too soon. There came lightning strikes all around them. The Morf ship exploded behind them with such a force all four were thrown from their feet.

The jungle sizzled with bolt after bolt of white crackling lightning. Through the trees, Morak could see at least a dozen of the round Morf ships flitting this way and that, raining down death everywhere.

"I know where we are," Chequita shouted, "this is our home territory. Over those mountains is the gorge containing the Golden City!"

They ran into the thickest areas of the jungle, mindless of living things or the thorns which tore at their clothing and ripped skin. A thick canopy hid their movements to some extent.

"They do not take kindly to one of their own dying," Isha explained to Morak between frantic puffs of air.

Suddenly, trees crashed to the ground all around them, and the air was filled with a heated, electric stench. Someone screamed and Morak turned to see Jaksim writhing on the ground, a smoldering wound across the priest's chest and right arm.

But before the Barbarian could move, Chequita Moya was also struck by the lightning. The dark-skinned navigator simply crumpled to the ground, soundlessly. Isha ran to him while Morak knelt beside Jaksim.

The Nakish was conscious, but a red foam escaped his lips as he turned anguished eyes on Morak. "It seems, Morak, those near you always die strange deaths." He coughed.

"You are not dead yet, my friend. And I think you shall still live." His voice was firm, but Morak's eyes were less certain as he examined the deep, burned wound on Jaksim. Gods, he was no healer.

"Morak," Isha called, "please come here." He joined her near Chequita, mindless of the death that still rained down around them.

At once, Morak could see Chequita had been injured much worse than Jaksim. His head hung at an odd angle, and blood spurted from somewhere beneath Chequita's crumpled form.

"Get out of here," he whispered, "get to the Golden City. I'm dead, my friends. Use my life to destroy the Brotherhood of Zartan Morf." He stopped, his dark eyes flashing from Isha to Morak, straining in their sockets because his head didn't work anymore.

"We will, friend," Morak said, "I swear it."

"Isha," Chequita gasped, "I've loved you for so long, yet never dared to tell you." He gazed above them, at the dancing lightning death, then back down to Morak. "Take good care of her, Morak, for she is Queen of Earth. Yes, leader of the free humans." He gasped, looked skyward again, and died.

"Oh, Chequita," Isha sobbed.

"Come along, Queen Isha," Morak said gruffly.

"Be quiet, Barbarian, a good friend has died today."

For a moment, they ignored the Morf lightning. Then both stood, Morak picked up the semi-conscious Jaksim, and they began again their nightmare run through the jungle.

All around them, fires burned and trees crashed to the ground, cut and splintered by the Morf attack. A close bolt singed Morak's left arm, and caused him to cry out in pain, but not slow his pace.

One of their number was dead, another half-dead, Morak thought, and nothing to do but run through this cursed jungle.

He always seemed to be running, and each time, to a place worse than before.

Sometime later, they came to the edge of a rocky outcropping with what appeared to Morak to be a cave entrance. Several meters of open space separated them from that goal.

Morak was in favor of continuing through the jungle, hoping to eventually outrun the alien attack. Even as he spoke, a Morf ship zipped into sight, unleashed lightning everywhere, and zipped off.

"We must use the cave," Isha said, ignoring Morak's urging for them to keep going.

"That is death," the Barbarian said with certainty. He pointed to three Morf airships in the distance.

Isha looked at the Barbarian. "Still, it's necessary," she said, "that cave leads to a tunnel, which, in turn, connects to the Golden City. If we can make the cave, we will be safe. Just inside are explosives with which we can obliterate the opening."

"Gods," Morak said, "death has followed me since I picked up this book," he fingered his pouch, resisting the urge to remove the book and throw it as far away from him as he could.

"And death will continue to be your companion until the book's secrets have been revealed and used."

Morak shrugged. "I will run as fast as you, Queen Isha. We will die, I fear, but we shall die together."

She glared at him, then looked back to the cave. "Now!" She whispered.

The two sprinted toward the cave, Jaksim bouncing on Morak's shoulder.

They were halfway across the open expanse when a Morf ship appeared suddenly at the edge of the forest. It hovered behind and above the two running figures and began shooting a great number of lightning bolts.

The two dodged this way and that. And the pilot of the Morf ship, Morak thought, used bad judgment. For his fierce attack around them raised dust from the rocky clearing, hiding their path from above. If the pilot had sense enough to use his weapon at closer range, and aim with single shots, he would have cut them down easily.

Morak dove, rolled into the cave, and came up against a sharp rock with enough force to cause a grimace of pain. Isha landed beside him, and they were just within the mouth of the cave. Jaksim sprawled a little farther along, where Morak had tossed his unconscious body.

"Hurry, Barbarian, we have to blow the explosives before the Morfs can follow."

Morak grunted, gained his feet, and lumbered off after the woman, Jaksim again over his shoulder. The cave turned sharply and light from the entrance ended in pitch blackness. He heard Isha swearing softly, followed by her hard breathing. He saw a spark, then light as a torch caught and flamed to life. Isha used that light to find a small, metal box. She carried it with her as they continued on, turning several more times, descending deeper into the mountain. Finally, they stopped.

"Ready yourself, and pray that everything works as it should." She twisted a dial on the box, then pushed a button. The cave shuddered, heaved, and rock dust settled on them, and Morak caught an odor of smoke.

"There, it's done," Isha said, "we should be safe." She leaned against the cave wall and took a deep, shuddering breath.

Suddenly, they were inundated in vampire bats, thousands of them. The scratchy wings, the chittering of the hideous creatures took them by surprise, and they took off running, Isha swinging the torch over her head.

They turned several more corners, and finally the bats were gone. "Are you hurt, Barbarian?"

"No, and I don't think those godless vermin were part of the Morf attack—I think they were roused by the explosion."

"I hope you're right. Now we must travel with care. There are traps within these walls, which will cause more explosions if we're not careful." As they walked, they passed several other cave openings, which Isha explained where alternate entrances. All of them were filled with explosives and traps. If the Morfs discovered any of several dozen other entrances, they would be useless to them.

A little further on, the walls became smooth and softly lit. Isha extinguished the torch and led them on confidently. "This is a seldom-used entrance, but I've been here before, Morak." Her voice was excited, almost childlike.

Morak frowned and wondered what was ahead. He still had the book, and its mystery, whatever that was. Jaksim was alive, although just barely. They were in the company of the Queen of Earth, or so he had been told. And they were headed for a place of safety, where neither the Morfs nor any other creature could reach them. Or so he had been led to believe.

So why was he so reluctant to enter this wondrous "Golden City"?

Half an hour later, following Isha through twists and turns, and a few more surprises for unwary invaders, they came to the tunnel's end. It opened out into a gigantic underground expanse. And there, filling the bottom of it, a glowing city so far away it appeared tiny.

It seemed to shimmer with an inner, golden glow, and Morak knew how it got its name; there was no other possibility. "The Golden City" fit. It seemed as if it were eternally at the edge of a glorious sunset. The buildings followed the cup of the cavern, growing taller and more elaborate near the center. Toward the edges were smaller buildings and large expanses of open, park like green, and even a few lakes. Bright golden globes hung from the cavern's ceiling and provided a good approximation of sunlight. He could see small, ant-like people moving along sidewalks. There were even a few flying machines in the air, the cavern was that big.

"That's it, Morak, my home. Home of a hundred thousand free humans. As complete a self-contained environment as our scientists could provide. You'll love it, I know."

She looked at him, her dark eyes shining. Morak said nothing. He wasn't so sure he'd love it, but he didn't know why.

Book Four

The Golden City

Morak, formerly a Barbarian from a land called Karan, stood at the window of his lush apartment somewhere in a place called Brazel. The dwelling was located within the huge underground expanse called the Golden City by its inhabitants, the free earthmen.

He turned at a sound. This room still bothered him. The bed was a large air-soft mound he found impossible to sleep on. To his maids' (yes, maids! *Three* of them) chagrin, he'd spread his bedroll on the carpeted floor, and found that, itself, almost too soft.

"Sir," a small, prim man asked demurely, "Mistress Isha would like to see you."

Morak sighed. He'd been in the Golden City three days, and the place was already beginning to bore him. He ushered the black-dressed servant out ahead of him and followed. Isha awaited Morak in a sitting room at her residence.

"Ah, Morak, thank you for coming. Your friend, Jaksim, has awakened. I'm about to visit him, and I thought you might like to accompany me."

Morak nodded. "Is he well? Have your healing magics cured him?" His deep voice rumbled through the smooth-walled room. Isha's residence would have housed an entire kingdom on Karan. This "sitting" room boasted a fireplace, books from floor to ceiling, and ever-present running servants.

Isha shook her black-tressed head. "Not yet, but thanks to our doctors, he soon will be. He was at death's door, and our healing apparatus is not as effective with his type of injuries. Come." She led him out of the building to another one she referred to as a hospital, although it didn't resemble any of the healing places Morak knew.

Isha allowed Morak some time alone with Jaksim. The Nakish greeted the Barbarian weakly. Tubes poked out of him everywhere, and his eyes were puffy and red. "Hello, Morak," he croaked, attempting a smile.

"You look awful, My friend. How do you feel?"

"I feel just as awful as I look. My healers tell me I'm doing well enough, I guess, considering I was at the very doorstep of the gods. And you?"

Morak shrugged. "I'm treated almost like a king. My every wish is granted. I have maids and hot baths and..."

"...and you are bored." Jaksim smiled again, "yes friend Morak, I know you. You'd rather be out slaying some nameless beast for the eyes of a winsome wench."

"Not much doing for wenches here," Morak commented. "When they see me, they run the other way."

They were silent for a moment, the mood changed. "Have you given them the book yet?"

Morak gazed at the paintings that adorned the otherwise empty white walls. Finally, he turned to Jaksim. "No," he said quietly, "although they make large of their refusal to ask me for it, in hopes I will be convinced of the rightness of their cause."

He went to Jaksim's side and looked down at the priest. Had Jaksim always been that frail? "My friend, I came to you with the book when I discovered others were willing to kill to get it. I knew I could trust you. So far, you are still the only one I would trust. Once again I ask for your advice. Should I give them the book?"

Jaksim closed his eyes, and for a moment Morak thought he'd fallen asleep. "How many people have died to get their hands on its pages? How many have suffered?" Jaksim asked quietly.

Morak thought back. He saw Carina, Tok, Dagrag, Jamet, Sumar, and the others. But mostly he saw Meesha, staring at him, calling to him, waiting for his help. But no help ever came. He, a warrior and a Barbarian, was gathered up and carted away, away from Meesha and away from Karan. Far away from an oath he would have died to fulfill.

"And now you place this burden on my shoulders, eh, friend? Well, I don't mind, it's the life of a priest. Have they been anxious to get their hands on it?"

Morak laughed. "So Isha tells me. But she has kept the scientists away, knowing I must make my own decision, and also knowing the Zartan Morf are up there, stirring around, yet not wanting to anger a Barbarian down here. It is a very amusing situation—or would be if not for the bodies stretched from here to Karan."

Jaksim sighed. "Yes, Morak, give them the book. Be done with it. Let the death in its name cease."

Morak grasped Jaksim's shoulder. He sighed deeply. "Very well, my friend. I will take your advice and give them the book, even though I suspect its use will lead to even more deaths. But that is not your concern. Your concern is to get well, and soon, eh?"

"I'm trying, Morak, I'm trying." Jaksim closed his eyes again. This time they did not reopen.

Morak turned as Isha entered the room. "Time to leave, Barbarian. He needs his rest."

As they strode along the hospital corridor, Isha asked him about the book.

"Send your lead scientist to my apartment. I will give him the book there."

The Queen of Earth smiled. "They've been working day and night, preparing for this moment, and afraid I'd fail to convince you."

"You didn't, Jaksim convinced me."

She grasped his arm, and Morak was surprised to see tears in her eyes. "Today, an historic promise will be fulfilled. Thank you, Morak."

"Don't thank me, woman," he said sadly. "Of late, I've not had much luck with promises. Take your book, and be done with it."

"Morak, getting the book won't finish anything. It is merely the beginning."

Somewhat confused, Morak made his way back to his residence. He disliked this place, with earth all around, pressing in on him. It reminded him too much of Simathica. He wanted to see the sky again, breathe fresh air.

As Morak entered the room, a tall, lean man strode toward him with long, purposeful steps. "Ah, you are the Barbarian." He stepped up to Morak, too close for comfort, and openly admired the Barbarian's stature. "Magnificent," he muttered, hand on chin, "a wonderful creation." Morak stepped back, the other blinked and looked up.

"And who might you be?"

"I am head of the scientific team attempting to create—or re-create rather, the jewel. I've come here for the book. You told Isha you'd decided to hand it over, right?"

Morak nodded. He didn't know if he liked this "scientist" or not.

"Good, good. You're doing the right thing, Barbarian, no doubt about it."

"I have quite some doubts about it," Morak said gruffly.

"Eh? Come, come, the book will do you absolutely no good. Most of its words would be meaningless to you." The scientist stuck out his hand. He waited. Morak gazed into the other's eyes, not moving.

"We have much work to do, Morak, and we've wasted entirely too much time already," the scientist said impatiently.

"You call me Morak. What am I to call you?"

The other looked startled. "Eh? Please forgive me. I'm Tucker D'air, physicist." He smiled sheepishly, and looked younger and more friendly because of it. "I apologize. In my work, Morak, common courtesy is often forgotten."

"Tell me, Tucker D'air, do you know how many people have died to get their hands on this book?"

"Wha—? No. Have people really died?"

"Yes, people have died. It is not only a book, but an epitaph. It carries the lives of many good friends."

Tucker D'air watched as Morak lifted the book out of his pouch, weigh it carefully for a short time, then place it in the hands of the scientist.

"I can only thank you," D'air said, "if we are successful, we may regain our freedom, and those who have died will have died for a purpose."

Abruptly he left, leaving Morak alone to brood. He felt an odd emptiness within, as if a part of himself were gone. The book was no longer his; it belonged to these, these strange people who waged a fruitless war against an enemy much too powerful.

He sat and thought, and brooded, for quite a long time before there came another knock at his door. He opened it and stepped back.

"Morak?"

It was Isha.

"The book? I gave it to Tucker D'air," he said.

"I know. I didn't come about that. I came to see you."

"Me? Why? You have what you wanted."

"We got what we needed," she said softly, "now it's time for me to get what I wanted." With that, she slipped out of her tunic, revealing smooth tanned skin, unbroken and glowing with an inner fire. She flowed up into Morak's arms, eagerly, demanding, her lips seeking his.

"Take me, Barbarian, use me as you will," she murmured against his ear. But she didn't give him a chance, she took *him*.

It was a fantasy world Isha led him into. He'd had many wenches in his time, but nothing like this. Isha was on him, an animal, leading him, pulling him into her eyes, into her body, taking him, using him, then, and only then, when her body was satiated, letting him go. To sink back on the bed, exhausted, unable to move. He tried to catch his breath, then she was on him again, now gently. Time stopped, pain and failures, and empty oaths all were forgotten, for a time.

Finally, they rested. Morak was exhausted, to be sure, but more relaxed than he'd ever remembered being. More at peace with the world than he could have imagined.

"Gods," he whispered into her sweaty hair after some time had passed, "you deserve to be queen of all Earth."

"And I," she whispered back, nibbling on his ear between words, "have never known a man like you."

Another eternity passed, as they regained their strength and thought their thoughts silently.

"You have the book," Morak said finally, rising up on one elbow to look at the glorious nakedness of Isha. "When Jaksim is recovered and you've defeated your Zartan Morf, will you then let us find our way back to Karan, back to our homes? Can you do that for us?"

"I'm sorry, Barbarian," her voice was suddenly cold, remote.

"Sorry? Why? Tucker D'Air told me you'll soon have more flying machines, and the book will tell you how to make your precious jewel. If you're right, there will no longer be a war. We belong there, it's our home." He lay back down, his eyes blankly searching the ceiling. "And I have some—promises—to keep. Yes, somehow we must return to Karan."

"No, Morak. It's not possible."

"Why? Do you think us unable to make our way back?"

She looked at him, at the disbelief in his eyes, and met that with her own seething anger. "You can't go back," she snapped, then more softly, "You can't go back, Morak, because, after we left Karan, the Morfs destroyed it." She looked away. "They destroyed all of it, every living thing, every person, they leveled every rock and mountain. All of it. It's all gone Morak, there's nothing left but sand and glazed glass. You can't go back, not ever."

Morak stared blankly at a wall and said nothing.

"Why? Why would they do that?" He said finally.

"The Isle of Simathica still had a functioning fusion reactor, Morak. If we learn to make the jewels, we could re-power it, deny them half the world. They couldn't allow that. I'm so very sorry."

"So we were nothing more than—pieces—in your little game." He looked at Isha and shook his head. "I begin to see. It's all coming clear now."

After a long silence, "I'm sorry, Morak. If I could command it, you would live out your life as a King in your kingdom. But I cannot." Her shoulders sagged, and she looked at him again, tears welling in her eyes. "I didn't want to tell you now, Morak. I wanted to wait until you had become accustomed to our way of life, until you were happy here. I'm sorry about that, it's my fault. I should have told you when it happened."

She sighed. "You are the last of your kind."

"Marry me, then, Isha," he said suddenly, desperately. "Gods, I thought I'd never say that. But if I have no home, no people, I want you for my wench."

"No, Morak, please don't ask me." She cried then, looking around her, searching for a way out, knowing what was to come.

"Why? Because you are a Queen and I am but a Barbarian?"

"No, Morak, no."

"Then there is someone else. Let me do battle with him, then, and win you as a man should."

"There is no one else," she said, tears streaming down her face.

"Then why, Isha, why? Do you feel nothing for me?"

"Damn my body, damn my cravings, damn, damn, damn," she cried.

Morak grabbed her shoulders and shook her. "No! You can't deny me. I have a right to know. Tell me why you won't have me!"

"Morak!" She shouted, "please don't ask. This was a terrible mistake. I must leave. Let me go." She tried to get up, but the Barbarian kept his hold on her shoulders. He found her efforts to rise admirably strong, and at any other time he would have commented on it.

"Not until you tell me why."

"You must let me go." She struggled, but his power was too great. "At my word, a dozen guards will arrive to kill you!"

"A dozen guards will arrive to die," Morak replied. "Tell me."

"I can't."

"Tell me."

"Damn it, you are a Barbarian!" She screamed.

"Yes, and I'll die one, with blood on my sword and heads piled around me."

"You fool."

He slapped her, hard, and again. She looked at him defiantly, then collapsed, sobbing into his arms, twisting sometimes, but no longer fighting. "I do love you, Morak, I do." she murmured.

Then finally, she sat up, her eyes steady on Morak's stone face. Her eyes were angry. "All right, you fool, I'll tell you, then. I'll tell you, and then you'll hate me. Fool. Think back, in all your wanderings outside of Barbaricum, in all the rest of Karan, you've bedded many women."

She stated it as fact.

Morak searched her face. "So?"

"Have you ever fathered a child among them? Even one?"

The Barbarian was startled. He thought about it. "I don't remember."

"Come, Morak, you don't remember if you have been a father or not? Try harder."

"Yes! I remember." His eyes were angry, and his upper lip curled in rage, "to my knowledge, there have been none."

"And there never will be, fool. Barbarians cannot intermate with women of Earth. You and your kind are not completely human."

"What do you mean?" He felt a sinking in the pit of his stomach. The sense of sudden loss became a sharp pain.

"You aren't *human*, Morak. The Brotherhood of Zartan Morf made Barbarians, created them; it was part of their plans to destroy the jewel on Simathica. Their plan using Barbarians failed, except for your part. Your kind remained on Karan, unknowing of your origins, and able to reproduce only among yourselves, fool, because you—are—not— completely—human." She cried in his unresponsive arms.

He held her absently, looking over the long black hair, staring at nothing.

"You are the last of your kind, Morak," she murmured into his chest, anger gone, "you are the last of the Barbarians. There will be no more, ever. If we were to marry, we could have no children." She turned her red, puffy face to gaze into his unseeing eyes. "That wouldn't do. I am a queen, I must have children. You understand that, don't you, Morak?"

He didn't answer. He didn't even look at her.

Again anger flared in her eyes, "you made me tell you, fool."

"Yes," he replied softly. His hands dropped from her shoulders. "Leave me now, I want to be alone." His voice was machine steady, and Isha's concern increased.

She dressed quickly. "If you need me, all you need do is

call." She left Morak to his thoughts, left him lying on the bed, eyes staring up at the ceiling, fists clenched tightly.

In her breast also, there was a stone-hard lump of pain.

Morak lay still and thought, or tried not to. After a time, it became dark and he slept.

• • •

Magatha, a god of Karan, spoke to him in his dreams. A booming voice, emanating from a mouth with pointed, hideous teeth, snapped at him. Morak writhed until a huge, bird-creature picked him up and they flew above mountains and oceans, landing atop the golden spires of a metallic nest. The bird landed, twisted, shrunk, became human, became the leader of thieves. The nest was filled with women and children, each holding a sharp, pointed knife, jabbing their own bodies in attempts to save themselves from the bird-creature's wrath.

Blood flowed, became a deluge and swept over Morak, tumbling him off the nest, off the mountain, and down, down, down downdowndown...

He woke, sitting up with a shout. He looked around wildly for a moment until he recognized his surroundings. It was morning. The lights eternal of the Golden City had been turned up, an inadequate artificial simulation of day. Then he began to shake uncontrollably. He held his head in his hands, eyes shut tightly.

There was a knock at the door. He looked up with feral eyes, then took a deep breath, lie back down, and said, "enter." But the voice was gruff.

One of the menservants entered, carrying a platter loaded with Morak's breakfast.

"Good morn, Master Morak. How are we today? A nice wonderful, bright day above, they tell me." While he spoke, he opened the diminutive table and began spreading out food.

Morak tried to ignore the small man.

"There we go—an excellent warm breakfast, fit for a king, if I do say so."

That was the wrong thing to say. "Shut up," Morak growled.

The servant chuckled and continued with his preparations. "What? Why that's no way to talk this fine morning. You must have slept poorly, eh, friend?"

"I'm not your friend. Get out, and take that gruel with you."

"Gruel? Oh my, now I'm afraid you've gone too far. The cook will be crushed, simply crushed."

Morak leapt from the bed, swept the table, along with its food, to all four corners of the room, grabbed the manservant by the neck, and shook him violently.

Suddenly he stopped, realizing what he was doing, and dropped the slightly blue man. The servant, grasping his neck, watched Morak with wide eyes. His legs scrambled as he gained his feet and hurriedly exited the room.

Morak sighed and lie back on the bed, his huge arms clasped behind his head. He spent a long time staring at the ceiling, dozing occasionally.

A maid came in, hesitantly, carrying her cleaning equipment. "May I come in, sir?" She asked softly.

A small, light-haired wench, she moved with humbleness and her looking pleased Morak. He nodded.

"You've made quite a mess," she said starting her duties. Then she stopped, smiled at Morak. "Are you hungry?"

"Yes," he said. She went away and returned with a tray of food.

"Take off your clothes," Morak commanded, "and feed me. I am a king, you know. The King of Karan."

"You really want me to..."

"Yes. If you've not a mind to please me, wench, find me one who will."

She looked down, smiling, and Morak noticed dimples. She said nothing. She set the tray on the edge of the bed, reached behind her, and suddenly she was naked.

She sat on the bed and quietly fed the Barbarian. She didn't flinch when he reached out and stroked a breast. "Your name?"

"Donya," she whispered, her large green eyes, amazed,

looking at his.

She fed him another bite, and her fingers lingered on his lips. She stroked his chin, and leaned closer, staring into Morak's eyes.

Suddenly, they were no longer interested in food. Morak took her, roughly, bruising her body in his lust. She cried out in pleasure, in pain, in joy. And held on.

Afterward, when their appetites and lusts had been fulfilled, a quick knock interrupted their peacefulness.

"Morak, I—" Isha stepped into the room, stopped when she saw the maid Donya entwined in the arms of Morak. "I—I'm sorry," she said, "I didn't mean to interrupt."

She didn't make a move to depart, but gazed steadily at Donya. Some communication passed between the two, for the maid pecked Morak on the cheek, then got up and quickly dressed.

She smiled and winked at the Barbarian before brushing past Isha and out the door.

"Morak...."

"Yes?"

"You scared that poor man almost to death, and look at your room. And yourself," she finished.

"Donya came here to clean my room," Morak said, "but we were—distracted."

"I see. Perhaps, then, the loss of your homeland did not affect you as I first thought."

Morak's jaws clenched. He said some things to Isha, slowly, in a monotone voice. He said things that a man should never say to a woman, but he said them anyway. Isha gasped. Her black eyes widened, her skin darkened. Sudden tears streamed from her eyes, but she said nothing. She turned and rushed from the room.

Morak rose as with a great weight, and went into the room for washing. Afterward, clean and dressed in the strange garb of this city, he found another maid cleaning up his room. This one was older, plain, rotund, and not inclined to—distraction.

Well, Morak wasn't either.

He gazed out the window until she left. Soon after, Jaksim arrived. Dressed in a white robe and slippers. He moved slowly and painfully. He came in and sat down on the edge of Morak's bed. He said nothing.

Both were silent for a long time, neither looking at the other. Suddenly, Morak's anger reasserted itself. "Well, what in the name of all the demons of the dark world do you want, priest?"

"You *have* changed, haven't you Morak. I was injured near unto death, but that was physically. With the loss of Karan, you are injured in here," he tapped his skull.

"I have no mood to be talked to," Morak replied, "nor do I have to listen to such rants."

"You aren't the only one who lost Karan. It was my home too. I feel the loss, the pain. What gods are there here for a priest to pray to? These—these people need only press a button and lights appear, press a button and talk with each other over distances, press a button and have food and water, press a button to watch tiny people in little windows entertain them. They have no need of gods. They *are* gods."

Morak snorted.

"Maybe not, but they might as well be," Jaksim conceded, "If you could but see it, there is a new world out there, new things to learn. I'm a priest, and gods or not there are people who will need me. And if you but open your eyes you will find people here who need you, as well."

Morak looked at the Nakish. "You are human," he said softly, "you can continue your blood. You can father children here, if you choose. With the destruction of Karan, all the Barbarians died, too. Beyond the end of my life, there is no future for my kind. Now go away." He turned his face toward the wall.

Jaksim was silent for a long time. Then he sighed. "All right, I'll go. But let me tell you this one thing. Isha loves you, and you've hurt her deeply. She didn't do anything to deserve it." A short time later, he left.

Morak sat silently for a long time. Then he began to cry. He held his face in his huge, rough hands, and cried. For the first time, perhaps, in his adult life, a Barbarian shed tears.

But it was a time to cry.

Sometime later, he took another bath and dressed. He went out and walked along the golden lit paths and streets of the Golden City, ignoring, for the most part, the people he met along the way. Some of them stared at him, but most went about their business not even noticing the huge figure in their midst.

Eventually, he came to a grassy knoll lit by suntubes to promote plant growth. He watched several children playing on the grass, laughing, screaming and tumbling in oblivious joy to the world.

When one noticed Morak, he came over, looking up a long way, and smiled. "Hi," he said, "how come you are so big?"

Morak was silent for a moment, then his stone face moved to make a smile. "I need all of this," he said, indicating his well-muscled frame, "to fight strange creatures that live in even stranger places."

The child's eyes opened wide. "Tell us about them." The other children joined the two. "Tell us, tell us about your strange land."

Suddenly, Morak sat on the grass and gathered the children around him. "It was a strange and beautiful land called Karan," he began. "It was mostly desert. Do you know what a desert is? Well, there were witches, and kingdoms, and Barbarians..." The children were enthralled and didn't notice the tears that rolled, untouched, down his cheeks.

· · ·

Across the street, Isha stepped out from behind some bushes and watched Morak and the children with those unwavering black eyes. She nodded to herself and stepped back into the shadows.

Tucker D'air caught up with her a short time later. "Lady Isha," he began with some impatience, "I find myself embarrassed to report we have a major problem."

"Don't be embarrassed, we don't have time for it," she answered shortly. "What kind of problem?"

"The book, despite its unscientific title, was all you promised it would be. I regret now that I initially opposed your expedition to retrieve it. We've been able to follow Colonel Darm's experiments on the mechanical aspects of the jewel with no problem. It's a simply marvelous work."

"So what's the problem?"

D'air tapped his foot in annoyance. "The book contains all the mechanical and engineering specifications. But the formulae— the mathematical properties of the jewel—were purposefully omitted from the book. There is some mention of depositing them elsewhere. If we are forced to reformulate those, it will take several months, if not years."

"These developments were not unexpected. This is something you should have taken into consideration," Isha said.

"Of course, but we had hoped for some clues, at least. I just don't understand why Colonel Darm didn't..."

"We will *not* disparage the name of Colonel Darm," Isha commented dryly.

"No, no of course not. I merely stated..."

"Just keep working on it, Tucker, you just might surprise yourselves."

"Anything's possible," he said, "but you realize we no longer have the computers that were available to Colonel Darm and his scientists. What we have available to us today are, comparably, quite primitive. We just can't..."

"Do your best," Isha said impatiently, "you must understand that you and those working on the jewels are fighting not just against time. We are all fighting for our very lives."

"We work day and night, Lady Isha. We understand the stakes and the consequences of failure."

As they talked, they had entered the residential area where many of the scientists lived. "It's just not like Colonel Darm," D'air said, "from all we know of him, all that he did, the formulae must be recorded somewhere."

"If those records were on Karan, they are lost to us forever."

As they talked, D'air and Isha passed by Jaksim's apartment, from which emanated a low murmuring. They walked past in silence, then suddenly Tucker D'air stopped, turned, and stared in amazement at Jaksim's quarters.

"What?"

"Shh," the scientist hissed.

He listened carefully for a time, then took out a notepad and began writing furiously. He knocked on the door.

The murmuring stopped. "Yes? Who is it?" Jaksim asked.

"It's Tucker D'air," he said excitedly, "and Queen Isha. May we come in?"

The door opened and Jaksim bowed. "Please do, you are always welcome." He stepped back and allowed the scientist and Isha to enter.

Once inside, D'air clasped his hands in front of him. "We overheard your voice in passing, priest. If we are not too impolite, may I ask what you were doing?"

Jaksim looked slightly embarrassed. "I was giving my daily prayer to the gods, whatever gods there may be in this place. It is a secret Nakish incant," he smiled, "so I regret I cannot share it with you."

"But," D'air began, then, "yes, yes, of course. I—we were just curious. How is your healing coming along? Nicely, I hope. Very well, then. Shall we go, Isha? Thank you very much, priest. We shan't interrupt you further."

"I am pleased for the time you shared with me," Jaksim said quietly, bowing, some amount of wonderment on his face.

D'air ushered Isha back out into the hall, pulling her around the corner. "What is all this? What's going on," Isha asked.

"Extraordinary! How soon," he said, "can you set up a listening device in the priest's room?"

"Eh? What are you getting at, Tucker D'air? What's this all about?"

"The priest's incant!" D'air exploded, then looked over his shoulder cautiously.

"Yes, what of it?"

He moved them further away from Jaksim's apartment. "Don't you see Lady? Colonel Darm *was* a genius. He developed a religion for Karan—the priest's religion..."

"I still don't see any connection with the jewel."

"It has everything to do with the jewel, Queen Isha, everything. His incant consists of the mathematical formulae for the jewel!" Again, he glanced over his shoulder.

Isha looked at the scientist with disbelief. "You're positive?"

"Of course I'm sure," he snapped, holding the notebook in Isha's face. "Ingenious. What a novel way to preserve critical information!" D'air spoke in a preoccupied voice, almost to himself. "As a religious incant, it would not be tampered with, or discarded, or diluted over time."

"True," Isha answered thoughtfully, "but I wonder..."

"Wonder what?"

"What effect this information will have on Jaksim when he finds out." She looked over her shoulder toward the priest's apartment.

"Hmm," Tucker D'air said, holding his chin. "We already have a Barbarian suffering from shock—it would be doubly dangerous to have both of them running around in such a state. Perhaps we should entertain the notion of eliminating the two of them. After we get the necessary information, of course."

"No!" Isha said sharply, anger in her voice. "I will not hear of such a thing."

"Yes, my Queen. But consider, such an action would solve a number of problems. We will soon have all we need from them."

"If we do that, we are no better than the Morfs. I said 'no'."

"Consider, Lady, what would happen if one of them should escape? They could bring the entire Brotherhood of Zartan Morf down our throats."

"This discussion is finished," Isha said coldly. "I will hear no more."

D'air bowed slightly. "As you wish, my Queen."

"The priest's room will be wired. When you have the necessary information, contact me at once."

"Of course, my Queen," D'air said smoothly.

• • •

Morak maintained his surly attitude toward most adults he contacted, but continued to play with the children for a time each day, either talking with them and telling fanciful stories, or wandering with them among the many parks within the Golden City.

One day, Isha came to him there, saw him with a girl-child on his right shoulder, and a boy similarly placed on his left. He laughed and ran with them until he sighted Isha. He stopped suddenly, the laughter dying in his throat.

He lifted the children down and told them to go play elsewhere.

"You seem to like children," Isha said quietly.

Morak placed his hand against a large tree. "I had hoped, someday, to be a father."

"I'm sorry, Morak. I'm so terribly sorry."

He looked at her. "Really, wench? You have what you need, why do you keep bothering me? Can't you let me live out my life in peace? After all, you must afford me some respect—I am last of the Barbarians."

"Are you finished?"

He looked away, then back. He nodded.

"You have a home here for as long as you wish. Your relentless efforts to deliver the book to us intact has earned you that. You must stay here until we defeat the Morfs, or until they defeat us. After that, if you still live, you are free to go as you please." She stopped, sighed, and continued. "I can't change things, Morak. Karan is gone forever. All I can offer you is the chance to be a part of what we're doing, a chance to pay vengeance on those who destroyed your homeland and your people."

Morak laughed. "And what can I do in this war between Thunder Devils and Lightning Gods? I'm a primitive beast." He looked down at himself, "I no longer even have a sword."

"Morak! You're a fighter, a leader. Do you think we could have survived on our trip here if not for you? Look at all you did to keep us alive. We need that kind of fighter."

The Barbarian bowed. "Well then, if my services are in such need, they are yours. Perhaps I shall yet have the chance to die in battle." His voice still held sarcasm, but his eyes were bright and steady, and they told Isha he spoke the truth.

"We have need of your services right now."

He looked startled for a moment.

"Jaksim found a listening device in his apartment. We told him why, and now he's tried to kill himself."

"What? Who would want to listen in on a priest?"

"I would," Isha said, "I ordered the listening device placed in Jaksim's residence."

"You! Why?"

"Yes, me, Barbarian. His secret priestly incants were the mathematical formulae we needed to construct the jewel. His holy words had nothing to do with his gods."

Morak was silent for a long time. He looked at the ground, then back to Isha. "You mean his religion was nothing more than a small piece of your puzzle?"

"A piece, yes, but not so small," she replied.

"And when Jaksim found out, it tore the reason for his living away from him."

Isha nodded.

"You seem to be very good at that. You should have let him die."

"We couldn't do that, Morak."

"So you have robbed him of his land, his religion, and even his death-right."

"It is not our way to allow death to be so freely given."

"Not your way? Not *your* way? We are not from your place; in Karan, each man and woman has a death-right. Can you know how deeply you have shamed Jaksim?"

"Even so, he is alive and once again in our hospital. Here, we hold life to be sacred and not for throwing away."

Morak spat. "There is much I do not like about this," he looked around, "this Golden City." He paused and gazed at the ground. "Take me to him. I'll do what I can."

"Yes, of course. But Morak," her arm touched his, "perhaps someday you will understand why I did what I did. There are millions of humans on this planet enslaved by the Brotherhood. It's my duty to free them, if I can."

"I understand, wench." He glanced at her, then looked away. "Now take me to him."

On their way to the hospital, the Barbarian maintained a silent rage. But before they went in, he turned to Isha. "Isn't it about time you told us the truth about Karan? All of it?"

"Why, I hadn't thought about it. Yes, I suppose it is time. Perhaps if you understand everything, your exile will be somewhat easier to bear. When you get Jaksim to agree, we will tell you all that we know."

Morak pushed the door open and gazed inside.

Jaksim was propped up on a hospital bed. His wrists were bandaged and his face ashen. His eyes were open, but he saw nothing. Morak entered and moved quietly to the priest's side.

Jaksim looked up at the Barbarian, tears welling in his eyes. "My friend," he said hoarsely, "take your blade and end my suffering."

"I'm sorry, Jaksim. I have no power to take your life. And I no longer even carry a blade in this, this graveyard city."

"They took my gods away from me, Morak," the Nakish said, tears streaming his sunken cheeks. "I could stand the loss of Karan, as long as I had my gods to pray to. But now they've taken everything." He leaned forward, head down. "Do it, Morak, just one quick twist of your hands is all I ask."

"No."

"You owe it to me," Jaksim said angrily.

"Perhaps I do. But no."

Jaksim lay back down, looking up at the ceiling. "Damn you then, Barbarian. Damn you and all those that came before you."

Morak said nothing.

Finally, Jaksim looked at the Barbarian. "I can't even make you angry with me."

"I can only be so angry, my friend. I don't have any anger left for you."

"I'll share with you some of mine," Jaksim said softly.

"They want to tell us the story of Karan."

"Who cares?"

"You do, my friend. You'll care about living, too, in a day or so. And I'll be here to see you don't do anything foolish. Now let's go listen to them. I have my own anger to nurture and I don't enjoy trying to cheer you up."

Jaksim smiled at that. He wiped his eyes on the sleeve of his hospital robe, and took a deep, shuddering breath. Morak helped hospital attendants arrange the priest on a wheeled chair, then he pushed Jaksim into a room with Isha, Tucker D'air and several other of the scientists.

"I hope you will choose to leave your anger—and other problems—outside this door," Isha began coldly, "we're telling you the story of Karan, how it came to be and why, because we owe you that explanation. Perhaps you have a right to feel anger toward us, but you are alive and all the rest of your people are dead. We are only part of the story. We did not cause your troubles, and we cannot end them. Here, you have a home. And, if you could but see it, a purpose to life. Come in, sit, and learn."

• • •

Isha waited until the Karanians were seated, then nodded to Tucker D'air, who took over. "A little over three hundred years ago, Earth was enjoying, perhaps, its greatest time. Human nations were at peace. The problems of overpopulation, climate change, and species extinction were either solved, controlled, or mitigated. Fusion reactions had given the population all the energy it needed without the perils of fossil fuels. It also opened up the benefits of space travel, where humans had access to unlimited resources." He stopped, staring at the blank looks on the faces of his audience.

"Maybe they don't understand 'fusion'," Isha commented.

D'air sputtered. "It's an energy source, the same thing that makes the sun shine. Oh, hell," he exclaimed, turning helplessly to Isha.

"Morak, Jaksim," she said softly, "we'll tell you the story in our words. We can answer your questions later."

The two nodded.

"Continue, Tucker D'air. Make your explanations as simple as you can."

"Very well," he sighed. "During this time of plenty, the Brotherhood of Zartan Morf attacked the Earth. The term 'Brotherhood' is somewhat misleading. We think they are hive creatures, incubated and born from eggs in a hive-like apparatus. They do not adapt to Earth easily, but their intelligence and technology are both very high."

D'air paused and took a deep breath, brushing a hand through his sparse hair. "They attacked on July 14, 2027 of the old years. Earth was taken by surprise, since peace had been, finally, widely achieved here, and many of the nuclear weapons stockpiled by various nations had been largely eliminated."

Pictures appeared on the screen in front of the two. This was something they could understand, and they examined them eagerly. They showed aerial battles between Terran aircraft and the familiar Morf atmosphere craft.

"The mental powers of the Morfs, their superior technology and numbers gave them easy victories over Earth's armies," D'air said. "Fierce battles were fought, entire areas of this planet were rendered uninhabitable—millions were killed. Oh, the Morfs lost their numbers, too. They lost battles, for they were not invincible. But they eventually won the war."

The picture changed to show thousands of human prisoners being herded into huge Morf spaceships. "They took thousands of our people, loaded them on these ships, and took them off Earth," D'air said. "We've never discovered what happened to them—why they were taken, or where. Some of our experts believe the Morfs took them to their own planet for use as slaves—or food—" He looked at the two, but saw no reaction.

"In any case, the Zartan Morf gained control over most of the

Earth, except for a few isolated places, including an underground geothermal test station—which became this Golden City—and a nuclear fusion research station, also underground, situated on a small island off the coast of Antarctica, an ice-covered continent at Earth's southern pole."

He paused, looked at Isha, then continued. "As with much of the Earth, the continent of Antarctica suffered major damage in the war as the Morfs attempted to destroy the fusion research station. The ice melted, leaving a desert land—and incidentally changing the face of the Earth itself because the melted ice flooded many seacoast areas."

A photo of a tall, black-skinned man appeared on the screen. Morak looked closely because the man resembled some of the inhabitants of the south areas of Karan nearest his own homeland.

"Lt. Col. Joseph H. Darm was in command of that outpost," D'air said. "It was his genius and foresight that thwarted a complete Morf takeover. He is regarded as quite a hero among our people, almost, shall we say, worshiped. He lived and died almost 300 years ago, but he has not been forgotten."

Isha broke in, "He and the other scientists on the island of Simathica developed the jewel, and used their fusion reactor to power it. With that kind of energy, the jewel spread its radiation over all of Karan, and much of the Southern Hemisphere."

"Had he time," D'air said, "Colonel Darm might have been able to defeat the Morfs. Three or four jewels such as his, placed around the Earth could have made the planet uninhabitable for the Brotherhood of Zartan Morf. Indeed," he continued, "the jewel's power was so great, humans living on islands and continents in the south were able to wage war an additional 100 years. We have legends of the exploits of New Zealanders in battle. But, lacking resources and technology, and suffering repeated attacks from the Morfs, their resistance eventually collapsed. Many people living in the Southern Hemisphere eventually migrated to the continent that had once been the ice-covered Antarctica because the Morfs couldn't reach them there."

He paused and looked closely at the two men from Karan. "I

don't know if you will understand entirely, but I hope you can see what we faced. An almost totally destroyed world, conquered and dominated by these—these aliens. And our only hope an island beside a destroyed continent and this underground city thousands of kilometers away. There are, of course, several other such underground cities around the world, but none that we know of had a scientific research purpose."

He continued gazing at Morak and Jaksim, then shook his head and resumed the story.

"Since Morf weapons were primarily thought-controlled and detonated, they could not get close enough to Simathica to attack the jewel installation; it was protected from all but the most powerful bombs. An array of automatic particle beam accelerators defended the underground base from most of those conventional atmospheric-launched and space-based weapons..."

He stopped, realizing he had again left his audience behind. "Isha," he protested, "how can we communicate? The gap is too wide."

Isha smiled. "Let me try. Morak, Jaksim, what Tucker D'air is trying to say is that Simathica was protected by a lightning god's weapon. Do you understand?"

They both nodded.

"You may continue, Tucker D'air."

The scientist looked from one to the other, cleared his throat, and continued.

"Antarctica, that is, Karan, had been changing during this time. The climate became warmer, the land settled into its desert role. The Zartan Morf couldn't attack, the humans couldn't get any information out—stalemate. And like any chess game played dishonestly, both sides began adding pieces in efforts to tip the balance. Colonel Darm, with his military genius and some of the world's top scientists, led the fight to preserve knowledge of the jewel. He wrote the information in a book. Your book, Morak, and placed it at the entrance to the laboratories. He titled it, *Tomb of the Dark Devices,* knowing that whatever civilization survived would soon revert to a more primitive state."

"But where did all the people on Karan come from?" Jaksim asked.

"Base personnel and their families, a few pilots who had been shot down, survivors from a few other experimental stations, and, as I said, several large boatloads of refugees from New Zealand and Australia and other areas in the Southern Hemisphere. It was not easy surviving those first few years. Water was scarce, and food even more so. Vegetation was introduced that could withstand the six months of night and day. Colonel Darm knew some would survive, and he planned ahead."

"And from whence came the Barbarians? And why?" Morak grumbled, almost afraid to know the answer.

Tucker D'air took a deep breath, glanced at Isha. "The Barbarians," he said carefully, "came from genetic experiments conducted by the Morfs on human captives—and something else, some other life form or forms. We don't know exactly what. Barbarians were created larger than humans, stronger, physically superior, but, in general, with the same shape and form of humans. The results of their experiments were loaded onto boats and launched toward Karan by the Morfs from afar. With some human DNA, Barbarians were immune to the effects of the jewel. Perhaps the Morfs thought the Barbarians would dominate Karan."

"But we did not," Morak countered, "Barbaricum was a land of small clans and families—not armies."

"As you say," D'air agreed, "the Morf experiments never truly achieved success, although we suspect Barbarians are more susceptible to their mental powers. We have speculated that Barbarians were supposed to conquer Karan, and then the Morfs, from afar, would have directed an attack on Simathica."

"Each side introduced factors," Isha said, "Colonel Darm and his descendants set up the kingdoms and the religions, especially the Nakish incants, to preserve portions of the scientific knowledge. Had priests from the other religions survived, it's impossible to say what knowledge we might have gained or what we might have accomplished."

"The kingdoms for survival, the religions for knowledge

preservation," D'air said, "Barbarians and..."

"There were monsters," Morak said, "huge, ugly beasts of various kinds. Some of them flew, others lived under the water..."

"Yes," D'Air said, "more chess pieces. The Morfs genetically engineered a large number of these beasts. Most of them did not survive. They were meant to destabilize the human element, but they, too, were primarily a failure. Although the Morfs kept trying, most of them died out. Only a few lived and grew large and became a threat. The Morfs were afraid if the humans survived, built cities, bred armies, they would someday find Simathica, and discover its secrets."

"The witches," Jaksim said, some small amount of eagerness creeping into his tired voice, "tell us about the witches."

"Ah, yes, the witches. They were the Morf's greatest hope. Bred into a select group of humans were some of the Morf mental abilities, altered and adjusted for their purpose on Karan. Their human blood made them more tolerant of the jewel's rays."

"But not entirely," Isha said, "they must have been born, and grew up looking like normal humans. But in time, the radiation would have caused physical deterioration."

"Yes," Morak said, "they had strange powers—and hideous features when old."

"And," Isha added, "an implanted compulsion to search out and discharge the jewel."

Morak nodded. "Which Dagrag did, with my help, and that of Tok, and Carina," his voice died out.

"There were many previous attempts similar to yours. All of them ended in failure, except yours. And that was the factor that caused us to hurriedly plan an expedition to Karan," Isha replied, "and luckily we took the Morfs completely by surprise and were able to find you—and the book—and get away before they could react."

"Colonel Darm," Tucker D'air said, "of course had no way of knowing any of the information he planted hundreds of years ago would ever get back to the free humans. Until just a few months ago, we were unable to even attempt reaching Karan by air or any other means. So the continent was isolated and abandoned for almost 300 years. It developed its own cultures. In many ways, its loss was a scientific and anthropological tragedy."

All in the room were silent as the screen darkened and the lights came on.

"A chess game," Morak murmured. "And we were just the pieces..."

"Tell me, scientist," Jaksim said, "will you only need a few of the jewels?"

"No, no, you don't understand. Colonel Darm's jewel was powered by a laser-fusion reactor. We no longer have the technology to create such reactors. The one on Simathica was the only remaining such reactor on Earth. No, we'll have to content ourselves with smaller, less powerful jewels. So we will need a lot of them. Regaining our planet won't be an easily accomplished task," D'air concluded.

• • •

The two from Karan were ushered out. Watching them go, Tucker D'air said, "Do you think it helped, our telling them everything?"

Isha shrugged. "I don't know. They're both suffering from severe shock. And I wonder how much they really understood?"

"Under such mental stress," D'air said intently, "they could do anything—they could reveal our location. Can we afford to take that chance?"

"I told you once," Isha said, "I won't consider what you're proposing."

"But we're so close, Queen Isha," his hand closed to make a fist, and his burning eyes met hers. "Don't let two savages destroy 300 years of work and hope."

"That's my responsibility," Isha stormed, "let me worry about it. You are dismissed." Clearly unsatisfied, D'air bowed and left the facility.

Later Isha went to see Morak, and found the Barbarian

brooding in his room. "It's a nice day out of the doors. It's almost Summer on the surface, so our engineers have increased the temperature a little. Why don't you join the children?"

"It's always a nice day here. Nothing ever changes." He looked at her, hands clasped beneath his chin. "It's strange," he said, "how empty one human, excuse me, Barbarian can feel. At one time I thought I knew some answers—once I had a world to live within. Turns out I actually had neither. Now there is nothing, and I don't know the inside of me any more."

"I know, Morak. It won't be easy, but I promise that if you give yourself some time, things will work out. I know they will. You'll find a place here, in this world, or out there in that empty world none of us knows anything about."

She paused and sat beside Morak. "Do you know," she said, taking his forearm in her hands, rubbing it up and down, "that Earth will be strange to us all once the Morfs are gone." Her eyes gazed off into space. "There will be cities to rebuild, new lands to conquer. Wouldn't you like to be a part of that?"

"I don't know," he replied softly, "a part of me does, but another part just wants to see the darkness of the end. Perhaps that will fill the emptiness. I don't know, I just don't know."

"I've told you I can't marry you, Morak. But I want you to know what you can have me, anytime you want, any way you want, until the time I am wed. Until that time, I will do whatever I can for you, and you only." Her voice was whisper soft, and her eyes dropped shyly.

Morak laughed. "Yes, you can do something for me."

"Yes?"

"Send in that wench, Donya."

Isha gasped, stood, stared at Morak with a surprised and hurt expression, and hurriedly left.

"You fool," Morak muttered, and lie back on his bed.

Ten minutes later, Isha returned with Donya in tow. She pushed the maid into Morak's apartment. "There. I told you I would do anything, and here's proof. Enjoy her."

Morak smiled, his eyes burning into Isha's. "Wench, did you

get to be Queen of Earth by lying so well?"

Her cheeks flushed. "I became Queen because I am descended from Colonel Darm. And after we regain control of Earth, the Queen—or King—will no longer have direct power to rule. That will be turned over to a body chosen by the people themselves."

"A strange way to run a kingdom."

Isha laughed. "Yes, I guess it is. A very strange way, but we prefer it. Now enjoy this—person. I've got work to do."

"Donya," Morak said gently, "thank you, but I won't need you now." Confused, the maid looked at both Morak and Isha, then quickly departed. "Now, what work was it you had to do?"

Isha's eyes widened. "Nothing special."

"Can you spare me a few moments?"

"Yes."

"Take off your clothes."

"Certainly. By the way, what is your fascination with that maid?"

Morak laughed. "Order us some breakfast and I'll show you."

She did and he did, and it was well into the night before she left.

• • •

The next few weeks went by slowly for Morak and Jaksim. The Barbarian began to feel trapped, and he thought about how he might escape from this Golden City, which seemed more of a prison than a home. Curse the Morfs, he wanted to be back on the surface—perhaps to breathe his last—but at least it would be fresh air, and under an open sun.

His daily walks suddenly took on purpose, taking him near the many exits from the Golden City. He learned there were hundreds of access tunnels to and from the giant cavern, some of them dozens of kilometers in length—but all of them protected by a varying array of devices, which, if they didn't kill an intruder, would destroy the tunnel. None of those would do.

Morak continued playing with the children occasionally, finding their innocence and uncluttered joy refreshing to the stale thoughts dwelling in his own mind, and the minds of those adults with whom he associated. Perhaps, subconsciously, he was attempting to repay his failure to rescue Meesha, a name which now brought a cold cringe to the pit of his stomach whenever it invaded his mind.

He felt trapped, closed in. It got to where he had trouble sleeping. He took to running and exercising to keep himself in shape.

One day, about a month after the discussion about Karan, Morak found a possible exit. He walked past the waste disposal plant, up to the bare rock earth walls of the cavern.

The day before, the city had been shaken time and again by saturation bombing from the Morfs. Isha had assured him it was nothing unusual—such attacks came several times a year, sometimes causing minor damage, but most often just annoyance.

What he found was a tunnel, where some earth had broken away from the cavern's side, undoubtedly shaken loose by the bombing.

Morak glanced around, then ducked into the tunnel. Its floor had a coat of dust. The upward thrust of the floor, and the puffs of cool, fresh air on his face gave him hope that this was, perhaps, a long-abandoned, and forgotten access tunnel that would lead directly to the surface, and hopefully, it was old enough to lead him to sunlight without traps.

Morak took some time to conceal the entrance from accidental discovery. Then he went back to his apartment.

And found Isha waiting for him.

"You've been gone a long time," she said.

"I took a walk," he grumbled.

She looked at him oddly. "Well, now that you're back, I want to show you something."

"Okay, show me."

She studied his face. "Is something wrong?"

"No," he said, taking a deep breath, "no, nothing's wrong.

What did you want to show me?"

"This," she held up her hand to reveal a red jewel hanging from a chain.

"An attractive bauble."

"Don't give me that," Isha laughed, "you know what it is."

"*The* jewel?"

"Of course. Why aren't you excited?"

"It doesn't look very deadly to me."

"Naturally, it's not powered. It would affect a Morf only if it was brought very close. It needs a laser to carry the radiation in a narrowed beam."

"As you say. And it's deadly to the Blue Skins?"

"Yes. It disrupts their mental powers, disorients them, makes them sick, and finally kills."

"But not you and me?"

"No, we're immune."

"So. Now what?"

"Now we go after the Morfs. We're calling in all our outside people, and we're continuing full speed in manufacturing the jewels."

"I'm happy for you," Morak said, "now you can fight them."

"Yes, don't you see. What you've done has given us all our dream. *You* did it, Morak, you and Jaksim. This is what we've waited hundreds of years for—a chance to destroy those beasts."

"You have my congratulations," Morak said.

"Ohh, Morak, you're impossible. Give me your sword."

The sudden change in direction startled him. "My sword? Why? You just gave it to me." He had a sudden suspicion that Isha was disarming him. In an attempt to cheer him up, she had presented him with a new sword last week, made of glistening tempered steel, and sharpened to a microscopic edge.

"Just trust me, will you? Now give it to me. I'll return it tomorrow. You couldn't have grown that attached to it so soon."

"I always grow attached to my swords," Morak said, reluctantly handing over the bright, shiny new blade made for him by the machinists just to keep him happy.

He looked at her eager, happy face, and relaxed. She wasn't trying to disarm him; she had a surprise in store. "Is that the only reason you came to see me?" He asked quietly.

Her eyes widened slightly. "Well," she murmured, "there was one more detail." The dress slid off her shoulders with one smooth motion.

An hour later she left, the sword sheathed under her arm.

• • •

Morak continued making his preparations to leave. He hid food and other supplies in his room. He wondered if he ought to take Jaksim with him, or even tell the priest of his plans. On the surface, Jaksim seemed all right, but his character had changed subtly. Just as, Morak knew, his own had.

Isha burst into his room two days later, just after Morak had finished hiding some food. "Don't you ever knock?"

"Sometimes," she said with a breathless grin, "but this isn't one of them."

Morak grabbed her, pulled her to him, and captured some of that sweet breathless breath, while touching her in other places.

"Goodness!" She said, twisting away, "wait just a moment. I have something to show you."

"I have something to show you, too."

Isha glanced down and bit her lower lip. "Well, okay, maybe yours is more important."

Morak laughed. "What have you brought?"

She held out his sword. The Barbarian examined it. The blade seemed the same as before, but he knew by Isha's attitude and excitement, there must be some difference.

"Thank you for returning it," he commented, taking the sword from her, drawing it from the sheath, and balancing it. "What's this," he said, noting an additional red jewel on the hilt.

"Press it," Isha said, barely able to contain her emotions. "Go ahead, it won't hurt you."

Morak pressed the bauble, and the blade was instantly outlined in a faint red glow.

"Just get that near a Morf, and you won't have any more trouble with him," she said, "your sword is now jewel-powered. It won't be as effective as our laser weapons, but since it's the weapon you're accustomed to, we felt it was best."

"Yes," Morak said, slicing the air with the blade, "that's very interesting." Interesting, indeed, since he planned to make his escape the very next night. The jewel would give him that much more of a chance to survive the outside.

"Have you been down to the city center recently?" Isha asked.

"No. Why?"

"Most of our outsiders have returned. We're arming them with jewel-powered hand weapons. With them and our local army, we're almost ready to launch an offensive. We have two more flying craft completed, and even a large laser cannon."

"That doesn't sound like the armament with which to win a planet," Morak said, wondering at the excitement glowing in Isha's eyes.

"No, of course not, but it's a start. We don't expect to win all at once. It's going to be a slow, uphill battle. But don't you see, Morak, before we couldn't fight at all. With the mental powers and technology of the Morfs, we were beaten before we began. Now we can begin to take some bites, small ones to be sure, but at least we can do something."

"Yes, I suppose you can."

"Come with me, then," she urged, "we're having a war meeting now. I want you to be there."

Morak considered the invitation. His preparations, now that he had his sword back, were complete. He only need wait until the still quiet hours of early morning when the lights were dim, and he would be gone, away from this place.

He still hadn't made his decision about Jaksim. Attending this meeting would give him the latest information about guards and military action.

"I'll go with you," he said.

At that moment, an urgent knock caught their attention.

"Enter," Morak said.

A tall man in white lab clothes burst into the room. "Queen Isha, it's the priest, the one from Karan..."

"What about him?" Morak said, advancing on the man.

"Why, he's dead. Shot. In the head."

There was a sudden silence. Morak was too stunned to talk, or even feel anything except an urgency to see Jaksim.

"When?" Isha asked.

"We found him just now, in his room. He can't have been dead for over an hour. We think he may have done it himself."

"No!" Morak said.

Isha turned to him. "Why not?"

"Did anyone teach him how to use the weapon that killed him?"

Isha looked at the doctor. "It was some kind of ray weapon. Half his skull was gone," the doctor said.

"There never was time to show him our weapons," Isha said slowly, "and the guns are so few. It's doubtful he ever saw one in action close enough to learn how to use it." Her voice trailed off.

"Someone killed him then," the doctor said, his large eyes growing larger, "he was murdered."

"Come on," Isha said, her voice icy cold. She kept thinking Tucker D'air had done it, but a conflicting part of her argued that the scientist had been much too busy lately to plan a murder. And besides, did he have the will to do such a thing?

They found Jaksim sprawled beside his bed, a large gaping wound where his head used to be, lying in a puddle of blood. His remaining eye was open in terror.

"First you took his land," Morak murmured, "then his gods, and now you take his life."

"No!" Isha said, "you're wrong, Morak. I don't know who did this, or why. But I'll find out, and whoever is responsible will pay with their own life."

Morak's face filled with an expression of animal anger as he faced her. "That is what you say—you've said many things. But what will you *do*?"

"I will do whatever is necessary." She looked at him, at the anger in his eyes. "Our people had no reason to kill Jaksim."

"Gods, wench, you had no reason to keep him alive, either." With that, he stormed out of the room, and back to his own. He began gathering his supplies, but a sudden weariness came over him, and he lay face down on the bed.

And he wondered why. Why so many of those he cared for had to die. He wondered at the fact that his whole life had changed so quickly. A cold feeling came over him that he was the cause of Karan's destruction. That, by taking the book, he, Morak, a simple Barbarian from the southlands, had set in motion events that led to the end of his homeland; the death of many thousands.

It was too much to be borne.

• • •

He got up, finished packing, and started on his quest to leave this city and make his way back to the surface, with a silent oath that he would kill anyone who came across his path.

The first person the Barbarian ran into was the same manservant he'd almost strangled to death. The little man took one look at Morak's eyes, paled, made a smooth turn, and started in the opposite direction.

"Hold!" Morak shouted, hurrying to catch up.

"Y-yes?"

"Tell me your name."

"M-master, m-my name is Meuton, sir."

"You're coming with me."

"W-what? Me? But I've got my duties."

"Forget it," Morak grabbed Meuton by the scruff of the neck and propelled him along.

"W-where are we going, sir?"

"You'll find out soon enough. Now shut up." Morak wanted to use Meuton to let Isha know he'd been successful in his escape. For some reason, he didn't want to just disappear on her.

The two crossed a residential section, and into the park.

There, Morak stopped when he saw several children who had become his friends over the past few months. He didn't want them to see him; it would only cause more problems.

But before he could turn away, he noticed a larger figure kneeling amongst the youngsters. Something about that narrow frame made Morak want to look closer.

He and Meuton circled the edge of the park, using some trees as cover until they were near the group. Morak still couldn't hear more than low murmurings.

But it was the tense posture of the man, the nervous mannerisms, the way he touched the children that made him pause. The man turned half toward the hidden Barbarian, and Morak noticed a pointed beard. A cold chill ran down his spine. The man stood.

He was tall and thin, and—his face turned to the light.

"Kam!" Morak shouted, roared. He burst from the trees, Meuton in tow, sword drawn. He couldn't believe what his eyes were seeing.

The leader of thieves here! He *must* have been killed when the Morfs destroyed Karan, Morak thought, he must have. Yet here he was in the Golden City.

How?

And suddenly, the oaths he swore many months ago came rushing back into his thoughts. His upper lip curled in rage; visions of Kam and Meesha, she tortured and used, rushed through his mind. It all came back in that one instant; a purpose to life, a challenge, an event he, Morak, could control.

It all came over him like a wave of that endless ocean.

Kam turned slowly, with confidence, with a power Morak no longer possessed, but once did. And slowly, Kam smiled. There was no fear of the sword Morak wielded menacingly.

"Kam, you vermin, know now, this day, you will meet whatever entrails that spawned you."

"My friend Morak. How amazing it is to see you. But I think I will not die this day." He pulled a small weapon from his waistband and pointed it at the Barbarian. "No, not today."

Morak stepped closer.

"And that's close enough, Morak. What this," he moved the weapon, "did to your priest friend can also do to you, or any of these children."

Morak stopped, the blade wavered then dropped. "So you killed Jaksim?"

"Of course. And I had planned to kill you. They told me you enjoyed the company of these children." He looked at the young ones, "Excellent choices. If only you knew the power that resides within every child, Morak—" He stopped himself, as if he'd said too much. "Anyhow, I knew I would find you here eventually. Unfortunately, I didn't have much time to make friends of my own. Such wonderful, innocent faces, don't you think, Morak?"

"Curse you to the pits of hell," Morak spat, "because you killed Jaksim, know that when I kill you it will be a slow, painful, lingering death."

"Come, come, Morak. We're old friends, you and I. We're also the last remaining citizens of Karan.

"That manservant there, you! Go to Queen Isha and tell her Morak requests her presence. Tell her it's an emergency." Kam grabbed the arm of a nearby child. "If you tell anyone else, this little one will die. Understand me?"

The child screamed. Meuton nodded.

"Now go."

Meuton looked from Morak to Kam. The Barbarian sighed, then nodded, and Meuton dashed off as fast as his short legs could take him.

"How did you survive Karan's destruction?" Morak asked. Talking should keep Kam from doing anything damaging, and might supply information he could use later.

"That's an interesting question, my friend. These Morfs, you know, I've come to respect them highly; their minds work much like mine. They like to save things, in the hopes that someday they will find a use for them."

"The way you found a use for Meesha?"

Kam looked startled, then laughed. "So right you are,

Barbarian. The Morfs chose to save me. After all, I almost secured their precious book for them. I was with them in one of their marvelous flying machines, and I saw them destroy Karan. They did a thorough job, Morak, a beautiful job. They thought I would be useful to them in infiltrating this Golden City—that's such a gaudy name, no doubt given by idealistic fools—and finding you. They want you, Morak. For some reason, they're interested in you, and they mean to have you, alive or dead, for study, I believe. And, of course, they mean to destroy this city before it can manage to become a nuisance."

He paused and smiled. "As for me, I've never been happier. They give me everything I want. They even," he glanced at the frightened cluster of children standing wide-eyed near them, "oblige my peculiar tastes in private hobbies. I'm very happy with the Morfs, Morak, yes indeed. And I would do anything they asked of me."

Morak half lunged at Kam, but the weapon in the other's hand stopped him. It was pointed not at him, but toward one of the children.

"Ah," Kam said a moment later, "I believe Queen Isha is approaching."

Morak turned to see Isha and Meuton coming toward them through the trees. "Morak!" She called, "what is this emergency? I don't see anything so pressing. This fool Meuton drags me out of an important meeting." She joined them, breathing hard, "and who is this?"

"His name is death," Morak said flatly.

"What is this? What's going on here?"

"My Queen, I am called Kam, son of Kam, by my friends," he bowed, "and I knew Morak on Karan."

"Kam?" Isha said, "it seems I've heard that name before."

"Yes, indeed, Morak must have spoken of me. I am a former King of Thieves."

"You!" She backed away and drew her weapon in one smooth motion. With someone less experienced than Kam, such a maneuver might have worked. But Kam merely pulled a child close to him, pointed his weapon at her head, and waited.

"I'm sorry, Queen Isha, but you'll have to drop your weapon. I would sincerely dislike killing this child." His voice was soft, but stone-cold, and his eyes bored into hers.

Isha's hand wavered, then the gun dropped to the ground. Morak let out a breath he had not been aware of holding. "What now?"

"I think we'll just take a nice walk to the surface," Kam said, smiling. "I have some friends waiting there who very much wish to know where this place is. Shall we go?"

"No!" Isha shouted, "kill us one-by-one, but none will go with you."

"Is that your feeling? All of you?" He glanced at each one, and although Meuton looked terrified, he stood fast beside his Queen and nodded.

"It is, regretfully, just as I thought," Kam said, left hand smoothing his beard. "It's unfortunate you are all so insufferably courageous."

He suddenly aimed his gun at a girl child nearby, and carefully shot her in the knee. The narrow red beam left a bloody hole. The child screamed and fell, grabbing her leg and writhing in a growing pool of blood.

"You fiend!" Morak screamed, the rage roaring from his entire body.

"Do you wish more to be injured? Or killed? I *will* do both unless you stop this nonsense and accompany me. I'll kill them all before you can stop me."

"Okay, okay," Isha said, "just don't hurt anyone else. We'll take you to the surface. Leave Meuton here to tend to the child, she's in pain."

"And she will continue to suffer pain," Kam hissed, "Meuton will come with us. Remember who caused that pain, Queen, by disobeying me. Remember that." He grabbed another child. "We'll take this one to ensure no further treachery."

They followed Kam's terse directions, not to Morak's secret exit, but to one of the more well-known, though less-traveled, caves. They avoided other citizens, and Kam gave none of them a chance to take any action.

Morak thought furiously as they went. His mind still reeled at Kam's sudden appearance. He had killed Jaksim, shot a child with no more than a casual interest.

Morak's rage seethed inside, but he calmed it as best he could. He needed to think. This was no time for Barbarian strength.

Isha, the boy's hand in hers, seemed willing to talk with Kam.

"How did you get here—inside our Golden City? Our tunnels are quite well protected."

"From outsiders, yes, my Queen. But when you summoned all your people at once, they did not all know each other. It was a simple matter to join them, each one thinking I was a friend of the other. A tactical mistake on your part, I might add."

"But why? You're human, you must have human feelings somewhere inside you. Why turn against your own kind?"

"I am my *own* kind," Kam said, a small, burning anger building in his voice, "and they take good care of me, these Morfs. Yes, indeed. It's my *pleasure* to obey them."

Isha merely stared at him.

"Now, my Dear Queen of Earth, you will guide us to the surface. No tricks, now. If you trigger something or make a mistake, you may kill me, but you will all die as well. You do understand, right?"

Isha gazed at Kam for a long moment, then she nodded.

They went on, through the mazes, past the deadly protective devices, some of them timed. All the way, Morak tried to think of something, some way to escape, to kill Kam slowly and with great pain.

That leader of thieves walked beside Isha and the boy child, the gun in one hand, Morak's sword in the other, his thin, pointed face smiling occasionally.

This was not the kind of conflict Morak faced on Karan—where death came suddenly more often than not, and choices were easy to make. No, this was a world too large for him to understand. And everyone, it seemed, knew more about it than he.

That, too, made him angry.

•••

They reached the end of the tunnels and came to the earthen cave leading outside. Kam became eager, but the others were not.

"I've got to rest for a moment," Isha said, "and this child is exhausted."

Kam's face showed impatience, but Morak was already sitting on a nearby rock.

"Don't get too comfortable, you won't be here long," Kam said, "and don't think your delay will change anything."

The four from the Golden City relaxed together, while Kam went ahead, searching for the end of the cave, and the daylight where he would find his allies waiting.

Isha began whispering earnestly to Meuton and Morak. The Barbarian nodded, got to his feet and joined Kam. Walked past him, in fact, and turned.

"You will die, you know," he said quietly. "No matter what happens—no matter how many innocent people you kill, you will die a most painful death."

Kam smiled. "It seems you swore that oath upon me once before, Morak."

"And I am still here to carry it out," he replied, teeth clenched, "one way or another. All your thieves, all the Morfs between here and Karan, were unable to stop me from delivering the book to these people—and nothing will stop me from killing you."

"You're a fool, Morak. If you would but join them, they would provide for you the way they have for me—you'd have your choice of many winsome wenches, yours for the asking. Or anything else. Anything." He leaned forward, "and, as friends, I'd share with you my little secret..." He glanced around, his voice dying out.

Isha looked up, her eyes boring into Kam's. Meuton and the child were gone.

"Where?" Kam shouted.

"I sent them back to the Golden City," Isha said calmly, "you can go after them if you want, but it won't help you and you will surely die."

Kam screamed, aimed his weapon at her, and pulled the trigger. The beam shot out and flashed the cave with a blinding light. Isha screamed and fell backward. Morak ran to her, but she was already rising, unharmed.

"You could have died," Kam breathed, a strand of spittle lashing out and landing on his lower lip and beard. "Your next foolish act will cost you your life."

Isha's eyes flashed. "It doesn't matter what happens to me, my people will be warned."

Kam grabbed her arm and flung her ahead. Keeping the gun pointed at Morak, he urged them along the cave almost at a run, until they came to the entrance and sunlight flooded their faces.

They found themselves on the surface, looking out over an endless jungle.

Morak had gotten his wish—he was back out in fresh open air. The Golden City lie far below. Along with his memories of Jaksim. And, perhaps, a piece of Morak himself—a piece that had died alongside the priest and Karan and the world he had once known.

Yes, Morak had escaped the Golden City. But he wondered what good it was going to do him.

A Morf ship appeared overhead and began to land.

Book Five:

The Quadrabred

Morak woke.

He shook his head, and for a moment, wondered where he was. Then he tried to move and discovered his arms tied behind him. A steady vibration under and around him caused his eyebrows to knit in wonderment.

There was something about that vibration...

Then he remembered. This was the aircraft in which he had found Jaksim. Then why was he tied up? He looked beside him, but there was no one.

More memories came flooding back. Jaksim was dead. And this was a different airship—one belonging to the Brotherhood of Zartan Morf. Morak wondered how long he had been asleep. As he studied his surroundings, he noticed one of the small, silvery aliens stood guard in the room. As Morak shifted, the Morf looked at him, calm and emotionless.

"You!" Morak shouted to his guard, "dog. My arms are in pain. Free me and fight like a Barbarian. Are you afraid to die?"

The alien remained motionless. Morak wondered about those small blue-skinned creatures. They had controlled Earth for three centuries; why were they suddenly so interested in him? To be sure, Morak had secured the fabled book, *Tome of the Dark Devices*, and delivered it to the free humans.

That's who they should be worried about, the humans. They had recently learned the secrets possessed by their ancestors and reproduced the mysterious jewels that were deadly to the Morfs.

Morak felt a sudden rush of anger when he thought of Kam, a human of Karan who had allied himself with the Morfs, and his successful infiltration of the Golden City. He had killed Jaksim, injured a child, and taken Morak and Isha, Queen of Earth, captive.

That devil-dog was even now revealing to the Morfs the exact location of the Golden City.

Morak strained at his bonds. He had sworn to kill Kam, but that leader of thieves had not given him the chance. Morak and Isha were herded aboard the Morf airship, given an injection, and told not to worry. Soon he'd lost consciousness and slept for he knew not how long.

Morak wondered about Isha; wondered if she still lived. The Morfs, he had been told, liked to save things. But the Barbarian knew they wouldn't hesitate to dispose of any human who had served his or her purpose. He wondered why Kam couldn't see that.

The Barbarian turned his head at a silent sound, a flicker of movement. A door had opened, leaving a space in the opposite wall. His guard withdrew, and in its place stood another of the small, blue-skinned, bald-headed creatures, dressed in a silvery skin-tight uniform. The two studied each other for a moment, silently. Morak got his first close unhurried look at the alien.

The small face was wrinkled and wizened, with large orange eyes now staring unmoving at the Barbarian. The tiny nostril tube ran back over the Morf's head and connected to the waist of his suit.

Morak became uneasy at the other's gaze, but he ignored the apprehension inside and stared defiantly back.

"They call you Morak," the Morf said softly.

"Yes."

"And you are a Barbarian from Karan?"

"Before you destroyed it, dog."

"Does your name have meaning?"

The question startled Morak. He shrugged. "My mother, a tall, large woman, once told me it meant 'Mountain.'"

"A strange name," the tiny voice said, "but not altogether inappropriate." He paused again, for a long moment. "These Earthians have painted us a very dark color."

"You destroyed Karan. I am told you have done other evil things."

A small, bell-voiced laugh filled the small cubicle, followed by, "any enemy is evil in his opponent's eyes. And as for the destruction of Karan—yes, it was an—unfortunate—accident. You realize we created the Barbarian race?"

"So I was told. Thank you."

"Ah, so there is a sense of humor dwelling in the depths of those rugged features."

The Morf's voice was, somehow, soothing to Morak. He lost much of his fear and anger, and began to view the alien in an objective manner.

"What are you going to do with me now?"

The Morf stepped further into the room and clasped his tiny hands behind his back. "Mostly we just want to study you. There are, regretfully, no more Barbarians. Besides yourself, of course. Your kind were created many hundreds of years ago then shipped to Karan—or rather, in that general direction. Our goal was to destabilize the human population living on that continent. Because of the radiation, we did not have sufficient proximity to gauge the results of our efforts."

"The jewel on the isle of Simathica was...removed," Morak replied cautiously.

"And for that, we thank you."

"Thank the witch, Dagrag. It was her doing, not mine."

"Granted, Barbarian. But her ability to reach the island and access the laboratory was primarily due to your efforts."

"Where is Isha?" Morak asked suddenly, angry at himself for not thinking of her earlier.

"She is here, safe, and being well cared for. You realize the capture of the Earthian leader is important to us, now that they have the secret of the jewel."

"I suppose. Can I see her?"

"I'm sorry, no. Not for a while at least. We will be landing in several hours, at a place once called New York by its natives."

"And then?"

"You will be taken to our scientists for study. You will also be made comfortable during your stay with us."

"You mean comfortably tied up," Morak stretched his arms out.

"We will rectify that as soon as we reach our base. Now that we know the exact location of the so-called Golden City, we can begin the process of its elimination."

"And how long will that take?"

The Morf smiled. "I can't say at this time. Now that we know the location, perhaps not long."

"Maybe you don't plan to ever release us."

"Nothing lasts forever, friend Morak. We shall see. Why don't you try to get some sleep? We've several more hours of travel." Morak sat back, his bonds forgotten.

"One more thing," Morak said, "do you have a name?"

Morak heard that bell-like laughter again. "I doubt you could pronounce it, our language is quite complex and involves speech sounds you have not had experience making. Hmm, let me see. Call me Taymakk; that is not too far removed from my real name." He stopped, looked thoughtful, then said, "should you require food or anything else, just ask the guard for me. I will come at once. Good day, Morak. We are quite happy to have you with us."

When Taymakk had gone, the guard returned. The door slid silently out of the ceiling and settled into place, leaving no evidence there had ever been an opening.

Morak was filled with a feeling of good will and friendship toward the aliens. He hadn't felt this friendly toward another person for longer than he could remember.

He smiled at the guard, feeling relaxed and at peace. Memories of recent events were dulled; the thoughts of Jaksim and Kam kept slipping away, not staying long enough to rekindle the anger. Even his nascent hunger became dulled. Finally, he yawned and decided to sleep.

• • •

He didn't recall falling asleep, but when he opened his eyes, the guard was gone. Morak turned his head, and standing beside him was Meesha. His mouth dropped open in astonishment.

"How!" He shouted. "Child, you're alive!"

"Yes, Morak," her voice was filled with fear. "You must help me. I'm so happy to know you're coming to get me. That man, Kam, is so terrible. So—evil and naughty. He does things to me, Morak. It hurts and I don't want to be here."

"Girl, use your witch power on him. You're not the quadrabred, but you *do* have witch power."

Sadly Meesha shook her head. "Kam is powerful also. And the little men with him would kill me if they knew. They watch me all the time. But, Morak, what do you mean by quadrabred? Tok told me last year that he is my father, Carina was my mother. But he told me nothing about witch power."

"Are you sure?"

The child shrugged. "I don't know. Sometimes he talked about another, not Carina or Dagrag. I don't know. It's so dark here, Morak, and I hate it. Please hurry."

The room went dark. The room became bright. Morak looked up and saw the guard eyeing him quizzically. Carefully, he feigned restlessness and pretended to go back to sleep.

Meesha alive! His heart soared at that news. She must have communicated with him mentally, just as soon as they got close enough.

Now his purpose had been renewed. He could save Meesha and end the life of Kam at the same time. Thank you, gods, he thought, for giving me this chance. Eventually, Morak did fall into a deep sleep.

• • •

In the course of time, the ship's vibration changed and that woke Morak. They had arrived at their destination. Soon the vibration stopped altogether and the door opened again. Taymakk entered, untied Morak, and led him out of the room in which he had, strangely, slept most of the way. The ship was filled with Morfs, all busy at their mysterious tasks.

They came to a ramp and started down, but Morak stopped halfway, staring out, not at the blue sky, but at the ancient tall thin buildings that surrounded them. Or rather, the bones of those buildings, as most of them were architectural dinosaurs, long ago abandoned to the weather and ravages of time.

"This is our capital on Earth," Taymakk said, "it was once one of Earth's greatest cities. It is more my home now than Morofia ever was. We don't use the old Earthian buildings much, however, so they have suffered over the ages. Many of them fell to ruin or were submerged when the sea level rose."

They continued down the ramp, Morak awed by the number of buildings and the Morf activity around them. An army of aliens, it seemed, swarmed around the aircraft, doing Morak knew not what.

He and Taymakk walked aross a large flat landing field, then passed into a walled corridor and from there into a large, domed building, its lack of right-angles setting it apart from the native constructions.

Inside the building, at the center of an open expanse, were several Morfs sitting at an ornate table. There was a taller, thin figure standing in front of the desk, and as Morak approached, he was not surprised to see Isha standing rigidly, anger emanating from her entire body.

When she saw Morak out of the corner of her eye, she turned, gasped, and threw herself into his arms. "I thought you were dead," she whispered into his ear. She looked into his eyes, her strong, thin fingers holding his face. "Don't worry, we'll find some way to escape. Don't let them..."

"Morak," Taymakk said softly, "this is our council of hive elders. They wish to question you and the Earthian leader."

The five elders gazed coldly as Morak and Isha turned to face them. The Morf on the extreme right smiled and said, "Welcome to our home on your planet." He looked much like Taymakk, except the blue skin was slightly darker, and the elfin face was even more wrinkled, if possible.

"What are you going to do with us?" Isha asked.

"In time, Queen Isha, in time. First, we have a few questions that must be answered."

"I'll answer no questions," she replied firmly.

"We have already begun our attack on the so-called Golden City," the elder said, "it will soon be ours."

"The Earthians are fighting back with the jewel weapons," Taymakk reported. "How large is your army?"

"You can't..." Isha hissed, "five thousand strong..."

She stopped, looked startled, and darted a quick glance at Morak. Her eyes were wide with helpless desperation.

"How are the jewels powered?" The elder asked.

"Laser beam," Isha murmured through clenched teeth, obviously against her will.

"Do you have fusion power?" Another elder asked.

Her mouth refused to open, but she could not stop her head from indicating the negative.

The Morf hive leaders seemed relieved at that revelation.

"Continue the attack," the elder told Taymakk. The other nodded, turned, and stepped away. He quietly conversed with several of his kind, then watched as they nodded and departed.

"You are Morak, a Barbarian?" Morak was asked.

He nodded.

"You were born and raised on Karan?"

Again he nodded.

"An interesting specimen," said another of the leaders, "it's unfortunate we do not have a female available for a breeding pair."

"Perhaps we could recreate the experiment..."

"To get a breeding pair? For what possible reason? The first experiment obviously failed," said another. "The island is gone. There is no longer a need for them."

"Perhaps," said another. "Yet they are an interesting sub-species."

"You can create more Barbarians?" Morak asked eagerly.

"Should we choose to do so," the elder said calmly, ignoring the burning light in the other's eyes.

"No, Morak," Isha said urgently, "don't listen to them.

They're only trying to trap you..."

"Silence," Morak snapped, "I want to hear more."

"There is little more to tell," the hive elder said, "if you join with us, we could take advantage of your, shall we say, unusual skills. In return, we would agree to recreate the Barbarian race here on Earth."

"This you would do?"

"Yes."

"They lie!" Isha screamed. Three Morfs came from behind them and took her, still screaming, from the room.

"Don't worry about her, Morak. She will be sedated and given some rest. We will not harm her, it's not necessary."

The hive elders turned to each other and talked in rapid, sing-song chatter that occasionally rose above Morak's ability to hear.

Finally, they told him, "Thank you for your assistance. You may go. Taymakk will be your guide in our habitation. We hope you will enjoy your stay with us. When you decide to join us, we will begin work on the Barbarian project."

"And Morak," another said, "if there's anything else you need—or want—just tell Taymakk."

Morak wanted to shout his acceptance of their offer right then, but something made him hesitate. Which surprised both he and the Morfs as they were clearly expecting him to affirm their offer. But suddenly his chance was gone and Taymakk led him out of the room.

They took a tour of the city once known as New York, riding on a small flying platform with a pair of handholds and a tiny rail that gave Morak no feeling of security. Taymakk looked at the Barbarian, smiled, and pressed a button that caused a metal cage to rise halfway.

Morak saw hundreds of the alien airships rising or landing. "These are our warships going off to battle the Earthians."

"Tell me," Morak said, suddenly reminded of something, "is it true that you can disappear and reappear where you choose?"

Taymakk's response was slow. "To a point, some of us can.

It's a trait we developed for the hybrids of Karan and have slowly been implementing it into our own genetic code..."

"You mean the witches?"

"Yes. We've managed to adapt the ability to some of us, a few volunteers, and with varying levels of success. We'll get better at it, over time."

Morak nodded. They saw a large number of humans, and Morak asked about them. "They're descended from the ones who chose not to do battle with us. They are free, not confined to an underground world."

The Morf spoke intently. "We did not want to battle the humans, Morak. But those that opposed us died or were forced to shelter themselves underground. The rest became our friends and now live peacefully among us. It is a benefit we offered to all humans, but as you know some few resisted."

The floating platform slowly settled to the ground and the two walked around for a while. Taymakk showed Morak the buildings occupied by both Morfs and humans. They ended at Morak's new place of residence, another circular Morf-style building.

"Everything in this room operates automatically," Taymakk said, "just ask and it shall be done. It's a very well equipped room, and it fully understands the human language."

Morak surveyed the large living space, the plush furnishings, a few green plants, the mostly-white color, and found it pleasing. He gazed out a large view window built into the far wall.

"Interesting." Morak turned and looked at the alien. "The Elder said I could ask of you anything. There is a human child somewhere in this city. She came in the company of Kam, your other—keepsake—from Karan. Her name is Meesha. I want her. I want her brought here, to me."

"Hmm," Taymakk looked thoughtful. "I'm not sure that's possible, friend, as you have not yet accepted our offer. But I'll see what I can do. Tell me about her."

Morak frowned. "She is a human child, in the possession of Kam. Surely that is enough information..."

"Kam is one of us. As such, we have given him many of the

small ones for his entertainment. Can you describe the one you wish?"

With a slight feeling of anger, Morak told him.

"I imagine it's a cultural anomaly of Karan to use children in Kam's manner, eh Morak?"

Morak kept confusion off his face, managed to smile and nod.

"Your friend Kam surprised us with this rather unusual method of staying young. However, it does seem to work. A culture without genetic science can do little else, eh?"

Again, Morak simply nodded, attempting to belie his totally confused nature. Staying young?

"Fine. I'll do my best. Tomorrow, we'll continue our tour with a visit to our scientific laboratories."

"When can I see Isha again?"

"As you were told, she has been sedated. She needs rest. Perhaps tomorrow. Good night, then, friend Morak." Taymakk turned and was gone. A door slid into place.

Alone, Morak explored the residence.

"I would like to eat," Morak said into the air.

A slot opened in the wall to his left. A tabletop slid out of the wall just below it. Within the slot, Morak found steaming food and a beverage. Although the tastes were strange, the food satisfied him.

Shortly thereafter, he became drowsy. "I want to sleep," he said, and watched idly as the eating table withdrew and a sleeping platform slid silently out of the opposite wall.

Morak had just requested the lights off when the door abruptly opened and two Morfs tossed something small into his room.

Whatever it was whipped around facing the door while backing farther into the room.

"Meesha?" Morak asked.

Silence.

Then, "Morak?" A small, terrified voice. "*Morak*!"

The Barbarian asked for the lights.

Suddenly, Meesha was in his arms, pushing herself against

him and crying, wailing in terror, sniffling in relief.

Morak held on to her tiny, stick-like shoulders and stroked her hair. He made soothing sounds. Finally, she quieted and lie in his arms breathing softly.

"Are you all right?" He asked finally.

"Yes. Now I am. Oh, Morak, I'm so happy you came for me. Can we go home now? This is an awful place." She lifted away from him a bit and gazed into his dark eyes.

"I'm afraid not, child. At least not just yet. Right now, I'm a prisoner just like you. Don't worry—I got you away from Kam, and he'll never touch you again. And as soon as I find him, he shall die."

Meesha threw her arms around his neck, the top of her head butting against Morak's chin. She shuddered, and cried some more.

• • •

Then, finally, they slept, fitfully.

When Morak woke again, it was still dark. He gently extricated himself from Meesha and stood. He started across the darkened room when he accidentally struck his knee against the edge of a planter. He winced in pain and grunted. The lights came on.

And...

He looked around. The apartment was no longer a safe, comfortable place to be. Suddenly, it was threatening, as would a prison cell. His pulse quickened. He wanted nothing more than fresh air and open sky.

He ignored Meesha's drowsy inquiry.

He went to the door. "I want to go out," he said, but the door did not respond. He knew then that all the Morfs had told him, their friendly manner, was a lie reinforced and made believable by their mental powers.

"What is it, Morak? What's wrong?"

"It's all wrong, child. The blue-skins have us trapped in here."

His mind, still feeling the pain in his knee, was clear for the first time since the Morfs had captured Isha and himself. He realized they were using their vaunted mental powers on him—and Isha—to control them and get information. His pain had broken their mental grip.

"We've got to get out of here," he grumbled. The promise to recreate the Barbarian race was nothing more than bait for a trap. He wondered how he had been so foolish not to see it before.

But that was in the past. Now he knew, and he had to escape, find Isha, and get both females to safety. Then, he smiled, he would begin giving these runts a taste of Barbarian vengeance!

He went to where he had seen the door slide into place and rammed his huge shoulder into the metal. He bounced back, and even after a dozen blows, he saw no effect. Except for the pain in his shoulder, which he didn't mind, knowing it helped lessen the Morf's mental hold over him.

He got an idea, went to the food cubicle and said, "I want to eat." When the slot opened, he grabbed it and twisted with all his strength. The panel was ripped off and came loose in Morak's hands. But the resulting space led nowhere, and was in any case too small for either him or Meesha.

Next he tried to rip the bed out of the wall, more in frustration than in an attempt to escape, but he only succeeded in twisting it at an odd angle. Finally, he sat down, breathing hard.

"I want to go out," he said harshly. Then, more softly, "I need to go out, the room is on fire." He waited. A light came on but the door still refused to budge.

"Morak," Meesha said, standing beside him and resting a hand on his heaving shoulder, "maybe I can do it."

"Well, child, I'm out of ideas. You are welcome to try."

Meesha gazed steadily at the blank wall where a door had to be. She concentrated, and Morak felt her fingers tighten on his shoulder.

A trickle of sweat ran down the side of her face, but Morak heard a grating sound, a loud pop, and the door bent and was flung outward almost violently.

Meesha let out a breath and relaxed against him.

"By the gods, child, you've power I've not seen in witch or blue skin. How...?"

Meesha took a deep breath. "I don't know enough, Morak. If only there was someone to teach me. It's so hard to learn by myself. I didn't know I could break a door until just now. Sometimes I feel so weak and powerless. This time..."

"I think your power is growing with use," Morak said.

He sprang to the opening and glanced out. In each direction, corridors curved in a half-circle away from them. He called for Meesha to follow, turned left, and trotted along, looking for some place to get out of the building, or somewhere to hide. He also had to find Isha—and, if the gods willed it, either escape or kill as many of these dog-creatures as he could.

It wasn't long before they came to other doorways along the corridor. With recklessness, he stood in front of the nearest door and said, "I want to go inside." The door opened to reveal a dark, empty room. He tried this method with several more doors. Some of them opened, but each revealed only empty rooms. Other doors ignored his request.

Until the fifth one. There, Meesha stopped him with a soft whisper and a hand on his arm. "There's someone inside. She's very sad."

Morak tried to open the door, but this time it stayed shut. He glanced inquiringly at Meesha. The child shrugged, "I'll try."

Again she concentrated, and this time Morak could feel something—almost heat—radiating from her thin body. A power becoming focused on the door. Suddenly it dimpled, bent, and collapsed to the floor.

Inside, chained to the wall in a standing position, naked, was Isha. She hung only semi-conscious. Morak went to her and tried to loose her bonds, but the material was plastic-like and slippery to the touch. Almost slimy.

He glanced around the room and saw a small heap of clothing. At the bottom of the pile, Morak found his sword. He used it to cut at Isha's bonds, but like his fingers, the blade, sharp through it was, kept slipping off.

He stopped in frustration, and looked closer at Isha. He held her face in his hands and shook her gently. Her eyes fluttered open.

"Morak," she said weakly, "how did you get here?"

"Are you all right?"

"Just so tired," she mumbled, her eyes rolling back into her head.

Morak pulled at her bonds. They stretched. At a loss, he looked once again at Meesha.

"Let her go," the child said in a small, timid voice. A voice, Morak recalled later, that was high pitched and somewhat like that of a Morf. The bonds dropped from Isha's wrists immediately and she slumped into Morak's arms.

"Morak!" Meesha shouted.

"Very good, Barbarian," came a voice from the doorway. Morak turned to see Taymakk and two other Morfs, each carrying weapons. "Your ingenuity surprised us all. Dress the woman, and come along, please." With Meesha's help, Morak quickly had Isha dressed. One of the aliens picked up Morak's sword and carried it with them.

They exited the building and Morak was surprised to see that morning had come during their search. They crossed a sunlit patio filled with Morfs and humans busy and relaxing—the two races occupying the same place, but separated just the same.

"We had hoped to convince you to join us, Morak," Taymakk said, "you and I, I feel, could have been good friends."

Morak scarcely heard the other's words. He was watching the guard who carried his sword. Those tiny blue hands were playing with the hilt, toying with the button that turned on power to the jewel. If the guard accidentally pressed the stud, it might give them a chance to escape.

Morak felt Isha's muscles tense in his arms. He looked at her and saw her eyes flicker open. He said nothing, but shook his head ever so slightly. Isha caught that move and promptly closed her eyes and relaxed in his hold.

If something should happen, Morak knew he had an ally.

Perhaps two.

They approached another building, this one square and cavernous—one of the ancient human structures.

"We like Earthians, you know," Taymakk said, "by the way, this is our food processing plant. That little one there, and Queen Isha, will be introduced to our plant in the very near future. If you're careful, Morak, you can avoid it."

There was a clatter. Morak's sword dropped to the floor. The Morf guard who held it gasped once, looked surprised, and collapsed, jerking for a while. Then he was still.

The other guard staggered, as did Taymakk. Morak dropped Isha to her feet, stooped to grab the sword, now outlined with the beautiful red and blue glow of the jewel. He made an upward cut arc, taking the other Morf guard's head off. Scarlet blood spurted high—and although it was a different color than his own, Morak was happy to see it; it had been too long since someone had died under his hand.

Meesha screamed. Morak whirled to see Taymakk grasping Meesha by the neck. Before he could move, the Morf was lifted invisibly and flung against the wall.

He slumped to the ground, semi-conscious.

Isha joined Morak with an alien weapon in her hand. They loomed over Taymakk as the alien regained his breath and slowly and carefully stood. "Unless you'd like to join your dog-brother," Morak said softly, "you will not resist. You will follow our instructions. Do you understand?"

Taymakk held his head and nodded. Isha relieved him of his weapon. "Please," Taymakk gasped, "please, turn off the jewel—I'll not give you trouble."

"Excellent, now take us someplace where we can rest and talk without being disturbed."

"My quarters," Taymakk said softly, the superior assurance of his voice gone. Morak held his sword away from the alien. In fact, he sheathed the blade to hide its presence from any other aliens they might encounter. It felt good to have a blade riding his hip once again.

They went into another of the large, round buildings preferred by the Morfs, and took a lift to the top. Taymakk said something to the wall in his own language and the door slid up into the ceiling. Morak shoved him inside, ushered Isha and Meesha in before him. The door slid closed behind them.

They sat on chairs provided by Taymakk's command.

"Morak," Isha said, "we can't afford to stay here. We've got to escape, get back to the Golden City and help them fight off these fiends."

"Not so fast, Isha," Morak grumbled, "perhaps we could do more damage here—by killing their leaders, destroying as much as we can before they stop us..."

"No," Taymakk shouted, lunging at Morak. The Barbarian drew his blade and the Morf staggered back as if struck a physical blow. Taymakk sat, glaring at the three intruders.

"Who is the child?" Isha asked, nodding toward Meesha.

"She is the one I told you about—the one from Karan, the one to whom I swore a death-oath."

"Morak!" Meesha shouted, looking surprised, "you swore a death-oath for me?"

The Barbarian nodded. "Of course, child. You were my responsibility, and more..."

Meesha flung herself into his arms, "thank you, Morak. I knew you would come for me, I always knew it, even when Kam was doing those awful things to me."

"He'll never do them again, I swear it," Morak said.

Isha knelt and stroked Meesha's golden hair. The child turned and smiled. "They said you were a queen. Is that true?"

Isha smiled, "Well, in a way, I suppose so."

Meesha smiled. "I'm happy to know a Queen." She extricated herself from Morak and bowed.

"And I'm happy to know you, Meesha. Morak has spoken of you often," Isha replied, returning the bow from her kneeling position.

"Now," Morak said, turning his attention to Taymakk, "It's my turn to ask the questions, and you will answer them. Perhaps that way, you will keep your head a short time longer."

"All right, all right. Ask your questions. But know this, Barbarian—you will not succeed You cannot escape from us."

Morak barked a laugh. "You may have created Barbarians, churl, but you do not know of our power. Soon, all blue-skins will fear the name of Morak of Barbaricum!" He stood over the small alien as he spoke, a towering rage of muscle and anger. Taymakk had no answer.

"Ask your questions, Queen Isha," Morak said, not taking his eyes from the alien.

"How many Morfs are there on Earth?"

"Over three million," Taymakk said, gazing disconsolately at the floor.

"And humans you have beguiled into serving you?"

"Ten million, and millions more to come."

"What do you mean?"

Taymakk looked up. "You have no chance, Queen of Earth. We have been breeding humans on Morofia for 300 years. They know not this Earth, only us. Their allegiance is to us. They will fight to the death any time we wish, against any foe we name. The Brotherhood of Zartan Morf plan to withdraw from this planet and let you battle your own kind. Then we will return once the battles between humans are finished."

"Devious," Isha hissed. "Our numbers are so small—our weapons so few." She slumped back into her chair, looking up at Morak. "He's right, we have no chance at all."

"You fought them for 300 years—why do you want to give up now?" Morak said.

"What use is there to fight, only to die?"

"Dying in battle is the greatest honor for a Barbarian. You now have a chance to kill those who've taken your world—what matter if you lose?"

"Yes, but we'll be killing fellow humans, not Morfs. Oh, what devious creatures."

"Yes, devious," Morak murmured, "yet perhaps we can be even more devious."

"What do you mean?"

"You told me the jewel on the Isle of Simathica was powered by some kind of sun light..."

"Yes, a fusion reactor. But I also told you we no longer have the technology to create such..."

"But what kind of power do these blue-skins use now? Might it not be as powerful as your fusion? Couldn't that be mated with one of your jewels? And wouldn't that kill them all within this foul nest?"

Isha's eyes grew larger as Morak spoke—and a slow smile brightened her face, and returned it to a beauty that made Morak's heart beat a little faster.

"Yes," she said, "Maybe you're right. I think Tucker D'air could plan such a thing—we could destroy them all before they left. Oh, Morak," she stood and kissed him, "you have saved our Earth!"

"Not yet, lady," he said, "We still need to get back to the Golden City—then return to take control of the Morf's source of power, and *then* use it to power your jewel."

"But it can be done, Morak. I know it can!"

"Morak, look out!" Meesha shouted. Something smashed over the Barbarian's head—launched mentally by Taymakk, who then sprinted for the door.

Morak slumped, dazed, and thus entangled Isha.

The door slid open. The alien scrambled out, seeking his freedom.

Morak saw Meesha step past him, twisted his head enough to see Taymakk jerk to a stop as the child reached toward him. The Barbarian got to one knee and pivoted to watch, a hand going to the back of his skull, feeling for blood.

But it was the child he watched. She seemed, somehow, to have a golden glow emanating from her. This time, she stood calmly, as if somehow confident of her power—whatever power that might be.

Taymakk made choking sounds as he was invisibly and slowly dragged back into the room. Meesha looked taller and much more mature than her few years, and the sense of power reflected that feeling.

Morak stood and staggered to the door. He took a quick look into the hallway, but saw no witnesses. He tried to get the door to close but was unsuccessful.

Meesha motioned him back. Her brow furrowed again and the door slid silently out of the ceiling to drop into place.

"You, blue-skin, will die," Morak breathed, turning to the alien.

Lines of greasy sweat marked the Morf's face. The tube running from his nostril, behind the right ear, to his belt, expanded and contracted rapidly as he breathed. Morak drew his blade and turned on the jewel.

Taymakk's eyes widened, and he breathed noisily as the radiation began to have its effect.

"Morak, no," Isha said, stepping between him and the alien. "We need him to get us out of here."

Morak looked defiantly at Isha for a moment, then nodded and sheathed his blade.

"You will do exactly as we say," Morak murmured close to the alien's face.

"I am Taymakk 109,981 of the Hive Landro, Morofia, cloned in the 9000th year of Tang-Yih," he said dully, staring straight ahead, looking at nothing.

"How soon will the renegade humans be landed?" Isha asked.

"I am Taymakk 109,981..."

Isha grabbed Taymakk's head in one hand and reached for the nostril tube with the other. "What would happen if I jerked this out of you? An even slower death?"

Taymakk looked at the floor. "They will be landed in two months from now, in a position to attack the Golden City as long as necessary. Reinforcements will be kept in this area, where local Earthians are even now making preparations to care for them."

Isha turned to Morak. "How do we get back to the Golden City undetected?"

"Hmm," Morak said, his forehead creased in thought, "the

Morfs are sending supplies to their warriors—perhaps we could go along in the guise of cargo..."

Isha looked doubtful.

"We don't have much time—they've no doubt discovered the two dead guards and they'll be looking for us," she said.

"Those individual flyers," Morak said, "how do we get to them?"

Taymakk looked sullen. "There is no way. You are trapped here—as animals waiting for slaughter. You can not make it back to your people—that is the truth."

"You lie!" Isha said, "we'll find a way. In fact, I've just thought of one. Morak, Meesha, listen closely. It will be dangerous, but I think we can pull it off..." She spoke intently to the other two. At first, Morak shook his head, but finally nodded reluctant agreement.

• • •

Morak used his sword to cut a superficial but bloody wound on Isha's left arm. She winced, then stanched the flow of blood with a strip of cloth.

Then she left with Meesha.

Morak then cut his own arm, wrapped it carefully, and told Taymakk, "that's to keep your devil brothers from gaining control of us."

"If you would but listen to me," the alien said, "we could show you a better life..."

"In your food processing plant?"

"That's not meant for everyone—only those we have trouble controlling—only those who will not live by our rules. It's nothing more than genetic cleansing."

"I am a Barbarian, unschooled," Morak commented, "yet even I can see the shallowness of your talk—and all the more reason you and all your kind need to die."

"Where have the females gone?"

"They've gone to surrender—and to lead them here to

recapture me."

"What?"

Morak smiled. "But I'll only surrender to one of your hive leaders. He must come alone—and accept my sword."

"Are you a fool?"

"Yes," Morak replied, "a most desperate one."

They waited. Soon the door opened, and in it stood Isha, the child, and a Morf. Morak did not recognize him, but the elders resembled each other in coloring and appearance of age. This one fit that description.

They stepped into the room.

"Your sword," the elder said, holding out a tiny hand.

Morak smiled, unsheathed his blade. Taymakk jumped to his feet to shout a warning, but Morak's blade sank deep into his body. Then he turned the sword on the elder, that steel still dripping scarlet blood, all before Taymakk had sunk, lifeless, to the floor.

"I will give you my blade, dog, the same way that one got it."

Isha pushed the Morf further into the room.

"Now you will do as we say, or you'll die and many other blue skins will die," Morak said.

"Never," the Morf replied.

Morak brought the sword close to the Morf and switched on the jewel. The hive elder looked startled and tried to move away from that glow.

"K-kill me if you must," he said, "I will not aid you."

Isha stooped and tied the alien's hands and feet. Then she picked him up and carried him from the room. Morak and Meesha followed closely.

They passed other Morfs, but the two paid them no attention. Isha had the elder over one shoulder, and the other hand held a weapon jammed against the Morf's temple.

They went as quickly as possible to the airfield.

They strode up to one of the air ships and pushed its attending Morfs out of the way. Several drew weapons, and more were closing in from behind.

Morak and Isha carried the elder up the ramp, urging Meesha

in before them. The child stopped, looked frightened while staring into the dark depths of the ship, but said nothing. After a moment of hesitation she went in. Morak and Isha turned at the entrance to see a large crowd of armed, angry Morfs facing them.

"We don't know how important this one is," Isha said loudly, holding up the struggling alien. "You have an opportunity to kill us now, but he will die also. We're taking him prisoner and returning to the Golden City. If we detect any ships following us, or if we are attacked, this Morf dies."

None of the aliens on the ground moved. The Morf in Isha's hands struggled harder but to no avail. They moved inside the ship, found the pilot and crew, and ordered them to evacuate the workers, close up the craft, and take off. Within ten minutes, the craft rose from its dock and headed in a southwesterly direction.

"Do you think we can get away with it?" Morak asked.

Isha Shrugged. "It's quite obvious they allowed us to escape. That means they have something planned. If we can out-think them we might have a slight possibility."

"Hmm, then we need to waste no more time."

Morak and Isha kept vigilance over the crew and their captive, alternating duty and quick snatches of sleep. Meesha had been unusually quiet, and finally dropped off into a deep, furtive sleep, punctuated by what must have been nightmares. Her body twitched, and she murmured almost constantly.

"Poor thing," Isha said to Morak, "she has suffered so much."

"Yes," Morak growled, gently stroking the child's soft hair, "and for that Kam will pay."

• • •

To the Barbarian, it was another endless journey as he watched the view screen—the jungles, the plains, oceans, and all of them over again several times, passed by below. And still the airship flew on.

"We're nearing Brazel," Isha whispered to him sometime later. Meesha joined them at the view screen.

"Are we almost there?" She asked in a quiet subdued voice.

"Yes, my child," said a familiar voice from the corridor behind them. Meesha whipped around and screamed. Morak's head jerked up and he turned. He saw Kam, leader of thieves, step into the room. The Barbarian pushed a Morf out of the way and jumped to his feet, sword in hand.

"You've returned one time too many, churl," he said, "this time you die."

"I think not, my friend. You see, all this time you thought these Morfs were believing your little charade, they were planning one of their own."

"What do you mean?" Isha asked, holding Meesha tight to her.

"What I mean, dear Queen, is that you've been out-thought again. That one is no hive leader—he is," Kam giggled, and Meesha whimpered, "a retired janitor. This crew are all volunteers. And this co-called cargo ship contains enough fusion explosive to wipe out this entire area of the world. It's armed and set to detonate automatically in two hours, and it can't be stopped by you."

"If that's true, what are you doing here?"

"I'm here, Queen, to accept the surrender of the Golden City, and to take you and other leaders into custody. And besides," he pointed to Meesha, "you've got something that belongs to me. I can stop the detonation sequence if you cooperate."

Isha's shoulders slumped.

"There is no other solution. You and your people fought valiantly, but you lost. Time to face facts, my dear."

"No!," she shouted, drawing the small Morf weapon. She burned a hole in the Morf captive, then turned the ray on the crew, cutting them down in a fast sweep. The aircraft lurched and the floor tilted.

Morak lost his balance and was flung up against a computer panel. The panel shorted, giving Morak a severe electric shock, throwing him to the floor, dazed.

Kam clipped a shot at Isha, striking her weapon and flinging it out of her hand. She screamed and almost dropped Meesha.

Kam chopped her on the temple, and she collapsed.

Unable to move, Morak watched the leader of thieves pull Meesha away, the little one screaming in terror. Kam shoved Meesha into an escape pod, then entered behind her. The door closed and the craft lurched as the pod was ejected. Then they were gone.

With difficulty, Morak regained his feet and went to Isha. Her eyes flicked open when he touched her. "Meesha?"

"He's taken her. They're gone."

Isha quickly righted the ship, then they made a quick search of the craft. They found no other Morfs or humans, but they did find the fusion bomb with its timer ticking off the seconds.

"We're dead," she told Morak, "no use kidding ourselves. But at least we made them pay a small amount."

"Do you think you can fly this craft?" Morak said.

"I don't know. What do you have in mind?"

"Come with me. I have an idea." They returned to the control room and dumped bodies to the floor. Some of the controls had been damaged by Isha's attack, but she sat down and studied them.

"I can't read them," she said finally, "I'll just be guessing."

"That's fine. But see if you can turn us away from land and out over the sea."

"Oh, I see. Yes, let's give this a try." They watched the view screen as the mountains dropped away and the rolling, white-tipped ocean waves returned.

"One hour twenty-five minutes until detonation," Isha said, glancing at a chronometer.

"Can you make this thing go any faster?" Morak asked.

Isha said nothing, but her hands played over the controls and the craft speeded up. They watched intently as the Morf cargo ship sped out over the open sea for almost an hour.

"Thirty minutes, that's it, send this thing straight up and let's go," Morak said. Isha made the adjustments and the craft began to rise higher. Morak pulled Isha from her seat and guided her back to the remaining escape pod. They climbed into the tiny craft and thumbed a button that flung the pod out and away from the other ship, which continued its rise up into the higher atmosphere. Isha fought the controls, and kept the tiny ship heading away from the cargo ship and back toward land. She piloted the pod close to the sea, speeding just above the tops of waves.

"Twenty minutes," Morak said, straining to see any sign of land.

"Fifteen."

Then a dark smudge appeared, splitting the sky and sea.

"We'll never make it."

"Yes we will, just keep going."

With five minutes remaining before detonation, they swept across a sandy beach and over trees. The pod lifted to cross a range of low hills, then higher to gain mountains.

The pod dipped into a valley, swerved among trees and hills, and peaks, just clearing them.

There came a brilliant flash. A hush. A stillness.

Then the small craft was slammed forward, and the last thing Morak heard was the buckling of metal. The last thing he felt was the heat of a hell-fire.

And his last thought was, "this is no way for a Barbarian to die."

• • •

The first thing he heard was the crackling of flames nearby. He opened his eyes and saw Isha lying like a doll against a burning tree.

But, for the moment at least, only the top of that tree was burning.

He shook his head and tried to sit up. He looked and discovered part of the escape pod across his left leg. A red puddle beneath it told him the leg was not in the best condition.

And come to think of it, the pain was pretty bad too.

"Isha," he called. She didn't respond, and he thought she must be dead.

But he had to find out. He looked around and noticed most of the tops of the trees were smoldering, but nothing burned in the small valley where the pod had crashed. Smoke filled the air—and something else. A hot, greasy rain of steam began falling, covering everything with rivulets.

Morak heaved and managed to move the metal a few inches before he let it drop. His leg was free, but he doubled over in pain. Biting his lip, Morak ripped cloth from his clothing and wrapped the large, gaping wound in his calf. Then he crawled over to Isha.

He could find no external injuries, other than numerous superficial cuts and bruises. He felt for a pulse, and discovered a thin, fluttery response.

"Isha," he whispered close to her ear, "wake up."

He shook her, and the woman's eyes fluttered, then opened. She groaned and tried to sit up, but was unsuccessful. "Morak? Are you all right?"

"I'll live," he said gruffly, "are you hurt anywhere?"

"I don't know. I'm, I..." She grimaced, grabbed Morak's shoulder to gain a sitting position. Her face was ashen, and her eyes were open wide in pain.

"It looks as if you'll have to go on without me," she muttered weakly.

"No," Morak insisted, "I'll never find an entrance to the Golden City on my own—and even if I do, how could I get through its traps?"

"Then I'm afraid we are lost." Her black-maned head dropped to rest on Morak's shoulder.

He was too weary to argue.

They slept, a fitful, pain-wracked sleep. Morak dreamt of Meesha, and in his dream he heard her tortured cries begging him for the mercy of death. He woke at the sound of her child-scream, to find it replaced by a loud wind howling through the valleys, and more hot, drenching rain. The freak storm came at them with an angry vengeance. The rain was hot enough to cause thick steam to rise from the jungle. He tried to go back to sleep, but it was some time before he succeeded.

Morak woke the next morning. The sky was free of clouds, but a thick haze had replaced it, muting the sun. The jungle was uncharacteristically quiet; an expectancy hung over the land. He checked Isha and found her still alive and sleeping.

He got up and limped over to where the largest portion of the pod lie. It was twisted and crumpled from being slammed between a tree and a large rock. But the ship's interior, designed to save life, had protected them from the worst of the crash. That, Morak thought, and Isha's piloting.

He heard a moan behind him. Isha had wakened and was attempting to sit up. Morak hobbled over to help. "How do you feel?" He asked.

"Something inside me hurts," she replied, "I don't know if I can make it—but we've got to try. We've got to make it back to the Golden City."

"But the trip might kill you."

"Death is better than living in a world controlled by the Brotherhood of Zartan Morf."

Morak had to agree. Their progress that day was slight. Early afternoon clouds gathered overhead, and large, greasy drops fell. The explosion had done something to the climate, he concluded; had altered, somehow, the very fabric of the planet.

The rain made everything slippery, and there were endless hills and rocks to climb over. At least the storm lacked the strong wind that had whipped at them the day before.

Morak's leg was a hindrance, and Isha could only travel for a few minutes at a time. That night, as they rested beside a small campfire, over which they had cooked some small animals Morak didn't recognize, Isha began coughing up blood.

The next day was no better, but the terrain became flatter and more jungle-like. The rain continued unabated, and the two were forced several times to skirt flooded areas. But it also provided them with a steady food supply, feeding on the small animals that fled the rising waters.

"Do you recognize anything?" Morak asked at the end of the second day.

"I'm sorry, Barbarian," Isha said between clenched teeth, pausing for breath between each word. She walked hesitantly, slowly, leaning on Morak for support. "I don't know where we crashed—and this cursed rain has changed everything." She bent over in another fit of coughing, and wiped away pink foam.

Morak knew she would not be able to travel the following day. And he'd be surprised if she lived two more days. His leg was a throbbing pain that seemed to have gotten infected.

• • •

That night, something woke Morak. The rain had stopped and the air was warm, humid and still. There came a distant boom. A few minutes later, a second one echoed past, this time accompanied by bright flashes reflected in low clouds.

The Barbarian looked at Isha. She was asleep or unconscious.

He got up and started off through the jungle. It wasn't easy, through the darkness and clouds. But he found the jungle itself gave off a slight, phosphorescent glow. He periodically marked his trail so he could find his way back.

The Barbarian traveled for several hours, guided by the occasional flashes and explosions.

The sounds of battle were closer now. He could feel the earth shake with the force of each blast. The flashes were no longer ethereal, but defined slashes into the night sky, accompanied by a sizzling, crackling sound.

He came to the edge of a clearing and saw several dark shapes moving there, and something hovering above the trees. Morak squinted and tried to see more.

Suddenly, a ray erupted from the hovering craft and licked at the ground in the clearing. There was an answering scream, and an answering beam of light that struck the top of the flyer.

During the exchange, Morak had recognized the hovering craft as belonging to the Morfs. And that craft now drifted his way, tilted and lifeless to his eyes.

But shadows in that clearing were also following the craft.

Morak looked carefully, and could see two more hovercraft entering at the far end of the clearing. The battle continued all around him.

He moved to the edge of the trees and kept abreast of the small machine. It finally drifted into the jungle just above him and hung up on a tree. He noticed that the hatch was open, and a lifeless alien hanging partway out. Morak looked around and saw approaching figures. He would only have one chance.

He leapt into the tree, wincing with pain as his left leg scraped a branch. He hooked a hand over the hovercraft and pulled himself up. The flyer tilted and he tumbled inside just as a ray from the ground singed his back. He pushed the dead alien out and slapped the button that closed the hatch.

Inside the small globe, two Morfs lie dead. The Barbarian tossed the bodies to the entrance, then shoved them out of the craft. He received a couple of ray blasts for his trouble. Though he was no pilot, the controls were standardized, and he had learned enough watching the pilots of previous craft to make it move and turn. The craft tended to float when not actively under the control of a pilot. He quickly angled the craft deeper into the jungle, back toward Isha. The craft listed heavily to one side, and Morak realized one or more of the rays must have damaged it. Also, he had no idea how long its fuel would last. In the heat of a battle, it was possible the Morfs would not pursue one man in a damaged flier. In the dark, Morak was able to follow his own trail where his passing had altered the jungle glow. Still, it was necessary to search for several hours before he found their primitive camp.

Just as dawn broke over the treetops, he drifted to a landing near Isha.

The woman did not respond to his attempts to wake her. Isha's pulse was thready and irregular. Morak placed her carefully into the hover-craft.

He took off, lifting the small craft as high as possible, and headed northeast, hopefully, he thought, toward the Golden City.

Low, dense clouds gave him an opportunity to fly undetected most of the time. Several hours went by. From time to time, Morak thought he heard the sounds of battle below him.

Isha groaned and tried to sit up, but was unsuccessful. Morak reached down and placed her in the seat beside him.

"You're still alive, I see."

"I'm weak, tired and I hurt inside. I don't know if you'd call that being alive." She took stock of her surroundings. "And you've learned to fly."

Morak smiled. "Can you see anything familiar?"

She gazed at the passing terrain. "With the clouds, it's hard to be sure. But I think—yes, over that way is an entrance. See that river? Follow it up canyon to the falls."

Morak followed directions, and suddenly knew they were close. Beams of death flashed at them from two directions.

He dropped the craft like a rock, stopping it just above the ground. The tortured machine began smoking and would go no further. It landed roughly and tipped over, spilling Morak and Isha onto the ground. Morak pulled her into the jungle just as their transportation destroyed itself in a fiery explosion.

If they were not now very close to an entrance, they would not make it at all.

Morak's leg was a throbbing mass of pain. He carried Isha as he darted into the foliage, trying to get as far away as possible from those who had destroyed the hovercraft.

A while later, he stopped to rest. Isha leaned weakly against him. "If I remember correctly, there's an entrance down in that little valley," she told him, pointing, "back to where the river is. At the end is a waterfall, and behind the waterfall, a cave..."

Her head slumped forward and Morak could not rouse her again.

He placed the woman carefully near a tree, then made his way into the small valley. He found the narrow river, now swollen by the unusual rains, and followed it upstream.

A noise from ahead made him stop. He crouched behind some bushes and took a careful look. At the end of the canyon, he saw a steep rocky wall, the center carved into a V shape by the waterfall. At the bottom, there was a small pond, fed by the waterfall. On the bank of that pond several Morf hovercraft waited, humming softly. At a point nearest the waterfall, four aliens were gathered, speaking and gesticulating.

Morak backed into the jungle and moved around past the hovercraft until he was parallel with the Morfs. Quietly as he could, Morak crept toward the aliens, until he could see them a few meters ahead. He drew his sword and turned on the jewel. He moved even closer, to the last barrier between the jungle and the pond. He tensed and launched himself, left leg dragging, into the middle of the aliens. He swung his blade as the aliens staggered back, their large eyes opening even wider in surprise and fear.

One's head came off and splashed into the pond. Another watched as Morak's blade sunk into his belly. A third tried to run, but stumbled, and Morak sliced him in two.

The fourth stepped back and drew his weapon. Although the Morf wavered slightly from the effects of the jewel, he pointed his rod directly at Morak.

The Barbarian, breathing hard, stopped and waited.

"You've killed one too many of us," the Morf said, "now it's your turn to die."

Morak said nothing. He lowered his sword and watched the Morf closely. The alien stretched out his arm, the weapon aimed at Morak's face.

The Barbarian waited until he saw the Morf's muscles tense, then he flipped the point of his sword into the ground, and up, flinging sand and dirt at the Morf. At the same time, Morak ducked to the left. A blue bolt of energy flashed out, but Morak had dropped to the ground and rolled toward the alien, who was frantically trying to clear his vision. The alien kept his ray firing, hoping to strike Morak out of chance. The Barbarian swung upwards with his sword, gutting the Morf before that deadly ray could touch him.

Morak got to his right knee and looked at the alien. "I've not killed nearly enough of you, blue skin," he said softly.

He went back and got Isha and took her to the pond. There, he wetted the woman's forehead and gave her water to drink.

She woke. "Are we there?"

"Yes. Now it's up to you to get us through." He watched as she coughed up more blood, and wondered if she would die in some dark tunnel, leaving him afraid to move one way or another. But the woman reached deep down inside her, deeper than the blood that oozed between her lips, and found a source of strength.

• • •

They ducked under the waterfall and entered a cave behind the rushing water. This was, apparently, what had attracted the interest of the aliens. They suspected it was an entrance to the Golden City, but could not find a method to access the tunnel beyond. The cave itself was shallow, but Isha moved her hand over various parts of the rock wall in a certain pattern, and a portion of it slid aside, revealing a dark passageway.

Morak assisted Isha as they entered the corridor. The stone slid back into place behind them, and the Barbarian began to feel trapped.

"Let's go," he said, anxious to end this trek.

"No, wait," Isha said between gasps of air, trying to hold him back. "Listen to me," she said, "we can't move for another two minutes. It's one of the traps; if we leave this area now, the entire mountain will be blown apart."

Morak shook his head. "I begin to understand how the Morfs were never able to attack your city."

She looked at him, her eyes wide with pain and fatigue. "We couldn't afford even one mistake."

"Hmm," he answered. Isha's head rested on his shoulder until the time they could continue. Slowly, they moved on down the dark tunnel, lit by a flickering torch carried in one hand by Morak. They stopped time and time again, along that journey, to let varying periods of time pass and to renew their source of light. To wait too long in one place was as deadly as moving on too quickly in another. Morak wondered if Isha had memorized each of their pauses, or if the rock walls held some unobtrusive clue.

Isha was lethargic between rests, but managed to stay conscious to give him murmured instructions.

Finally, some eternity later, they came out of the cave and into the cavern which held the Golden City.

It looked the same to Morak, at least at first. Later, he would notice signs of battle damage. He waved the last torch as he carried Isha down toward the city itself. People came running up, each holding a weapon at the ready. But when they discovered who Morak carried with him, they were overjoyed to welcome them home. Those who had been fighting a grim battle shouted and screamed to have their queen back among them.

The two were quickly rushed to the hospital and placed under the powerful healing rays. Isha, Morak was told, had extensive internal injuries. She would likely live, but it would take a while for her to recover. Morak, himself, suffered from a severe infection to his left leg, but that was the type of wound the machine was best at healing. He expected to be up and walking within 24 hours.

The next afternoon, Tucker D'air came to see him. The two talked in general for a while, recounting for each other their respective situations.

"We've been under attack for several days," D'air said, "casualties are heavy, especially among our surface fighting forces. We haven't yet been able to speak with Queen Isha, and we need information."

Morak didn't respond at once. How could he tell these people what he knew? That, unless there was some miraculous stroke of fate, the Golden City would be overrun—if not by Morfs, then by humans fighting for their alien masters.

"What are their numbers?" D'air pressed, "do you know their plans for attack? Did you notice any weaknesses?"

Morak looked away from the scientist and took a deep breath. "If you do not act quickly," he said, "you will have no chance for survival."

"What do you mean?"

Morak told D'air about the Morf plan to use humans, raised on the alien home world, for battle. D'air turned away, walked to the wall and slammed a fist into it. "My God! It's an insidious plan. We'll end up fighting our own kind while they await the results from afar."

"Just so," Morak said, "but your queen and I have an idea which might help balance the odds." He told the other about the plan to connect a jewel through the alien power plant.

"Yes," D'air said thoughtfully, "it just might work if their power source isn't too different from those we know. It will mean removing one of the large jewels we've been using to keep the Morf's out of range here..."

"How soon can you leave?" Came a voice from the doorway. Both men turned to see a white-skinned, wobbly Isha supported by a nurse.

"Isha," Morak said.

"My Queen," D'air added, "you shouldn't be up so soon—you're still very ill."

"I'll get up when I damn well wish," she said irritably.

"I'm afraid not," D'air said, "I am going to personally take you back to your room." He moved toward her.

"You'll have to fight me," she said in a thin, high-pitched voice, a sad parody of her former commanding tones. "I've no time to be gentle." Her eyes were rock steady. D'air hesitated.

"We need a live queen," he said, "you don't know how much word of your return has helped our spirit. Our fighting forces know if anyone can pull off a victory against the Brotherhood, you can. Now, back to your bed."

"Tucker," she shouted weakly, "I will do as I please. Those fiends must be defeated, no matter what the cost." She started into the room. "Has Morak told you—"

She would have collapsed had not D'air caught her.

"Tomorrow," he said gently, stroking her hair, "we can talk of this tomorrow."

Morak was surprised to see tears in Isha's eyes when D'air lifted her in his arms. "Curse my weak body," she said in a hoarse whisper.

"Strong body," Morak said, striding forward, "of steel forged harder than any man's sword. But you *must* rest and allow it to recover." At that moment, he had never loved any woman more. Karan had been a place where only the strongest lived long. But he knew that even there, Isha would have been a queen.

• • •

The next morning, Morak was awakened by the sound of dull booms and the building shaking. He got up and tried his left leg. The muscles were still stiff, and the wound itself looked pink and jagged, but there was little pain, and everything worked.

He went to find Tucker D'air. Outside, he found the Golden City a mass of activity. No one was standing still, and few were walking.

It felt good to have a leg that worked again. The slap of a sword against his hip made Morak anxious to fight more of the aliens. He was beginning to enjoy killing the tiny creatures. Their weapons and powers made fighting them a challenge.

It took him a while to find Tucker D'air. The scientist was supervising the transport of a huge jewel—almost as large as the one Morak had seen on the Isle of Simathica.

"Be careful with it!" D'air shouted as one of the transporters stumbled. He looked at Morak. "Good morning," he said.

Morak nodded.

"At least it will be a good morning if these oafs don't drop the jewel. It's precisely tuned, if it's jarred too much, the radiation won't emanate the full effect." He watched anxiously as the jewel was carefully loaded into a large padded crate, and secured.

"Where are the children?" Morak asked suddenly, looking around, finding at last that which had been nagging at his subconscious.

"They're safe, friend. For many years now, we've had a contingency plan to save the children—and pregnant women, along with some of the older citizens—by taking them to another underground location known only to a few."

"That is good news."

"Good news, yes, if we succeed. That does it," D'air said, inspecting the crate, "we can leave any time now." He paused, looked at Morak, "did you feel the explosions this morning?"

"Yes. A Morf attack?"

"In a way. They foolishly tried getting through some of the tunnels—blew up a few mountains, I understand. They know where we are, but getting to us will cost them. Now, let's go see Isha."

The Queen of Earth was propped up on a hospital bed, and obviously unhappy. She was also obviously in much better shape.

"Get this slop out of here," she shouted at a harried attendant.

She looked up at the two men. "Well?"

"We came to say goodbye," D'air said, "we're leaving for the Morf stronghold in New York."

She turned away. "I order you to take me along," she said softly, her words carrying no conviction. But she had to say them.

D'air tried to laugh. "You may be Queen, but your doctor says no, and right now, she's in charge of the royal body."

"Tucker don't," she said, turning wet eyes to him, "you know I'm not a royal queen, I'm a fighting queen."

"I'm sorry. You're in no shape right now to fight anything larger than a fly."

"And you, Barbarian, do you abandon me here also?"

Morak shrugged. "I'm not in charge. But I'm going along. They need someone who knows the city and the Morfs."

There was a long moment of silence.

"Well," D'air said hesitantly, "so long."

Isha grunted.

D'air and Morak went to the captured Morf airship they would use for their trip to the alien capital. D'air and the crew made their final take-off preparations. The airship was located in a deep ravine near the Golden City. Thick jungle growth hid the ship from almost all angles, and the terrain prevented close scanner searches. But still, there remained a strong possibility that the ship might be discovered, and through it, the closest entrance to the Golden City. It was a chance they had to take.

Morak stood on the ramp as D'air ordered the camouflage

removed. The Barbarian was looking around when he saw something moving through the jungle. His eyes widened, and he called to D'air. The other looked up, and Morak pointed.

Coming through the dense growth, in full battle dress, was Isha. She was flanked by two nurse attendants, but she walked unassisted.

She stepped up to Tucker D'air and stated in a loud, firm voice, "Isha Montoya reporting for duty." Morak noticed that her eyes were two orbs of steel that would not be refused.

D'air looked at her, looked away, ran a hand through his hair, then looked back.

Neither said a word, but some communication passed between them. D'air jerked his head toward the ship's entrance. "Get aboard," he growled, "we leave at once."

Isha smiled and hurried aboard the ship. As she passed, she glanced at Morak, still smiling. She winked but said nothing. The Barbarian had not failed to notice the pain, triumph, and sheer determination fighting for dominance in her eyes.

Seconds later, Tucker D'air came up the ramp. "She would have us believe she is recovered," he told the Barbarian quietly, "but truly she is not. That means we must both watch over her carefully." He looked as if he had eaten very sour fruit, "as if we won't already have enough to do."

Morak laughed. "Ah, well, we will probably die anyhow—but Barbarians have never died alone—they take an honor guard of their enemies with them to the dark realms. Let's go, I'm eager to kill more blue skins."

Already aboard was a selection of the leading scientists and a contingent of the best-trained warriors. As Morak watched them board the craft, he wondered how this pitiful force of fifty or sixty humans could wage a successful battle against the thousands, perhaps tens of thousands, of alien blue skins.

Morak and Tucker D'air were the last to enter the craft. They stepped inside and the ramp pulled itself up and the hatch slid closed. The expedition to save earth rose slowly into the sky. At other entrances, kilometers away, several other captured Morf airships also rose into the sky with the same destination in mind. These were decoys and possible reinforcements should any of them make it to the target area. In addition, ground forces would launch an attack on Morf forces surrounding the Golden City in an effort to create sufficient confusion to keep the enemy occupied. Overall, their chances of success were deemed poor to non-existent.

Tucker D'air, Isha, and Morak held favored positions behind the pilots' station, watching them operate the aircraft. They took a route they hoped was not frequented by many of the alien ships.

"How do you feel?" Morak asked, leaning close to Isha.

"That is not your concern, Barbarian," she snapped. She glanced at him and her face softened. "I'm sorry, Morak. I am not well, but anger and hate will keep me going. And the pain inside will keep the Morfs from controlling me." She paused. "But why are you here? This isn't your fight, you've done your part—more than that."

Morak gazed out the view window. "Kam still lives, and perhaps Meesha as well. I've sworn an oath to kill one and save the other," he said simply. "And I have other debts to pay," he added, "Jaksim and others you've not met, and Karan itself. It's a battle and I'm a warrior and fighting is something I do well. And when this is over, if we are successful, what place will there be in this strange world for the likes of me? I am the last of my kind—when I die, there will be no more Barbarians. And when the Morfs are gone, perhaps there will be no more battles, and that will end my chance to die a Barbarian's death."

"That's important to you, isn't it? But what if you don't die in battle this time? What if you are condemned to live on?"

Morak shrugged. "I don't know. I just don't know."

• • •

The ship flew on for hours, undisturbed. Tucker D'air and Isha were both happy their ruse seemed to have worked. And both were worried that the Morfs were fully aware of their efforts and had prepared a welcome that would spring a fatal trap as they arrived. Tucker and Morak visited the scientists and troops, huddled uncomfortably in a cargo hold. They ate, slept, ate again. Night came and went.

"We're nearing our target area," the lead pilot said finally, turning to look at Tucker D'air for further direction.

"Okay swing out over the ocean past the city, bring us in from the north—and keep this ship low. We don't want to show up on their sensors. Hopefully, they won't expect us to arrive from the north. We'll walk the last few kilometers."

Thirty minutes later, the airship had landed and deposited its volunteers in a forest. They worked first to cover the ship with foliage to hide it from above. They swallowed, and carried with them, pills that caused stomach pains. With this, and small jewels placed on their bodies and powered with batteries, they hoped to nullify most of the Morf mind powers.

They began their trip to the New York area, passing through forests that were sometimes filled with the remains of buildings and decaying roads, 300-year-old ruins. They went slowly because they carried the jewel, and because of Isha. She kept pace with the others, but her face was set in a grim mask of determination.

As they approached the edge of the inhabited city, the task force came to cultivated land. They saw no people or machinery until just beyond the first line of ruined buildings.

Morak, Tucker D'air, and one of the others watched from behind a wall of worn stones as a number of humans toiled quietly in a field.

The workers were alone, each tending a separate section of the field.

"Maybe they know where the Morf powerplant is," D'air said.

"Let's find out," Morak replied, and before the other could say anything, "wait here, I'll be right back."

The Barbarian entered the field, a wary eye searching for evidence of Morf overseers. He came upon one of the men working silently, a tall, thin, middle-aged man.

"You. Tell me where the Morf powerplant is located."

The man looked blankly at Morak, and there was no sign of comprehension, no spark of intelligence in his eyes. Indeed, there was no expression at all on the man's face. He looked Morak up and down, then went back to his farming. A chill ran up the Barbarian's spine.

He grabbed the man's arm and shook him. The farmer dropped his hoe and stood, almost limply, in Morak's hold. Slowly, the man put himself together and showed his first reaction. Fear.

At the same time, Morak noticed a small, round, metal tube protruding from the man's neck, behind the left ear.

"Who are you?" he said.

The man shook his head, pointed to his mouth. He seemed surprised at Morak's speech.

"Where is the Morf powerplant?"

The man frowned, then turned and pointed southeast, toward the sea.

"Why can't you speak?" The man indicated the metal tube, then used his hands to suggest an explosion.

Could it be possible? Morak decided to take his captive to Tucker D'air, allow the scientist an opportunity to examine the man.

Morak pulled the other with him, and got to the stone fence when the man stumbled and struck his knee hard against a large rock.

Tucker turned to look as the man grimaced and grunted deep in his throat, an unwilling sound, his eyes wide in fear. There was a short, sharp blast, and the Barbarian was hurled past the fence and into tall grass beyond it. He was stunned and dazed, but otherwise unhurt.

He got to his feet and saw Tucker D'air standing over the man's body. There was no sign of a head, only the jagged stump of a neck, and a body that twitched slightly and still oozed blood.

Tucker was muttering when Morak rejoined him. "We have not yet touched the depths of their depravity," he said grimly. One of the scientists examined several other human workers. They found each of them equipped with similar explosive devices. Should the wearer speak or move from the general area of his or her daily routine, the device would trigger, thereby eliminating a recalcitrant worker without the need for guards or overseers.

They continued, skirting the fields, ignoring the many other humans, both men and women, they passed. They did not once come upon a Morf, nor did an alien aircraft fly in their direction.

Eventually, they came to the sea. They followed that for a time, and rounding a bend, saw it—an artificial, metal peninsula stretching seaward, almost completely covered with low, domed buildings. From each of the domes came a steady hum and a muted yellow glow. It was built at the remaining edge of what had once been known as the Isle of Coney.

"That's got to be it," D'air said, "let's go."

"Wait a minute," Isha said, "you don't think they will let us just walk out there and hook up the jewel, do you?"

D'air looked impatient. He was a scientist, not a strategist; he was getting tired of all this sneaking around. "What do you suggest?"

"We approach by sea..."

"Not another raft," Morak groaned.

Isha smiled. "Yes, a raft. You have some experience with rafts, my friend?"

Morak grunted in reply. "Well, if we must, let's get on with it. Someday, maybe, I'll even become accustomed to floating on oceans."

They went to work, using materials they had brought with them, and rapidly put together three inflatable rubber rafts large enough to accommodate the task force and their equipment. As dusk fell, they hid their work near the water and then withdrew into the woods where they prepared and ate a cold and rather tasteless meal.

Afterward, Isha told them "we'll leave just after midnight. That should give us enough time to do what we have to do before dawn."

Morak checked his battle gear—the sword, his throwing

knife, and the one used for cutting. "Take this also," Isha said. He turned to see her holding one of the ray weapons.

"Do you think that wise?" He asked, patting his sword hilt, "this is the weapon I know."

"It's simple," she said, "you hold it like this, point it, and press the trigger." A ray shot out into the ground, leaving a large hole and a puff of smoke. "Small bursts are better than long ones—the power pack will last longer. This weapon gives you the option to kill at a distance."

Morak took the gun and tried it, aiming at the limbs of several nearby trees. Without comment, he took the holster from Isha and strapped it on opposite the sword, and pocketed several extra power packs.

The night was full of busy sounds as the warriors checked their equipment and made last-minute plans. The air was damp, and smelled of the sea and forest.

· · ·

With little noise, three rafts slid into the gently lapping waves, filled with men and women, one Queen, a Barbarian and a jewel. They paddled outward, toward the artificial metal peninsula housing the Morf power plant.

No one talked. There was no need. Each one knew this was their only chance to drive the aliens from Earth. One among them, the last of his kind, watched the sea moodily. Yet, within, there was the tight excitement he always felt just before a battle.

The wondering, the waiting; that was the hardest. It wasn't too soon for Morak when the raft bumped the side of the Morf installation. They were as close as possible to the end of the peninsula, near the largest power dome.

Morak climbed out of the raft, Isha pressed against his shoulder, followed by other members of the task force. The jewel and scientists were on one of the other rafts, still hidden by the night, awaiting the verdict.

Morak looked around, saw no movement, and motioned for

the others on his raft to join them. Seaward were two of the glowing domes, including the largest. Back toward land were five more. As quietly as possible, the humans exited their rafts and quickly began unloading their equipment.

From beside one of those domes, Morak saw movement. "Look out!" He shouted, just as a bolt of energy ripped out and slammed into one of the Earthians. The man screamed and fell back into the water.

Isha returned fire, leaving a bright glow at the edge of the dome. Several others fired shots. "Spread out," Morak said, "keep low." He began running toward the landward domes. When he reached the nearest, he turned to see Isha and two others following.

A ray burst out and burned a hole in one of the men's chest. Morak returned fire and heard a thin scream.

Behind him, toward the seaward dome, sounds of battle reached their ears. Morak and Isha continued toward land, hoping to create a diversion and draw fire away from the peninsula.

Morak and Isha went one way around their dome, the other man went opposite. The Barbarian advanced slowly, bent low and holding his ray gun at the ready.

Several shadows moved ahead of him, near the next dome. Both he and Isha fired, and Morfs screamed and fell. They moved on, past that dome and closer to land. They lost sight of their companion, and sounds of battle diminished behind them.

Morak stopped to catch his breath, and to give Isha a chance to rest. "If we get to land," he breathed into Isha's ear, "we'll try to get into the midst of them and create our own battle. They will be less likely to reinforce those near the power plant."

Isha nodded, head bent. She was breathing hard.

Back in the distant forest, two military technicians had remained behind, where they had landed the Morf aircraft the day before. They had orders to fire two of the craft's missiles into the heart of the city at exactly twelve-thirty. Isha checked her chronometer, swore softly, and gazed at the night sky.

One missile roared overhead and landed near the Morf population center with a loud and brilliant explosion, shaking the ground. The other was not to be seen. It had either failed of launch or had been destroyed by Morf defenses.

"Nothing to do about it," Isha breathed, "they must have located our landing spot. Let's go, we're running out of time." Before continuing, however, she talked with Tucker D'air via a tiny radio. The task force was under attack, but all the rafts had been unloaded, and they were fighting their way to the largest dome.

Isha and Morak made it to land without confronting any other aliens, although they hid once while quite a number of Morfs rushed past in several vehicles.

"Why don't you wait here," Morak suggested, "I'll go on and do as much damage as I can..."

"Forget it," Isha looked at him defiantly, "I'm going with you."

"Earth needs its queen. No one needs a Barbarian; this is my chance to die in battle."

She looked at him with softer eyes. "*I* need you, Morak. And somewhere out there is a child who needs you."

Before he could reply, Morak saw several Morf airships drift overhead, on their way to the power plant. He took aim and unleashed his ray at one of the ships. It did no visible damage, but the other Morf ship slowed and turned back, searching for the source of the attack.

"Let's get out of here," he shouted. The two ran for the nearest buildings as bolts of deadly energy rained down upon them. Morak and Isha ducked into one of the ruined Earthian buildings. The dim light from outside was enough to show them the piled-up bones of human bodies. They kicked their way through the remains of ancient slaughter and exited through the back.

And into the midst of Morfs. Morak didn't know what they were doing there; assembling to reinforce the power plant guards, perhaps, or a meeting of a scientific contingent maybe. Few of them were armed, but that didn't stop the Barbarian and Isha from cutting them down ruthlessly.

The small courtyard was soon silent and still except for a few twitching arms and legs.

"Follow me," Morak said, cutting through another of the buildings and down several dark streets until they arrived at the main alien habitation area, built on land that had been filled in after the sea level rise.

They hid in shadows and changed to fresh power packs while watching frantic Morf activity going on around them. It seemed their goal of a surprise attack had been at least partially successful.

Morak took careful aim at a group of Morfs on a second-story ledge who seemed to be giving orders. He fired carefully, swinging the ray to cut down as many of them as possible. Isha's ray joined his, at the opposite side of the habitation. Morf screams filled the night air. The aliens began firing in panic, not knowing where their target was, sensing enemies in their midst, but unable to pinpoint their location because of the confusion. And because Isha and Morak kept moving.

They ducked from shadow to alley, picking their shots to create maximum panic. They entered buildings and fired from different floors, attempting to create the impression that a much larger force was in the midst of the aliens.

In that time, several dozen Morfs died.

But more and more rays were finding them hidden in the shadows. The more mature and experienced Morfs were relaxing, ignoring the activity, and mentally honing in on the two humans.

Three times in the past minute, Morak ducked back just in time to avoid death. The odor of burning flesh was thick in the air, and the two were forced to retreat as the Morfs mounted a sustained attack.

"Let's go," Morak said, pointing away from the activity, "we can't do much when they know where we are."

Isha bent over, hands on knees, gasping for breath. She looked up, her face stained with sweat. "You go ahead—I'll catch up in a minute."

"No," Morak replied, helping the woman down the stairs of a building. They hurried to prevent Morf warriors from flanking them. Morak led them deeper into the alien residence buildings, but they saw none of the Morfs for several minutes.

Morak ran with his sword drawn, knowing it would be a more dangerous weapon in a confined area. He turned on the jewel and they continued down a long, well-lit corridor.

They turned a corner and came to a lobby—one packed with Morfs. They were all turned away from Morak and Isha, except for one, who was speaking to the others. He noticed the intruders, his tiny mouth opened and his eyes stretched to their maximum width.

Suddenly the lights went out. Isha's weapon burst forth, giving Morak still-life glimpses of aliens dying in agony.

With a wild shout, he waded into the midst of them, his glowing sword slashing, thrusting, and cutting its way through alien flesh. Several Morfs tried to cut down the Barbarian with their weapons, but more often than not, they ended up killing their own as the Barbarian moved as the wind in the darkness. Isha helped, too, picking off a number of Morfs from her hiding place in the doorway.

The confusion, Morak felt, was helped by the jewel in his sword. It affected not only the judgment of the aliens, but also their physical and mental abilities.

Soon the room was full of Morf heads and other severed and burned body parts. The floor was slippery with blue alien blood. Sometime during the melee, Isha joined him, and they fought their way to the other side of the room. They dashed down the corridor, ducking and weaving to avoid Morf blaster fire.

They turned another corner and stopped, breathing hard.

"Remind me never to get you mad at me," Isha gasped. "Where to now?"

"I want you to attack their main building, try to get at the hive elders. I'm going to the human area."

"Meesha?"

Morak nodded. "And Kam."

"Are you sure that's wise?"

Morak smiled grimly. "I have no other choice. This I must do."

Morak gazed at Isha, the tangled black hair, the dark, fiery eyes, the heaving chest. "But you be careful, and don't get hurt."

She gave him a smile, which quickly died. "Find the child and forget about Kam, Morak. Killing him won't help our cause."

"No. He must die—I swore his death before I left Karan, more than once since then. I mean to keep my vow."

Her eyes searched his for a long moment, then she nodded. "Good luck, my Barbarian."

Morak suddenly grabbed her and they kissed deeply, with the realization that they probably would never see each other again.

"For a free Earth," Isha said, saluting him with her ray gun. Then she was gone.

• • •

Morak watched her out of sight. "And for love," he murmured. Two Morfs ducked into the corridor and shot at Morak. The Barbarian slid sideways, returning fire, watching as one of the aliens twitched and went down.

He sprinted the opposite way along the corridor, around several more corners, and eventually out into the night. Morfs and humans were everywhere, moving with frantic haste. An occasional random ray blast indicated confusion still reigned.

Morak moved carefully and quietly away from the activity and into the human habitation area. Here, the air was silent, except for distant sounds of battle. He hoped Isha was all right, and would be able to continue the diversion until the scientists had time to connect the jewel. If they, themselves, still lived, Morak reminded himself.

Ahead was a group of humans moving in the darkness. Yet they moved strangely, in a way Morak somehow recognized. But he couldn't tell for sure; it was too dark. He hid behind some bushes and a low fence and watched as more and more of the dark, hulking shapes arrived and congregated silently in the garden clearing and in the streets, moving and shifting softly and almost restlessly.

Without a sound, suddenly, all those shapes turned and began shuffling toward Morak. Before he could find a way to escape, they were all around him—humans dressed like the farmer of the day before. A cold chill rippled down Morak's spine.

He backed away, only to find himself up against a building. The humans pressed closer, closer. Not threatening. Just pressing.

"Back, you godless demons," Morak shouted, jabbing his blade toward them. The multitude showed no reaction, but pressed closer toward him, pushing forward.

Morak hesitated. He was there to kill Morfs—and Kam—not innocent humans. Before he could decide, one had impaled himself on Morak's sword, and the dead weight of the man's body dragged the blade from Morak's hand.

He wrenched it free, but it was too late. Dozens of humans were suddenly atop him, their hands outstretched, eyes blank. The Barbarian ducked away, pushing through the crowd.

And...

"Softly," said a woman. And with that sound, her head exploded, slamming Morak back against the wall.

Sounds, words, grunts preceded explosion after explosion as the closest of the humans opened their mouths and spoke. And died. The force pressed Morak against the wall. He bent, trying to protect himself, but they didn't stop. As one row of men and women crowded against him, only to have their heads blown apart at the sound of long unuttered words, another row took their place.

The wall was plastered with brains and skull bones of humans, and the ground at Morak's feet piled high with headless bodies.

Morak felt himself losing consciousness, and he knew it was only a matter of time before one of those unfortunate people got close enough to kill him. The bombs implanted inside their heads were not intended as offensive weapons, but fragments of skull bone sliced into Morak's skin. He protected his head as much as possible, yet the attacks continued.

He reached down and tried to draw his beam weapon. He was forced to his knees as humans pressed in upon him and spoke. He was covered with blood and human gore.

"To hell with you all!" He shouted finally, grabbing one of the bodies at his feet and using it to shield him long enough to draw the gun.

He pulled the trigger and swept the ray back and forth, back and forth. Silently, except for the one utterance allowed them, the humans dropped, most cut in half by the burning ray. Those alive groaned and their heads exploded.

Morak worked his way to the left, reached down to grasp his blade, then continued to the edge of the humans. Then he was away, running down a dark street and around several corners.

He stopped, pressed against a wall, and slammed another power cartridge into his weapon.

• • •

About two kilometers to the northwest, Isha had blasted her way to the vicinity of the hive elders—the main governmental buildings of the Morfs.

Almost 20 of the aliens lie dead, and Isha herself sported a red welt on her left forearm. But something was not right—she saw too few Morfs. She had expected to be dead by now, overcome by hundreds of the aliens.

Yet only a token force had opposed her—and not very effectively at that. The thought disturbed her that she and Morak had failed in their attempt to create a diversion, that the main Morf forces were at the power plant mopping up the last of the Earthian invaders. Where else could they all be?

"Tucker?" She whispered into her communicator.

No answer. There hadn't been for some time.

She tensed as a Morf guard exited the capitol building. She aimed carefully and squeezed the trigger. The ray sizzled the air and burned through the chest of the Morf.

Isha ran crouched toward the doorway. She darted to the left as several rays chipped the roadway around her. Reaching the door, she snapped it open and lunged through, dropping to her belly and rolling. Three guards and an elder were busily gathering papers at the huge table where she and Morak had been questioned only a short time ago. The range was extreme, but it was possible they hadn't seen her. She depressed the trigger and moved the ray in an arc. The three guards went down, cut almost in half, with high pitched screams. The elder, on the other side of the table, tried to duck behind it, but Isha followed him down, keeping the trigger depressed until the Morf had virtually vaporized.

"*That* is human vengeance," she whispered, her lips curled in anger.

Behind her, the door opened.

• • •

Morak, sword in one hand, ray gun in the other, darted in and out of shadows. There were no more humans about, no Morfs. He saw two buildings ahead, on the right, and in one a window glowed with light. He saw several shadows moving about within.

But there came a sound behind him. Morak whirled, gun aimed at the small, moving figure he first thought was a Morf.

"Meesha?" He mouthed silently. But he hesitated. It was indeed a girl child, with long golden hair just like Meesha. She walked silently out of the shadows. But no, it was not Meesha.

Morak smiled. The child came closer. Morak saw more were joining them. He would tell them to hide, then lead them to safety when he was finished.

The smile died as the first child came close enough for Morak to look into her eyes. Her dead, lifeless eyes. Her automated movements. His blood ran cold when he saw the antenna sprouting from behind the bright yellow curls.

"No!" He shouted, "no!"

There were dozens of small, slowly moving shadows, all coming toward him. The girl, seven years, no more, reached out a hand toward Morak. She sang.

Her head exploded, knocking Morak back against the building. His eyes wide with terror, he backed away and began to run, away from the children, as fast as possible.

His flight took him in the direction of the lighted window. Without a thought, he flung himself at the window, crashing through it.

He rolled and came to his feet, looking wildly about him. A totally surprised Kam sat half disrobed on the room's only furnishing—a large bed. Beside him were two children—both naked—one a boy and the other—"Meesha!"

"Morak! Oh, Morak, you came for me again!"

Kam jumped to his feet, eyes wide in disbelief. "You! It can't be!" He shouted.

"Yes, devil spawn, it's me."

"But how—how?" Kam shook his head. "No, no. You're dead. You have to be dead; we laid waste to a third of the earth to kill you."

"But you, hell-spawn, still live, but not much longer," Morak said, advancing slowly, ray gun held at the ready. He glanced at Meesha and the boy child, at the red scars on their thin bodies. He noted the dullness in the boy's eyes, the lack of fear, eyes somehow more terrifying than those he had escaped from outside.

"So this is how you live your evil life?"

"As I told you, Morak," Kam said, edging away from the Barbarian, back along the side of the bed, "my alien friends give me everything I want."

"Now I give you death," Morak shouted, lunging at Kam. His sword pricked the other's right arm, but Kam reached behind him, grabbed the small boy and impaled his body on the end of Morak's sword.

Horrified, Morak stopped, gently lowered the weapon, and eased the boy onto the bed. Kam acted, grabbing Meesha and dragging her screaming toward the window.

"Stop!" Morak shouted, "you will not take her again."

Kam halted. Smiled. "Let me live, Barbarian, and I'll share with you my secret."

"I have no need..."

"It's the secret of youth, Morak," he held Meesha close, blocking Morak's aim.

"You talk nonsense." Morak kept his weapon aimed, hoping for an opening.

"No, no, Morak, listen to me. This is what you don't know. I am not Kam son of Kam—no, *I am Kam*! I am one-hundred-fifty-seven years old, my friend. I've found the secret of—"

Morak clipped off a shot, but Kam ducked and held Meesha higher. "Stop, or I'll break her neck."

Morak hesitated.

"Once you have my secret, you can live forever, too."

"All right, dog, tell me your precious secret." Keep him talking, wait for an opening. He will *not* take Meesha away again.

"It's the children, Morak. They are filled with the full measure of youth—all you need do is take into yourself that which they can share, Morak, their blood, the sweat from their brow, the tears. Pain brings those forth and it is filled with the stuff of youth. Consume it, and you can live for ever."

Morak shook his head. "Nonsense."

"It's not nonsense. I'm *old*, Morak. Look at the youth in my face."

Morak half-listened to Kam. He watched Meesha intently. Her face was frozen in concentration. Kam was pressed against the window frame which Morak had crashed through.

Something about that broken frame seemed not quite right. And he was sure Meesha had something to do with it.

"But this one, Morak, oh, she is very special. Meesha has power, great power, more power than even she suspects. And in the drinking of her life, she has begun passing on this power to me. That's why I can't let her go, Morak. You understand, don't you? I need her to become as powerful as these stinking Morfs. Someday, my power will exceed even theirs, and then I'll rule them. This child is the key."

The window frame came loose and crashed around Kam's head and shoulders.

Startled, he released Meesha, and the child scrambled away. Morak fired, but the leader of thieves had fallen back, out the window, and into the night.

Morak leapt to the window and saw Kam race around a corner of the next building.

Morak turned. "Are you okay?" He asked Meesha.

"Yes, I guess so." She flung herself at the Barbarian. "I'm so happy to see you again, Morak. I want to go home. I want to see Carina and Tok!" She wailed against him.

Well, he felt like crying too.

"Come on," he said gently, "get dressed. We can't let Kam escape."

"Please, Morak, no. I'm afraid. He'll get me again."

"No he won't, I swear it." He knelt, gazed intently into Meesha's too-big eyes. "Yet understand this, child. You have powers that can be used against Kam. Don't fear him, he is nothing against you. Understand?"

She nodded. Morak smiled, wiped tears from her cheeks, then helped her dress. Then they exited through the window and followed Kam.

• • •

Isha turned to see who stood in the doorway—wanted to see her executioner. But it was not the squat form of a Morf that stood outlined against the almost-dawn, but a tall, thin figure, breathing hard.

"Who?" She asked softly. It couldn't be Tucker D'air...

The man stepped into the room, and Isha saw the pointed beard and the wild eyes of Kam. The leader of thieves looked at the Queen of Earth, half smiled, then pulled the trigger of his weapon full in Isha's face.

Seconds later, Morak guided by Meesha entered the same room. Morak pulled the child to the right, and down to the floor. "Stay here," he whispered. He almost tripped over Isha's body. Startled, he knelt and felt for a pulse while his eyes glanced over the empty room.

There, he found it, a thin, thready pulse. She was alive, for the moment. "Isha," he whispered, that hissed sound echoing through the empty room. He reached out a hand to her face, but his fingers touched only a thick goo. He fired his ray at the floor near them. From the burst of light, he could see her. Meesha gasped. He looked away.

"Barbarian," the gravelly voice called to him from the floor. It bore no resemblance to Isha's voice; did not even sound human. "Morak." There was a long pause.

"I'm here. Don't talk." He tried not to look too closely at her ruined face in the dying glow of the ray blast, trying to keep his heart from crying out.

"Do," the voice took a raspy breath, "what you must."

"I love you Isha, I..."

Her hand grasped his wrist with an almost inhuman strength. "Finish—my—job."

Her hand fell away. Morak sat near her for a long time, rocking back and forth on his heels, gazing out into the dark shadows of the deserted room.

Silently, softly, Meesha came to him and put her arms around his shoulders. Now it was his turn to cry.

Later, he saw the small communicator lying at Isha's side. He sighed, picked it up, and tried calling Tucker D'air.

He was surprised to receive a reply. "Morak," D'air's voice crackled, "we're pinned down. We can't connect the jewel. We can't hold on much longer."

"Finish my job," Isha had told him, her dying breath.

"I'm on my way," he said into the communicator.

• • •

He and Meesha made their way back to the artificial peninsula. At first, they saw no aliens, which was strange. But as they drew closer, more and more of the blue skins crossed their path.

For the most part, Morak and Meesha hid from them, using his sword only when necessary, and the gun not at all.

Once at the metal dock, however, there were far too many

Morfs to hide from. The air held several of their large aircraft, firing an unceasing barrage of lightning bolts.

"Come with me," Morak whispered. They made their way to the edge of the facility. He needed to hurry; it would be light in a matter of minutes.

As he suspected, the artificial peninsula was equipped with an access catwalk about halfway down. He put Meesha on his back and told her to hold on tight. He climbed down to the walkway.

Once there, they made good progress as the Aliens were concentrated on the top level. The closer they got to the main power station, the louder the sounds of battle became. They watched as a human warrior screamed and fell over the side, to splash into the water.

"Wait here," he told Meesha.

"No, I want to go with you."

"You'll get hurt or die up there."

"No, I won't. I'm needed up there." Her voice held an insistence and her eyes were fixed on the dome above, and he decided it wasn't a good time to argue.

Morak held the ray gun in his mouth, because he knew he would need it right away. On that count, he was correct. He came over the side into a skirmish line of Morfs, facing away from him.

He pushed Meesha down, then opened fire, cutting the aliens down before they knew they had been flanked. Morak and Meesha dashed for the largest dome, dodged fire, then ducked inside.

On the way, they'd passed too many human bodies. What they saw around the dome was only a few of the original task force returning Morf fire.

Inside the building, Morak was met by one of the scientists.

"Tucker D'air is down inside, but it's hopeless. There's no way to connect the jewel."

"Their power is too weak?"

The scientist shook his head. "Too strong. It killed three of our experts and almost burned out the jewel."

"Morak!" D'air ascended some stairs and hurried to meet the Barbarian. "Where is Isha?"

Morak shook his head, unable to say anything.

D'air stopped as if struck. "So we've lost. Finally."

Morak looked around him. "They don't seem to be attacking with much determination."

"They don't want to damage their power plant, Morak. All they need do is wait for a little while, picking us off one-by-one, then they can easily retake it with few or no losses. All we can do is damage this plant, which would cause them a minor inconvenience. We're safe here for a little while longer, but we're running out of time."

"Take me to the jewel," Meesha said suddenly.

"Not now, child," D'air said, noticing Meesha for the first time. "Morak did you see any possibility—"

"I said take me to the jewel." D'air found himself forcibly turned toward the girl. His eyes were wide, he opened his mouth but no words came out.

Morak preceded D'air's reply. "Do as she says. There is no time to explain."

Tucker D'air stared at Meesha for a moment, glanced back at the Barbarian, then shrugged. "This way. Although I don't see why we should bother..."

"Just do it," Meesha said impatiently.

Down they went into the heart of the power plant. The installation was buried deep in the ocean. D'air explained that huge amounts of water were needed to cool the strange reactor.

The uncrated jewel sat lifelessly while two more scientists gazed through a small window into a glowing room.

Meesha went to the thick, armored door and reached for the handle.

D'air stopped her. "Two men went in there, and did not come back."

"Let go," she said. Tucker D'air felt himself pushed back by some invisible hand. Morak picked up the jewel and watched as Meesha caused the massive door to swing open. He started to follow, but she stopped him.

"No, if you went farther you would die." She smiled at him.

"Give me the jewel."

It was a heavy load for a child, but she balanced it in one hand easily. Morak knelt. "You be careful in there."

"I will, Morak. I love you, you know." She searched his eyes, "you've saved me so many times." She kissed his cheek, then was gone.

The door closed after her, despite Morak's attempts to keep it open.

He watched through the thick shielded window, his heart beating rapidly. This reminded him too much of a similar room on Simathica. Of a jewel. And a powerful woman. Perhaps the quadrabred could do such a thing, judging from the hand-written notes appended to the *Tome of the Dark Devices* by the sole surviving scientist on Simathica just before his death. But Meesha, Morak had been told, was one generation short of the Quadrabred. She was...

He watched as Meesha went to the main power conversion output device. The jewel left her hands and floated over to the intense beam of white-hot energy.

It stopped, positioning itself above the roaring beam of power. There came a deep rumble and the whole building shook. Suddenly, the dome around them groaned and echoed the sound of ripping steel. Back on the surface, the dome split open, cracking ceramic, glass, and less flexible metal.

A red glow burst forth from the room. Morak chanced a look and saw Meesha, hands outstretched, by the will of her child's mind, bending the path of the alien energy away from its conduit and up into the jewel; and from there, a red glow spread out, through the top of the cracked dome, and beyond into the newborn morning sky.

Meesha turned to Morak and smiled. She waved. Unlike Dagrag, the radiation from the jewel did not seem to affect her.

He had a feeling she would be all right. She wasn't a witch of Karan that grew ugly and evil from the radiation of the jewel. Her power was strong and pure.

And it suddenly came to him that Meesha had to be the final

step in the quadrabred experiment that Tok and Dagrag and Carina had begun; there must have been another, one unmentioned to Morak, a first witch-wife of Tok's.

If so, they had lied to him to conceal the child's true worth.

But then again, maybe a fourth generation wasn't needed. At least not in the way he had imagined it.

He looked into the room, gazing through the small shielded window. His eyes opened wide in disbelief.

The figure standing amid the death and radiation and smiling, was no longer small and childlike. Dagrag had gone into a similar room an ugly, misshapen witch, and the jewel radiation had dissolved her.

Meesha had gone into this room a small, thin child. Now she turned and calmly walked to the door, the jewel behind her still emitting its radiation. Morak saw...

She had gone in a winsome, frail child. She came out a tall, thin, beautiful young woman. Fully mature.

"Morak," she said, "the change is complete. The jewel power was all I needed to regain my memory and full knowledge. This," she looked down and indicated her matured body, "was the missing information—that which Tok needed to complete the quadrabred experiment. It took the jewel power to finish the transformation. He had originally intended to bring the Simathica jewel back with him, to use on me, but Grandmother Dagrag couldn't overcome the compulsion to discharge the jewel."

Morak stared, speechless.

Meesha touched his cheek with her soft fingers. His unbelieving eyes widening in an astonished face. "I'm yours," she said, answering his unspoken question, "that is if you want me. I've always known it. I'm yours forever, just as you are mine. We are the last of our kind, Morak. There is no need to speak of love, because it is a silent bond between us stronger than any spoken oath or man-made metal."

Slowly, he nodded. He took her hand in his own. "Wait here," he whispered into her soft, silken, golden hair. "I've one more thing to do."

"I know. My love. Hurry back to me."

• • •

Morak exited the ruined building and made his way quickly back to land. He saw no living Morfs, but dozens of bodies were piled about, lying in hideous positions, undoubtedly felled by the jewel's radiation.

He made his way, unopposed, to the airfield, to a series of huge buildings he had not been allowed to inspect on his tour with Taymakk. He searched for a back entrance to the first building. He found it, finally, but hesitated. He noticed small beams of light, shifting and moving from under the door.

Under other circumstances, he might have found another, less obvious, way to get on the other side of that door. Once, he had been a crafty Barbarian moving easily like a night shadow through a world he understood.

Now...

Now, he kicked the door open and rolled through it, beams of energy heating the air just above his head. He fired back, wildly, realizing the area was a huge spaceship hangar and full of Morfs—literally thousands of them—loading themselves and equipment into six massive star ships. Bodies were strewn about, those who had succumbed to the radiation. Others were in the process of dying. The rest moved with frantic speed.

The high, domed roof was closed, except for a crack at its center. Morak noticed through blasts that the crack was slowly opening, revealing a dim glow of morning light.

That's why there hadn't been much opposition. They were all leaving, and once in their star ships, they were somewhat protected from the full impact of the radiation. Thus protected, they were leaving the Earth. Once in space, they would be safe, and they could send down their human warriors to do battle for them.

Morak was kept busy rolling and twisting, trying to avoid sudden death to think much, while sending out his own beams. One of the Morf rays clipped his right leg, causing the Barbarian to wince in pain. Another singed his head and twice along his left arm. The air around him was so hot, his body ran with sweat. The air smelled of ozone and his own burning flesh.

Yet he kept his own weapon firing, dropping Morfs from railings and from behind crates. His maneuvers finally brought him up behind a room at the edge of one wall, providing a moment of protection. He rolled to a stop, gasping for breath.

More Morfs than he could count were running toward him. He aimed his weapon, pressed the trigger and swept the beam back and forth.

Morfs dropped, screaming. The remainder retreated, shooting at him from safe positions.

This gave Morak a chance to examine the ships and the frenzied yet orderly efforts of the aliens to board them.

Instead of shooting at the nearby armed aliens, Morak tried to wreak havoc by picking off those boarding the ships.

He killed Morfs carrying boxes up the ramps, thereby causing panic and confusion. He spotted one of the hive elders at the extreme opposite end of the huge hangar. A well-aimed ray caused that Morf to stumble back into his brothers, his chest burned to a black crisp.

Then Morak's weapon went dead. It died in mid-shot, and he had no more power packs. The nearby Morfs wasted no time before beginning their advance—some of them disappearing and reappearing again closer.

Morak rolled behind the building, checked his sword to be sure the jewel was still on, then got to his feet and waited. He would die, it seemed, a Barbarian's death.

He felt a puff of air behind him, turned without a thought, and ran his blade through an alien who'd suddenly appeared and was still leveling his weapon.

He heard others approaching, waited until the last second, then leapt into the midst of them, swinging his blade.

"Die, you demons of darkness," he shouted as the Morfs desperately tried to regroup and shoot the Barbarian, rather than themselves. But Morak moved quickly, darting here and there, swinging his great blade that left dead Morf piled upon dead Morf.

Behind him, he heard a meaty explosion and glanced back to see the remains of two Morfs who had reappeared in the same space at the same time.

Abruptly, one of the alien's rays struck the hilt of Morak's sword. The blade was flung from his hand. He glared at the blue-skins and awaited his Barbarian death.

Silence. Through the crowd of alive and dead Morfs strode Kam. Morak, on his knees, looked up at the leader of thieves.

"So it seems you win after all," the Barbarian said bitterly.

"Yes, indeed, my old friend, it does. In some ways, I'm regretful—we've had a long and eventful association, Morak. Soon, I will be the only Karanian left. My friends here," he said, indicating the Morfs, "have promised me a place on their world, training their humans to do battle back here on Earth."

He paused, checked his weapon, "they've also given me one more gift." He then aimed the gun at Morak. He raised an eyebrow and smiled. "It's time."

One wall of the building collapsed. The Morfs screamed as the full, unshielded power of the jewel bathed them. Morak glanced up and saw Meesha floating over the collapsed wall. The Morfs writhed, convulsed, and dropped, twitching to the ground where they died.

Kam fired a shot at Morak. The Barbarian grabbed his side and went down. The King of Thieves turned and aimed at Meesha. Before he could press the trigger, Kam noticed a deep, bass rumble. He turned and saw the spaceships closing up, abandoning any who were not yet aboard. All the Morfs outside the ships were on the ground, most of them still, but a few twitching feebly.

"No!" Kam shouted, "wait! You must wait for me!" He ran toward the ships, to the ramp of the nearest one. The two farthest ships were slowly rising. They barely cleared the opening in the roof. The rumble became mixed with a high-pitched scream, and the starships lifted into the sky and were gone.

The next two rose into the air as Kam stumbled up the ramp of the fifth one. He watched as one of the ships wobbled slightly, hit the side of the building then crashed through the wall and crumpled outside. The other made a successful escape.

The remaining two did not move, but the sounds from them became louder and louder. Kam, his screams no longer audible, pounded at the airlock doors of the spaceship. His arms were raised, his mouth open in a scream of fear and rage, when the airlock began ponderously to open.

Before he could squeeze inside, Kam lurched, his eyes bulged, and he looked down to see the point of Morak's dagger protruding from his chest.

That thin blade slowly withdrew and Kam seemed to deflate as blood spurted from the wound. He turned to see Morak behind him, holding the knife. The Barbarian ran a finger through the blood at the dagger's tip, then used it to paint a line down the center of his forehead.

"Let the Earth be done with you," he said quietly, his brown eyes boring into Kam's empty ones. Then Morak spat full into Kam's face. The leader of thieves turned back to where the airlock was again closing. Then he collapsed and slid partway down the ramp, one arm outstretched.

But Morak didn't notice. He'd already turned, and, running quickly, went to where Meesha awaited him. They exited the building, knowing from the vibrations in the air there was going to be a gigantic explosion. And soon.

They moved rapidly back toward the ocean, and ran into Tucker D'air and the remainder of the task force. Before anyone could speak, one-half of the Morf spaceport exploded. The humans took cover as debris shot past them, and more dropped from the sky like a clattering rain.

"So," D'air said when the air cleared, wiping his hands, "the Brotherhood of Zartan Morf no longer darkens the skies of Earth, nor foul its lands."

"Those who could, have left," Morak said. "The rest..." he shrugged.

D'air looked at Morak. "Thank you, Barbarian."

"Meesha deserves the thanks," he said.

D'air glanced at the woman beside Morak. "Our land is yours, all we have you may share, for as long as you live."

"Thank you, sir," Meesha said softly.

One of the other scientists looked at Tucker D'air, bowed, and said, "King Tucker, chosen heir of Queen Isha, what are your orders?"

"Damn," D'air said.

• • •

Much later, after days of searching, they determined no Morfs were left alive, at least not on Earth. Several thousand had escaped in the spaceships. And there were Morf space stations in Earth orbit that were evidently still inhabited and functional.

But the jewel worked effectively, as did its sister in the southern hemisphere, once they fought their way onto New Zealand and from there to Simathica where they were able to repair the fusion generator and re-connect a replacement jewel.

There was no way of telling when the Morfs would attack again, this time in the form of humans dropped from space, but hopefully there would be time for Earth to prepare.

People began arriving from the Golden City to re-inhabit the portions of New York remaining above the new sea level.

Meesha and Morak were the first ones married, and their union turned into a huge celebration of victory.

The Morf-raised humans still alive were confined until they could be re-indoctrinated and studied.

They found thousands of bodies, but no living humans with bombs in their skulls.

"The Morfs probably detonated all the bombs before they left," D'air told Morak. The thought made Morak sad—he had hoped there would be some way to save those poor people, especially the children.

Morak lived with Meesha at the top of an abandoned building. Yet after a time, he grew restless, moody.

He was happy when Tucker D'air came by to talk with him.

He accompanied D'air to the Earth-king's office to study some maps when a military general burst in. "King Tucker, we've just tracked a Morf ship carrying a human attack force. It attempted to land several kilometers from here, but crashed."

"Any human survivors?"

"Yes, sir. About half were killed, but the rest are still alive. Some are injured. We've freed the survivors from the ship and they're on the way here."

"Very well, call me when they arrive." He turned to Morak. "This should be interesting. Would you care to join me for their arrival?"

Morak nodded. Anything to break the boredom. Certain, he was happy with Meesha, especially as the woman's powers matured and she discovered new capabilities. But while she was delighted with her progress, Morak had no more battles to fight.

He felt out of place in this new world, useless. Of course, he and Meesha would have no children. Once they died, there would be no one left from Karan. They were not Adam and Eve. He was the last Barbarian, she the first, last, and only Quadrabred.

Morak stood and followed D'air, who was still getting used to being King of Earth, to watch from a railing as vehicles full of humans descended into New York. Humans born and raised on Morofia, and trained to fight their own kind on Earth.

Meesha suddenly appeared next to him. She could always find Morak, and he smiled. "I missed you," he said.

She leaned against him, watching.

The prisoners were removed from the vehicles and escorted to the habitations where they would be studied and hopefully re-indoctrinated. They looked just like the guards around them, as they strode sullenly past. Morak leaned over the railing to get a closer look. One of the Morofian humans saw him, and shrank back in fear, with words of warning to his fellows.

"It seems they recognize you, Morak," D'air said, frowning. "Curious, isn't it?"

Indeed, each of the prisoners was looking at Morak as they filed past, some of them pointing. And each of those eyes was filled with recognition. And not a little fear.

"It is strange," Morak said, "it's almost as if—as if they've seen Barbarians before."

"What do you mean, my love?" Meesha asked.

"I'm not sure," Morak said, frowning. "Perhaps it means that there might be Barbarians among the Morfs. But that's not possible."

D'air looked at Morak. "I wonder—"

"What?"

"Look at you two—so different. Yet both of you are the results of Morf experiments. Isn't it strange that two of their failures freed Earth? Isn't it odd that both of you, with no need to get involved in our battles, won those battles for us?"

"I am a warrior," Morak said simply, his eyes gazing up, spaceward. "Somewhere out there, it seems there may be others like me. Other failures. You know, Kam said these blue skins hated to waste anything. Perhaps..."

"Perhaps what, my Barbarian darling?"

"Perhaps there are other failures somewhere out there that can help to bring the blue skins to their knees."

"What are you thinking? You want to go out there? To their planet?"

Morak looked into Meesha's endless blue eyes. "Only if—"

"Of course. We'll go together. We'll always be together. We have a lot to learn about ourselves. Don't you agree? Besides, if they have Barbarians, perhaps they also have witches, and we can recreate the quadrabred experiment."

Morak thought for a long moment. "Perhaps. Besides, there will certainly be many more blue skins to kill."

Tucker D'air watched the two for a moment. Then he nodded. "We have several of the Morf starships. With the thanks of a free Earth, one is yours."

"Thank you," Meesha said.

"Yes," Morak agreed. The two men looked at each other, then they clasped hands.

"And if you succeed, remember that you—and Meesha—and

any of your kind you may find among the stars—will always have a home here."

"Thank you, my brother." He and Meesha stepped away from D'air. Morak looked up into the darkening sky. Stars were appearing, and Morak had a feeling he would find Barbarians among them.

"You created us," he said to the stars, "for your own pleasure. As mere pieces in a game." He pulled Meesha closer to him, "but now the game is over; now is the time to taste the true power of your playthings."

Tucker D'air, unable to hear Morak's words, but seeing the death reflected in those eyes gazing starward, shuddered and looked away.

###

About the Author

Mark West is the pen name of a best selling writer of non-fiction. West is the author of the novel "Inanna and the Giant" as well as the soon-to-be-released novel "Messages" during the fourth-quarter of 2020.

"Inanna and the Giant" is currently available in print or as an e-book from Amazon. "Messages" is also available from the same venue.

Find out more information about these novels and other books at www.minref.com, the finest in small press publishing.

We would appreciate a review on Amazon when you finish one of our books. Thanks!

www.ingramcontent.com/pod-product-compliance
Lightning Source LLC
Chambersburg PA
CBHW020551020726
47494CB00006B/2026